A Day to Remember

A Novel of Alzheimer's

Gretchen Nelson Ezaki

Ezaki

ISBN: 9781522088950
Independently published

Dedication

There is no question that this book must be dedicated to my late mother, Bettie Jayne Nelson

> who lovingly protected and nurtured me in infancy;
> carefully guided and trained me through childhood;
> devoutly prayed for me during adolescence;
> gently released me as a young adult;
> wisely counseled me when I began my family;
> and unknowingly provided the inspiration and contents
>   for this novel.

I'm grateful for everything she taught me, including the painful lessons at the end of her life of which she was unaware.

Preface

Credit for this book cover goes to SelfPubBookCovers.com and specifically to SelfPubBookCovers.com/mary60. Thank you. It was very easy and perfect!

A Day to Remember is the book I wanted to read while my mother suffered from Alzheimer's. Unfortunately, it didn't exist. I knew falling in love with a fictional family, whose life struggles paralleled my own, would be encouraging and therapeutic, because when my mother behaved oddly, I responded with frustration, anger, or embarrassment, but if an Alzheimer's victim outside of my family did the exact same bizarre things, I could laugh or enjoy a sweet sentimental moment. Often, I became consumed with my mother's illness and missed the joys of life. I needed a reminder that, even though life is hard, life is good.

I hope this book will be therapeutic for others who are living too close to Alzheimer's to view it objectively. May this story be a reminder that, even when life is painful, love and beauty are close by.

Table of Contents

Contents

1954 Prologue

Mary clung to her mother's leg and buried her face in the prickly yarn of the wool-knit mourning suit. She rubbed her cheeks back and forth as if the coarse threads of the black skirt could scratch off the events of the past week. Warm, spring sunshine caressed her shoulders with its lie of drowsy contentment, and song birds twittered a carefree tune, whiling away the morning. Mary shuffled around into her mother's protective shadow to hide from their lure and deceit. The cool, smooth silk stocking under Mary's fingertips was the only familiar sensation, offering a hint of reassurance that not everything had changed.

Pinching her eyes tighter and squeezing her stubby fingers into her mother's thigh, Mary tried to escape the solo soprano voice as it floated across the groomed lawn of the cemetery, blending with the birdsong, bringing comfort and renewed tears to the group assembled there.

> *"Amazing grace, how sweet the sound,*
> *that saved a wretch like me,*
>
> *I once was lost but now I'm found,*
> *was blind but now I see.*

When we've been there ten thousand years,
bright shining as the sun,

We've no less days to sing God's praise
than when we'd first begun."

The pastor dipped his graying head and murmured a prayer. Then, spreading his arms wide, the voluminous sleeves of his ecclesiastical robe swaying in the light breeze, he broadcast a benediction of hope. At the final amen, two cemetery workers emerged from the crowd. One steadied the head while the other cranked the handle at the feet of the shiny, black casket. Slowly, George Miller was lowered into the ground on March 30, 1954. He was twenty-nine.

Mourners milled around and shared awkward small talk in hushed voices. The spiked heels of women's pumps sank into the soft sod, necessitating slow, exaggerated steps like the march of Clydesdale horses. Most of the assembly drifted in groups of two or three toward the center of the gathering, where Mary's mother, Greta, stood next to the rectangular chasm that was her husband's new, permanent residence. Friends offered condolences, their eyes focusing on one of Greta's pearl stud earrings or the small dimple in her chin. They patted the top of Mary's head and attempted, unsuccessfully, to ignore the morbid hole confronting them with their own mortality.

A small group of George's coworkers approached, bowler hats held in honor over the breasts of their brown business suits. They mumbled incoherent words to their polished shoes, nodded sympathetically, then rushed off, eager to return to their busy offices and ledgers and memos, where young men do not die.

Around the periphery, small, scattered groups formed. Subdued voices and indiscernible words mingled with the whisper of the breeze and birdsong. A common theme existed among the separate, independent conversations: everyone was amazed by Greta's composure. Most people praised her strength of character, which she would need as a young, single mother. Others, who relished gossip, failed to detect a grieving widow in her demeanor. They questioned the depth of her emotions, and speculated on possible causes. Greta accurately interpreted the insinuations behind the conspiratorial whispers and glances her way. She ignored them.

With her brown-bobbed head erect on her five-foot-four frame, Greta politely thanked friends for their sympathy and declined their offers of assistance. Strength was her friend today. Weakness might be the first step down a slippery slope too steep and deep to ever recover.

Resolutely, and nearly successfully, Greta battled the ever-present threat of tears. The occasional, silent drop which succeeded in escaping and rolling down her cheek was covered, and almost hidden, by a single layer of dark netting on the black felt pillbox hat that matched her black knit suit. Contrary to what observers assumed, her stoic expression and rigid stance were unrelated to courage or strength. They resulted from fear: fear for her young, vulnerable daughter. Her maternal radar was intently focused on identifying and avoiding any situation or comment from a bumbling well-wisher that might hurt her child. And crying — well, she refused to give in to crying, because her hands were occupied, preventing her from dabbing her eyes or blowing her nose. One arm was returning Mary's hug around her right leg while the other hand alternately rubbed the little girl's back or ran reassuring fingers through her fine, amber hair.

Greta's mother approached. "It's time to head back now." Placing a hand on the small of her daughter's back, the middle-aged version of Greta ushered them to the waiting limousine. Greta picked up four-year-old Mary, stooped, and entered the plush and depressing interior of the shiny, black vehicle. Mary snuggled into her mother's lap, nestling her head against Greta's breast. Long before they reached the church where the funeral service had been held and Greta's parents' white Buick waited, Mary stumbled into a troubled sleep.

Carefully, Greta climbed out of the limo and maneuvered into the backseat of her parents' car, cradling her exhausted daughter. Greta laid Mary across the brown vinyl, resting the fair head in her lap. Greta's father slid behind the wheel as her mother settled into the passenger seat.

"I'd really like you to think about moving back home," Greta's mom repeated one more time. "We miss you and we want you with us."

Greta's strained, tired face and puffy, red-rimmed eyes appeared an easy target for persuasion. But, at her mother's comment, her jaw clenched with determination and her eyes hardened with irritation.

The car's engine revved to life and pulled away from the church. With forced restraint Greta answered, "Mom, I told you. I want to stay here. George and I dreamed of making California our home. I'm not ready to leave and let go of the plans we made."

"Blood is thicker than water. At a time like this you need family."

As if reading a prepared statement Greta recited, "I appreciate your offer and your concern, but I plan to stay here."

Catching her daughter's hazel eye in the rear-view mirror, Greta's mother persisted, "Well, I hope you'll reconsider after everything settles down. If you change your mind we have room for the two of you. I want to make sure you know that."

Greta broke away from her mother's insistent gaze. How could she explain? Family could not bring George back. If she had to go on without him she wanted to go on here, in central California, where they'd created their life together. As long as she was frugal she should get by. The life insurance claim awarded by George's employer was enough to dismiss the mortgage on their small house. Thrifty use of her remaining funds would allow her to wait until the fall, when Mary started kindergarten, to look for a job. Hopefully, without a house payment, she would be able to support the two of them.

Greta gazed out the rear side window without seeing the pastel tulips and early roses coloring the front yards of the well-kept, middle-class neighborhood. The warmth of the sun on her arms and lap, intensified through the car window, reminded her of the lazy summer days of childhood. When she was young her family often camped at Lake Tahoe, exploring the wooded areas and boating on the lake. During high school, she spent summers hanging out at the river with friends where daring kids drank and smoked and others swam or fished. Those had been good times. Sparks, Nevada held many pleasant memories, but they were only memories. Happy, surreal images with the struggles conveniently faded.

Life had changed. Nevada offered Greta nothing now. Contrary to her parents' belief, Greta was convinced that staying in the little house in Clovis, California was the best thing for her, and especially for Mary. The child had never lived anywhere else. All Mary's memories of her father were in that house, and at less than five years of age, those memories would become few and dim. Greta was determined to keep them as numerous and vivid as possible. Besides, Greta had no desire to live near her family.

The following days and months passed slowly, but they did pass. Grief beckoned to Greta, tempting her to stay and linger as with a dear friend, but Mary needed care and a routine, so every morning Greta forced herself out of bed and into clean clothes. By August, the pain in Greta's chest had subsided into a barely discernable ache. It was strong enough to dispel any feelings of deep happiness, but no longer capable of eliminating all enjoyment. To outside observers, Greta appeared to be recovering quickly. Her face was once again framed by pin curls and a pleasant lilt had returned to her voice, although no one could claim to have seen her smile with her old enthusiasm. Mary, who skipped from place to place and rode her tricycle in circles in the driveway, seemed to have fully recovered from the trauma of losing her father. Out in the bright sunshine Mary giggled and played, but during the loneliness of night, an unnamed monster woke her and gloated that everyone had abandoned her in the vast, empty darkness. Most mornings, Greta found her daughter in a fetal position, cowering under the covers of the double bed in the master bedroom.

Bzzzzzzz. Greta startled to the unfamiliar cry of the alarm clock. She hit the silence button and threw back the blanket, uncovering the lump next to her. Rumpling the tangled mop of dark blond hair and kissing the exposed cheek, Greta said, "Rise and shine my big kindergarten girl."

An hour later, a large, tense fist clutched a small, trembling hand as Greta and Mary trudged in silence to the first day of school. At the classroom door Greta stopped. Mary hesitated. The bright bulletin boards and smiling white-haired teacher encouraged her to come inside. Mary pulled on her mother's hand so they could explore the room together, but Greta held firm, stationed on the exterior of the threshold. Leaning forward on tiptoes, but retaining a grip on her mother, Mary peered into the classroom. In one corner, several boys built then destroyed a tower of cardboard blocks. Across the room, large, bright pillows lay scattered on the floor in front of an overflowing bookcase. Mary wanted to go there and recline on the blue velvet of the largest pillow. She could pretend it was her magic carpet. She would hang on by the golden tassels dangling from the corners and fly around the world.

The experienced teacher followed Mary's gaze. "Let me show you the exciting books I have for you to look at." Mary let go of her mother and took the offered hand leading her toward the bumpy wonderland of pillows and books. The teacher stopped after two steps and said, "Give Mommy a big hug. We'll see her when school is done."

Greta watched with glistening eyes as Mary ran ahead of the teacher and jumped onto a large blue pillow.

"Excuse me. Can we get past?"

"Oh, I'm sorry." Greta stepped aside from the doorway, losing her view of Mary.

The woman waved a hand in dismissal. "Must be your first. It gets easier with each one. This is my fourth and she's been begging to come to school since she was two. Bye sweetie," the mother yelled to the swaying blond pigtails skipping across the room. Swiftly and unemotionally the woman turned, proceeded to the front gate, and exited the school.

Greta remained fixed on the cement walkway outside the door. She looked up and down the exterior hall. In front of each classroom a few other forlorn mothers dallied. The thought of talking to teary-eyed strangers made the knot in Greta's gut turn sour, but her feet refused to begin the solitary walk to an empty house.

Greta inhaled a feeble breath, surrendering to time and change. She turned, left the doorway, and wandered over toward the school office. A crowd of crying children with frazzled mothers spilled out of the main door. Crossing the breezeway to distance herself from the noise and confusion, Greta scanned announcements posted on a bulletin board. An official notice on school letterhead announced a job opening for a full-time secretary. Greta perked up. She read it again, paying closer attention to the details. Application due date--next week. Requirements included typing a minimum of fifty words per minute and knowledge of shorthand. Greta's pulse rate spiked, circulating a surge of optimism. In Nevada, Greta had attended secretarial school, then worked for two years before getting married. She used to type seventy words per minute and was the second best in her class at shorthand. Rushing out the front gate, Greta trotted home. She pulled her typewriter out of the closet and began refreshing her skills.

Three hours later, Greta ran the four blocks to school,

arriving breathless, mere seconds before Mary emerged through the classroom door. Mary skipped to her mother and excitedly chattered about the other children, the different areas of the classroom, and about her teacher who was the best teacher in the whole world. Greta pretended to listen as she watched the door to the school office. When the crowd of distraught mothers and children finally dispersed, Greta smoothed her skirt, straightened her back, and with Mary in tow, entered the office to enquire about the job posting.

7:30 a.m. The Beginning

The Wedding Day

The morning arrived gently. Diffuse December sunlight shone on the thin, floral-print curtains, creating barely discernible patterns on the soft pink walls. Deanna yawned and stretched, lazily rolling onto her back. The minor shift brought her inches from the bedroom wall and convected cool air against her left side. At five feet eight inches, Deanna's lanky frame hardly fit in the tiny twin bed. A queasy tickle rumbled through her stomach. Massaging her abdomen, she opened her blue eyes to an overwhelming aura of pink. She was under a puffy, hot pink comforter and blush colored sheets. Her long, straight brown hair fanned out across a pillowcase printed with pink-hued wildflowers, which coordinated with the curtains.

Around the top of the walls, pictures of last decade's pop stars cut out from *Teen Vogue* and *Seventeen* magazines created an uneven patchwork border. Small sections of N'Sync and The Backstreet Boys peeked through, nearly covered up by Kelly Clarkson, Regina Spector, and Jason Mraz.

On the desk to the right of the bed, Deanna's square, pink and white polka-dot pressed cardboard jewelry box overflowed with red, green, blue, and tie-dye rubber bracelets. Each bracelet represented a cause she supported in high school, although to be honest, gaining the attention of high school boys—and Mike Murphy in particular—was the cause to which she had devoted a majority of her time. A countless number of nights had been spent in this room with her friends, plotting ways to gain Mike Murphy's attention. The next weekend, they would gather again, crying because their attempts had failed. He'd rarely acknowledged them, and when he did, it was worse. He'd returned their devotion with scorn and ridicule. Deanna shook her head and let out a soft, snorty chuckle. Mike Murphy. How could she have been such a silly teen as to have thought herself in love with him?

Here she was, daydreaming in her room again. The room where she'd alternately dreamt of today and despaired that it would never come. Deanna reached out and tenderly stroked the small framed photo propped on her desk. "Oh Hank, I know you don't believe it, but you never had any real competition for my affections," Deanna said to the image of her fiancée teasing her with his mischievous smile. He wore jeans and a blue striped button-down dress shirt as he leaned with crossed arms against a tree in front of the Fresno State administration building. Deanna had snapped the picture with her cell phone one afternoon as they'd walked across campus shortly before they began officially dating—which meant before he graduated and while the anti-fraternization clause in his contract was still in effect.

During her teen years Deanna had created many phantom lovers, some demonstrating genius intelligence, others executing unsurpassed athletic feats, but all with Mike Murphy's face and voice. The substance of her imaginary Mr. Wonderfuls did not resemble the conceited, self-absorbed teenager they looked and sounded like. While Hank lacked the athletic prowess and dashing looks she had envisioned, he resembled her perfect creations in character and integrity. Hank was considerate, intelligent, and focused. He enjoyed laughing and joking as much as anyone, but he preferred an esoteric, theoretical discussion over a comedy movie, and definitely over a night out drinking beer and playing poker with the boys, which, from the latest Deanna had heard, was still Mike Murphy's favorite pastime. Mike was not a bad person, just shallow. Even in high school, with the intensity and insecurity of maintaining his status at the top of the popularity hierarchy, he had not intentionally mistreated or taken advantage of others. He'd just had simple, myopic ambitions; his life had focused on himself.

Deanna had been a nobody in high school. Her extracurriculars involved rushing home after her last class to care for her forgetful grandmother. When yearbooks had been distributed during first period the week before graduation, Deanna had tuned out the school announcements coming through the PA system overhead and opened the book, heading to the senior photos. She'd looked for her picture—most likely, her only picture. Flipping several pages at a time, she'd quickly gotten to the middle of the alphabet. The first picture on the page showed Courtney Nelson posed on a fallen tree over a stream, her flowing patterned sundress fanned out in the breeze, and the tips of her simple flip flops dipped into the cool water. It was a nice picture. Next to Courtney was Marcus Nolasco. He wore a poorly-fitted dark gray suit and wide red tie. His stiff, forced smile convinced Deanna it was his parents' idea that he wear dress clothes rather than his usual attire of jeans and a t-shirt. Deanna scanned up and down the page for her picture. It was not there. Every other year, she had been sandwiched between Courtney and Marcus. Deanna checked the next two pages. Then she went backwards. In the middle of the M page, she found her picture. Under the photo it read DeAnn Miller. DeAnn Miller? Who was DeAnn Miller and why was her name attached to Deanna's picture? It should have read Deanna Nilsson? Deanna's mom was Mary Miller. Since Mary had been thirty-five and established in her career when she married, she'd never changed her last name, but Deanna had her father's last name. Correspondence from the school usually included both surnames. Deanna was disappointed the school would confuse her last name with her mother's, but she could understand how it had happened. Transposing Deanna into DeAnn, however, was inexcusable. Obviously the students creating the yearbook, as well as their advisor, had never met Deanna during her four years of high school.

Deanna had left for college determined to make it a very different experience than high school and arrived at Fresno State with an unquenchable sense of freedom. For the first time, she was moving away from home, and relinquishing the responsibility of looking after her grandmother. It was Deanna's independence day—her own personal Fourth of July. The thrill of freedom lasted about a month, until her first exams to be exact. Then, Deanna's carefree irresponsibility had switched to shock at the increased rigor of college. But Deanna had stepped up to the challenge and proved her ability on future tests. The decreased personal space of the dorms, however, impeded studying, so she'd discovered a secluded study carrel tucked behind the stacks in the library, offering a respite from the intrusive, fishbowl existence of coed life. The periodic solitude helped Deanna establish a balance between enjoying campus life with new friends and completing class assignments.

The next year, Deanna had moved off campus. She'd rented a one-bedroom apartment with Jenna and Katie, two girls from the dorm. The tiny apartment was nearly as cramped as a dorm room, but the girls enjoyed the mature feeling of shopping and cooking for themselves, even though, during the entire fall semester, no one had cooked anything that required more than one pan. Unconsciously,

Deanna began referring to Fresno as home and her childhood residence as her parents' house. Deanna also enjoyed the intellectual stimulation of her classes.

"Welcome to the Tuesday afternoon discussion section of twentieth century American literature," the teaching assistant facilitating the class said. "You're in luck, because our reading list is long, dense, and excellent. By the end of this course, I predict, ten percent of you will switch your major to American lit. Half of you will wish you could. The other forty percent, well, you're probably science majors. I can't begin to predict what science majors will think or do. All I know is they have much worse ahead of them than this class. Seriously, if you are not thrilled by American literature at the end of this semester, I will quit my position as a TA." The students said nothing. In the near silence, the friction of feet scuffling against the cement floor and pencils doodling on notebooks became audible. A loud, unexpected squeak pierced the room as someone in the back row shifted his weight. Ignoring their responselessness, the instructor continued, "Not really. I'm quitting anyway. This is my last semester."

The instructor stepped around to the front of his desk. Leaning his weight against it and casually crossing his right leg over his left, he rubbed his hands together like a mad scientist in anticipation of beginning an experiment. "Now for introductions: my name is Henry Floyd. I'm called Hank by everyone except telemarketers and a few senile family members. I'm a graduate student hoping to actually graduate this semester. Of course, I graduated once before, but it didn't last very long. I came straight back the next semester. This time I'm hoping it will stick a little longer, but you never know; I am a lit major, after all. My master's project is complete, flawless, and outrageously boring. It's on its way to the graduate dean's office right now to see if they will confer an advanced degree upon me or doom me to facilitating undergraduate discussion sections for the rest of my life."

Most students slumped in their chairs and zoned out, or scribbled on their crisp, new notebooks. But Deanna sat up, focused, and took in everything she could about this interesting young man teaching her class. On first impression, he appeared quite average. Good looking enough, but not someone who would stand out in a crowd. He was average height and build with light brown eyes and light brown hair that probably was blond as a child, but had faded to nondescript over the years. Falling almost to his shoulders, its inconsistent wave and bohemian unkemptness gave the impression it was a short style that should have been trimmed a month ago.

He was thin but not too thin. If he worked out, he could have developed broad shoulders and an athletic physique, but he obviously preferred reading to weight lifting. The jocular tilt of his head and mischievous twinkle in his eyes were by far his best features. Deanna was captivated by his wit. It was cute, clever, and self-deprecating. After the cruelty of high school humor and the crudeness of dorm room jokes, it was refreshing to laugh without demeaning anyone or feeling violated.

Hank went over the usual stuff: course objectives, assignment due dates, plagiarism laws, and the obligatory self-introductions. Everyone introduced him or herself, trying to sound intelligent and sophisticated, even though no one listened to what anyone else said.

The following Tuesday, Hank greeted three students by name, and Deanna was one of them. She struggled to listen during that class. Her mind wandered to all sorts of romantic places, speculating about why he remembered her. She hoped it was because she had impressed him. However, she knew it could just as easily be that she had annoyed him. Most likely, he had an unemotional and irrelevant association with her name. Perhaps his sister shared her name. Or, the family dog.

Deanna dove into her literature class, relishing the

content as well as admiring the instructor. She read books, some new and some she knew well, with an educated quizzical view which added to her enjoyment. She uncovered depths of human motives and emotions behind the actions of the characters, and plots and settings shrouded in symbolism. But, best of all, every Tuesday afternoon, she could count on Hank smiling when he saw her and filling her afternoon with his clever witticisms. Deanna knew he was a much more worthy object of her infatuation than Mike Murphy had ever been. However, every Tuesday morning before class, she concealed her jitters from her friends and roommates, as well as her thrill at his smile when she arrived. It would have hurt too much to be teased.

"You really progressed this semester. It's refreshing to see a student grow in understanding, and appreciation of literature," Hank praised her when she came to pick up her final paper, a literary analysis of *The Adventures of Huckleberry Finn.*

Smiling artificially and nervously intertwining her fingers, Deanna replied stiffly, "Thanks. I learned a lot in this class." Unsure of what to do next, she looked around the office. Two desks were pushed against each wall. A corkboard or whiteboard hung above each. An arrangement of yellow silk flowers sat on a tidy desk. Pinned to its corkboard were inspirational sayings calligraphied onto parchment. The board next to it contained more Chinese restaurant takeout menus than notes. Hank's whiteboard appeared to have randomly scribbled words or phrases in three clumps. A few torn scraps of paper were taped to it as well. On closer inspection, Deanna realized it was divided into three columns. The left contained notes about classes he was teaching, the center was for classes he was taking, and the right was designated for non-school related reminders, including an appointment slip for the dentist.

Breaking the extended silence, Hank said, "I don't have control over the final grades, but I've given my recommendations to Dr. Lopez. I hope he listens to me better than my students do."

Deanna's attention returned to the attractive man in front of her. "What do you mean? Everyone loved listening to you."

"No, I was just a boring TA droning on about obsolete books."

"You were not. I'd already read several of the books we discussed, but I missed all of the most important information until you pointed it out."

"Yes, you listened. That's why you're on the 'recommended for an A' list." Hank made imaginary quotation marks in the air. "One out of twenty students listening to me, hmm, that's not a great percentage. I may not be a math major, but I know that's only five percent. Not going to win me teaching assistant of the year."

"Everything you said was fascinating. I'm sure everyone listened as attentively as I did."

"Stop," Hank said, holding his palm up to Deanna's face like a crossing guard on a busy street. "We regress to speaking in hyperbole. Remember, that is not allowed in my class. The reality is, you listened consistently, most students listened sporadically, and a few ignored everything I said." Hank shook his head and released a defeated sigh. "It's hard to convince students that hundred-year-old books can clarify their beliefs and shape their worldview." Smiling at Deanna he continued, "I really appreciated your comments and insights. It seemed like you got a lot out of the course."

"Oh, absolutely. I loved this class. In fact, I think this has been my favorite college class so far. If I wasn't committed to being an education major, you would have convinced me to switch to literature," Deanna said, remembering his opening-day speech.

"Education, huh?" He tipped his head, pursed his lips, and squinted at her, sizing up this new revelation. "Yeah that fits. I bet you have a bunch of little siblings you love to boss around."

"No. I'm an only child, and I think I should be

offended by that comment." Deanna crossed her arms in mock offence.

"Not at all. I happen to like bossy women. You should consider it a compliment."

Hank flashed a flirty smirk. Deanna's breath caught in her chest, preventing her from arguing her point further. After a gap during which Deanna's heart raced as she forced herself to inhale and exhale in a regular pattern, she replied, "I may not have bossed around brothers and sisters, but I was a slave driver to my dolls and stuffed animals. My grandmother says that even as a toddler I played school instead of tea party. I lined up my inanimate pupils against the wall and paced back and forth at the front of my imaginary classroom, teaching shapes and colors. Unfortunately, I didn't know my shapes and colors at the time, so my dolls are very mixed up."

Hank laughed deeply and honestly. "Poor, confused dollies." He paused and looked down. "Um." Straightening the edges of the stack of unreturned essays he cleared his throat to speak but took some time before producing any words. "Maybe we could continue to discuss literature even after this semester is over?" Glancing up with a hopeful expression, he clarified, "I mean, maybe we can talk over a coffee sometime? Or…um…that is, if you want to."

Deanna's heart accelerated to double time. Her palms turned slick with sweat. She hoped he was asking her out. Afraid to act as if this was a potential date, in case it wasn't, she shrugged and replied, "Yeah, sounds great." She attempted to sound indifferent, but her voice came out shrill and clipped. With a spastic jerk of her head, she swung her long brown hair out of her face. "Did you have a book in mind?" She wanted to take back those last words as soon as they were out of her mouth. If he had been asking her out she just turned it into a friends-only thing.

"Well, actually, we don't need to talk about literature at all…that is… unless you want to. I mean…yes, of course… we certainly can discuss a book since I'm a lit teacher. What are you reading now? Maybe I've read it," Hank babbled, recovering his composure a little.

"No. No, we don't need to discuss literature," Deanna interjected, hoping to undo the blunder she made. "I'd love to talk with you about anything, but not over coffee. I'm not a coffee drinker. Everyone said that would change when I got to college, but I still can't stand the stuff."

"To be honest, I'd rather take you to dinner than coffee, but that seemed like a little too much to ask for; too high of stakes for the first approach." The twinkle was back in his eyes as the corner of his mouth turned up into the teasing smirk she had admired during the last few months.

"Dinner works for me. I may not drink coffee but I do eat dinner every single day," Deanna said coyly. For the first time since entering the office, her facial muscles relaxed into a genuine smile. Her nervousness was gone, replaced by a powerful feeling of flirtatiousness.

"Great," Hank said. "How about tomorrow at six? We could meet at The Old Spaghetti Factory."

Deanna nodded eagerly. "I love Italian food. That sounds perfect." At a loss for anything else to say, and fearful of saying the wrong thing and causing him to retract the offer, Deanna gave a departing nod and smile. "Well, I'll see you tomorrow." Pausing in the doorway she asked, "Do you want my number, just in case something changes in the meantime?"

"I've already got it." Hank stopped suddenly and blushed slightly, and very uncharacteristically from what Deanna had experienced during the past semester. "Oh, no. Now you've caught me. You see, I have access to student records. I, sort of, looked up your number, in case you didn't come by to pick up your paper, or you came with a group so I couldn't talk to you." He sheepishly dipped his head, his brown eyes gazing beseechingly through the strands of his shaggy hair, pleading for mercy with the endearing expression of a lovesick puppy dog.

Deanna turned to leave. "See you tomorrow at six," she

said over her shoulder. She crossed the campus with a bounce in her step and a radiant glow on her face, oblivious to the curious glances of her fellow students.

"Are you up yet, honey?" Mary carried a long white gown protected by a clear plastic garment-bag as she entered her daughter's room. Deanna snapped back to the present. She'd slept in her old bed last night and awoken with butterflies in her stomach this morning, because today was her wedding day. This evening she would be Mrs. Henry "Hank" Floyd. Pushing the puffy pink comforter aside, Deanna jumped out of bed and hugged her mom tightly. No more daydreaming; reality was better.

Fifteen Years Before

Steam rose from an oversized, white mug in Greta's right hand as her left hand fumbled to cinch the belt on her threadbare, terrycloth bathrobe. Abandoning the futile attempt, Greta padded in fuzzy yellow slippers from the kitchen to the front room.

"Hi Grandma."

Greta startled, nearly spilling her tea. Then, she smiled warmly. "Oh, you're up already."

Deanna was sprawled on the couch, wrapped in her favorite pink fleece Disney princess blanket. She tipped her head and scrunched her bright blue eyes in a question. Then she laughed a tinkling laugh of carefree innocence and resumed watching a Saturday morning television show. Greta deposited herself into her recliner. She half-heartedly tried to figure out the convoluted misunderstandings of the teens on the screen while sipping tea and continuing to manipulate her robe to cover the large swatch of exposed blue nylon.

A commercial break interrupted the program. Deanna popped upright and asked, "Is my cinnamon toast ready?"

"Are you asking me to make cinnamon toast for

breakfast?" Greta prompted. Setting her mug on the doily covered end table beside her chair, Greta prepared to get up and do her granddaughter's bidding.

"You didn't make it yet? You said you would."

Greta stopped, poised at the edge of the seat. Giving her granddaughter a squinty-eyed, doubtful look, she asked, "When did I say that?"

"Earlier. When I came in your room. Remember?"

"No. I don't remember."

Deanna giggled. "Yes, you do."

Instantly, Greta's body tensed in hyper-alertness, as if Deanna had doused her with cold water. "I don't think so. You were asleep when I got up."

"Un huh." Deanna contradicted her grandmother cheerfully, assuming this was playful teasing. "You wanted me to climb in bed with you so you could keep reading, but I wanted to watch TV. You promised to make cinnamon toast as soon as you got up."

Remaining rigid on the lip of her chair, Greta reviewed her morning. She'd woken up, read a few pages in her book, then headed to the kitchen to make tea and wait for Deanna to rise. She had neither seen nor spoken to her granddaughter since last night when Mary and Dean, her daughter and son-in-law, dropped Deanna off and left to celebrate their anniversary weekend together.

"I did not see you earlier this morning," Greta reiterated adamantly.

Deanna's face puckered in confusion. Slowly, her expression brightened and she chuckled. "Oh, I get it. You didn't see me because you were looking at your book."

Greta's eyes widened in concern. Deanna's story was untrue. It had been late last night before Mary and Dean finally left. They hadn't begun packing until after dinner. By the time they'd dropped Deanna off, she'd stumbled groggily through Greta's house like a drunken sailor and went straight to the extra bedroom and climbed into the spare bed. Deanna had not made an appearance earlier this morning and there had been no previous conversation. Why was her granddaughter lying, and persisting in such an absurd lie?

Greta rose to her feet. With a severe expression, she admonished her granddaughter. "You are not telling the truth. I'm going to make cinnamon toast and I hope you will drop this ridiculous story before I return with your breakfast."

Greta entered the kitchen and popped bread into the toaster. In the past, when Deanna fibbed it was always to avoid punishment. When confronted with the truth, she would dissolve into contrite tears and confess through trembling lips with jagged breaths. Greta reached up into the cupboard and grasped the plastic bear filled with a mixture of sugar and cinnamon. An alternate possibility occurred to her. Perhaps Deanna had dreamed the nonexistent conversation of this morning. That seemed more likely than fabricating and sticking to a detailed account of an insignificant event. In Greta's subconscious, just beyond awareness, a hazy possibility loomed that she might have forgotten the conversation shortly after it transpired, but the thought was obscured by a thick fog of denial. Greta cut the toast into triangles and delivered it to Deanna on a small, pink, plastic plate. "I think you must have dreamt that we talked this morning. You were still asleep when I got up." Greta finished with a confident nod.

Deanna snickered. "Silly Grandma. It wasn't a dream." Deanna pulled her knees up to her chest. The taut blanket over her legs created a fuzzy table of sorts. Balancing the plate on the fabric between her knees, she munched and directed her attention toward the television.

"Deanna, this is not funny anymore," Greta scolded.

Deanna turned her head, pointing her face toward her grandmother while keeping her eyes glued on the TV, where two teenage girls crouched behind potted plants and eavesdropped on the boys they were stalking. "What?" Deanna mumbled through a full mouth.

Greta pointed a condemning finger at Deanna,

prepared to confront and correct. Suddenly, the hidden possibility that her memory might be the culprit broke through to Greta's consciousness. Nothing came out of Greta's open mouth. Her eyes widened in fear and her extended finger trembled. Dropping her hand and her head, Greta retreated to her familiar cushy recliner. Deanna laughed at the slapstick comedy and farcical plot, oblivious to her grandmother's labile emotions, while Greta repeatedly replayed the morning in her mind. No matter how hard Greta tried, she could not remember seeing Deanna earlier in the morning. And no matter what logic she applied, it was unlikely her granddaughter made up the elusive conversation.

The Wedding Day

"Deanna." Mary tapped on the bathroom door. "I'm heading down to the church to set up. Aunt Audrey is going with me. Are all of the little holiday baskets for the pew ends inside the boxes in my car?"

"See you when you get back," returned Deanna, ignoring her mother's question since Mary knew the location of wedding supplies better than anyone else. Deanna stepped into the shower of the jack-and-jill bathroom that connected her bedroom to the guest room, which had turned into the wedding storage closet.

Mary and her sister-in-law, Audrey, crossed the garage and seated themselves in Mary's blue Toyota Avalon.

"I wasn't sure about a Christmas wedding when you first told us, but it's making the season more exciting rather than taking away from it. In fact, I think I'm enjoying the preparations for Deanna's wedding more than I did my own children's," Audrey rambled in her usual rapid, stream of consciousness narration. "I'm not sure if it's because I'm not paying for anything, or just that it is so nice to have another wedding in the family. It's been such a long time."

Mary gave a noncommittal "umm" as she backed out of the driveway and turned onto the tree-lined street. She drove through a hazy December mist toward the main drag of her rural town. Deanna had chosen to hold the ceremony in the small, historic Methodist church they'd attended when she was little, before she'd followed friends to a larger church with an active youth group and Dean and Mary had followed her. The long center aisle and rich, dark wood altar railings were Deanna's vision of the perfect wedding venue. Mary had urged her friends to come early for a good seat because the sanctuary would barely accommodate the expected two hundred guests. The church was on the opposite side of the town from their house, which meant about a mile away. Mary drove while Audrey delivered a running monologue. "Do you have a plan for where each item goes? Did you look up the proper way to secure them? The internet makes figuring these things out so much easier. Of course, not everything on the internet is right. We'll have to just do some trial and error to see what works best." Audrey twisted around to inventory the wedding decorations in the back seat.

"Do you realize it has been almost ten years since my Elaine got married, and of course fourteen since John Junior's wedding? We tried to talk John Junior into waiting a little longer, but he wouldn't listen. You know how kids are. Besides, we didn't realize at first that they couldn't put the marriage off. Kids don't seem to follow the same rules nowadays that we did, but I'm glad things have worked out for John Junior and Monica. And their girls! I know all grandmothers think they have the cutest grandchildren in the world, but you have to admit, John Junior and Monica's children are the three cutest girls you've ever seen. And the oldest has turned into such a lovely young lady. Not that Elaine's kids aren't cute, mind you, but there is something special about John Junior's children." Audrey had always been a talker. Whenever Mary was annoyed with her husband for being too quiet, he blamed it on his sister. Dean claimed his sister had spoken for him since the day he was born, eliminating the need, as well as preventing the opportunity, for developing the skill of speaking for himself.

"Yes, your grandchildren are cute," Mary agreed dryly.

Audrey continued, oblivious to Mary's lack of enthusiasm. "Do you think Deanna will have children soon? How much school does she have left, anyway? John Junior had one year of college left when he and Monica got married but he was able to finish and now he is doing very well. He just expanded his office and is hiring two more paraprofessionals." Audrey shifted a bolt of tulle off the top of one of the boxes in the back seat in order to examine the contents.

"Deanna has one semester left to finish her teaching credential," Mary answered, even though Audrey's prattle would continue with or without responses. "And, I think they plan to wait a while for children. Hank wants to teach at the college level, but can't find anything permanent without a doctorate." Mary remembered being in Hank's position. It seemed like only a few years ago that she had been struggling to enter academia, and now she was on the cusp of retirement. "I had trouble finding something permanent even with a doctorate. I hope he has better luck than I did."

"But you've taught at the college for years and years now," Audrey said, giving her sister-in-law a sideways glance.

"Yes, but I took the job because it was the only one I could get. Women with doctoral degrees were rare at that time. Plus, I went straight from college to graduate school, so I was young and had no work experience when I applied. Universities wouldn't touch me. I only got hired because the college was brand new and desperate for faculty."

"Well, you must like it since you've stayed there your entire career."

Mary tipped her head and puckered her brows, considering. "Yeah, I suppose I do. I've been there so long I know all the faults of the community college system, and sometimes I forget the benefits." Returning to their earlier conversation, Mary said, "Hank is applying to PhD programs all around the country, and where he gets accepted is where they plan to live next fall. It could be as far away as Connecticut."

"Oh my! I don't think I could handle it if my kids moved very far away. And you only have one. I don't know how you'll be able to stand it!" Audrey closed the top of the box, replaced the bolt of netting, and untwisted so she was looking out the front windshield of the car.

"Right now is a terrible time to be looking for a teaching job in California, anyway. Between the recession and the state budget issues, most districts have frozen their hiring. It may actually be easier for Deanna to find a job in a different state. Plus, I think they want to begin their married life with a great adventure."

"Adventure is fine and dandy, but it can't replace family."

Mary stopped talking to concentrate on driving. Making a left turn onto the usually quiet Main Street was difficult today. Evidently, last minute shoppers were early risers when it got down to the last weekend for holiday purchases. Mary wondered for the hundredth time why they'd scheduled the wedding on the Saturday before Christmas, and Audrey droned on like a talk radio station playing in the background. Audrey's constant prattle grated on Mary. Mary reminded herself that behind Audrey's rambling lay a generous heart which was fiercely loyal to family. And, since their family was so small, maintaining positive relationships was important. Audrey and John were Deanna's only aunt and uncle, and their children her only first cousins. They were, also, their only relatives in California. Mary had a large extended family in Nevada, but she saw them infrequently. She knew them primarily through Christmas cards.

Mary glanced at Audrey's profile. Her jaw bobbed up and down as she blabbered on, oblivious to Mary's lack of interest. There was a definite family resemblance between Audrey and her brother, Dean. Both were tall, thin, fair-skinned Nordics with pale eyes and delicate noses, although Dean's hair was darker. But that was where the similarity ended. Mary had to pry information out of her husband, whereas her sister-in-law's chatter was impossible to stop. Mary estimated Audrey must utter a thousand words for every one Dean spoke.

Inside the church, Audrey strung cascades of white netting from one pew to the next, showcasing the center aisle. Mary fastened a small basket of holly greens and red berries onto each pew end, securing the netting in its place, and creating a festive holiday ambiance.

Audrey reached the final pew at the front left of the church. Turning to Mary, she asked, "Will you and Dean be the only ones in the front row? John and I can sit here with you if you'd like. That way you won't be alone while Dean escorts Deanna in and gives her away."

It was a kind offer. Mary had not considered how she would feel sitting alone during the bridal procession and beginning of the ceremony. Now that she thought about it, she would be rather exposed, isolated on the front pew. Mary nodded. "Yes, I'd like that. Thank you for thinking of it. Up until last week I expected to have my mother next to me. But you must have heard we decided it would be too confusing for Mom. Besides, if she comes then both Deanna and I will spend all of our time hovering over her and worrying about her instead of enjoying ourselves." Mary pointed to the long, empty bench. "It does leave a rather big pew for just me, though."

"Yes, Dean told me on the phone a few days ago." Audrey practically clicked her tongue. "I have to admit, I was extremely surprised. After all, your mother helped you raise Deanna. I know you had to put her into a home a few years ago, but I didn't realize she was doing so poorly that she couldn't attend her only granddaughter's wedding."

Mary bristled at the condemnation. But, she pinched her lips together and attempted to ignore Audrey's scolding.

Mary wanted peace and harmony today more than she wanted to defend her decision to institutionalize her mother. Why did people uninvolved in making painful decisions always feel justified in expressing an opinion about them? Tapping her fingers on the back of the wooden pew, Mary took a deep breath before replying. "Well, Mom has had Alzheimer's a long time now."

"It hasn't been that long, has it?" Audrey said doubtfully. "Plus, I've heard that they have medication for that nowadays." Audrey considered her memories of Greta and amended, "I guess I did notice some forgetfulness at Elaine's wedding, but it didn't seem very bad, and I never saw anything before that."

Mary focused on Audrey with the same intensity she used when a student challenged her authority. "Mom was diagnosed with dementia several years before Elaine's wedding--the doctor didn't call it Alzheimer's at first--and it was a couple years before the diagnosis when I started to notice something was wrong."

"What! Deanna was still little then." Putting her hands on her hips, Audrey challenged, "Didn't your mom babysit Deanna back then?"

"She did, but in reality, I'd say they babysat each other after Deanna was in about fourth or fifth grade." Mary disregarded the unfair judgment she was receiving. Today was Deanna's wedding day. She was not going to ruin the day with a family fight.

Focusing above Audrey's head, Mary cued a frequently replayed scene from her life. "I remember the first time I noticed a problem with Mom's memory. It was Deanna's eighth birthday. I remember it clearly."

Fifteen Years Before

It was the night before Deanna's birthday party. Greta cut the tops off two large plastic bags and dumped the candies and cheap plastic trinkets onto the beige tile of the island in

Mary's kitchen. On the opposite side of the island, Mary added powdered sugar, cocoa powder, milk, and butter into a medium-sized Pyrex bowl.

It had already been a long night. Mary had put Deanna to bed before beginning the preparation for the party. But Deanna was too excited about the party to fall asleep. Mary had brought her two cups of water and read three extra chapters from the latest Magic Treehouse book before Deanna had finally been relaxed enough to tuck in for the night. By the time the cake was done baking, both Greta and Mary were yawning. Mary squinted to bring the wall clock into focus. Then she groaned. It was almost eleven pm and she had been running since six a.m.

"I bought a Lion King play set for Deanna's birthday," Greta said conversationally as she sorted the colorful mound in front of her. She pushed the little wrapped candies to the left and the toy trinkets to the right. "I also got a dress with those two lion cubs on it, Simba and the little girl lion— whatever her name is. It's the cutest thing you ever saw, with a pink and purple African motif." Greta paused, anticipating a reply from Mary. When none came, she stopped her task of party prize assembly and scrutinized her daughter. "What? Don't you think she'll like it? I know she's excited about *The Lion King.*"

Mary shrugged, added more powdered sugar into the runny brown frosting, and resumed stirring. "Yes, she loves *The Lion King* right now, but…"

"That's why this is an African safari party. It's the only thing she talks about lately. We're planning to see the movie on opening day, you know."

"Oh, she'll love the dress and the party tomorrow, but I'm afraid she could change her mind about a Disney movie very quickly. If one girl at the party says 'only babies like cartoons,' that will be the end of Deanna's love of *The Lion King.* She's turning eight and eight is a rather unpredictable and changeable age." Mary dipped a finger into the frosting, checking the consistency as well as tasting the sweet treat.

"Eight? Is she really eight? I thought she was turning seven." Greta gave a brisk shake of her head, as if attempting to expel the inaccurate number.

"Seven was a good year," Mary said wistfully. "If I could keep her seven a little longer I would. But no, tomorrow my little girl will be eight." Cradling the bowl of frosting in the crook of her left arm, Mary tapped the top of the cake with her right hand. "I think the cake is cool enough to frost. Do you want to do it or should I?"

"Me, of course. Cakes are a grandmother's prerogative," Greta stated emphatically. Then, Greta reached down and retrieved her faded denim tote bag. The bag had served her faithfully for decades, carrying typing and calendars back and forth from home to school during her years as a school secretary. Greta set the worn bag on the tiles next to the party prizes. She reached in and dramatically pulled out a small pastry bag, as if she was a magician pulling a rabbit out of a hat. "I don't know how you would be able to decorate the cake, even if you wanted to."

"With your pastry bag," Mary responded snidely.

"No!" Greta squeezed her decorating accessory protectively against her chest. With the pastry bag closely guarded by one arm, she stretched her other arm across the bar and grabbed the bowl of frosting from Mary. "Until you get your own, I decorate the cakes."

With a mischievous glint in her eyes, Mary slid into good-natured provocation. "I'll buy the cake before I buy a pastry bag."

"That's the problem with your generation: too fast to buy new things instead of buying the right things and taking care of them."

Mary cut in, finishing the oft-repeated lecture. "I should have a few good, sturdy, basic pieces--for the kitchen as well as clothing and furniture--and take care of them so I have them forever and ever to pass down to my great-great grandchildren who will not want them and will have no idea what to do with them." Greta clicked her tongue and shook her head at her daughter. It was truly a different era.

Greta covered the cake in a smooth layer of chocolate frosting then added a bright pink ring of piping around the top and bottom like two circles made out of small, overlapping seashells. She changed the decorator tip on the frosting bag in order to write on top of the cake.

"Should I write 'Happy Birthday Deanna' with a big seven below the writing or should it say 'Happy 7th Birthday Deanna?'" Greta peered at the cake, attempting to picture both possibilities. Cocking her head to the other side, she said, "I could put 'Happy Birthday' on top, 'Deanna' on the bottom, and a large number seven in the center."

Mary froze, keeping her hands submerged in the soapy water along with the pans and mixing bowls she was washing. Cautiously she corrected, "Mom, she's eight. Remember?"

"Eight! Really? All day I've been thinking she's turning seven."

Mary's stomach constricted, forming a hard knot. Could her mom have really forgotten their conversation so quickly? Mary's grandmother, Greta's mom, had developed Alzheimer's before passing away a few years ago, so Mary's mind immediately made the unpleasant leap to that insidious disease. Mary calculated the math in her head. Her mom was born in 1926 and now it was 1994. Sixty-eight years old. Young for dementia but not too young. Resuming her washing and attempting, unsuccessfully, to relax, Mary said, "Mom we talked about her age just a few minutes ago. Don't you remember?"

"We did?" Greta looked up. Doubt, mingled with a hint of fear, flashed across her face and into her enlarged eyes. Then, her expression hardened. Her eyes squeezing to narrowed slits. Insistence and denial won. "You're mistaken. You might have been thinking about it, but we did not talk about it." Greta returned her gaze to the cake and demanded, slightly manic, "What do you want me to write on the cake? I think I'll put happy birthday in an arch around the top with a big number seven in the center and Deanna's name below." Greta leaned over the cake, poised to begin writing, hoping to ease her sudden tension and restlessness with activity.

"Let me finish the cake, Mom," Mary said, drying her hands on a tea towel and reaching across the kitchen bar for the bag of frosting. Her slow movements and calm voice belied the gnawing in her stomach as it escalated into a quivering, nauseous mass.

"Fine. I'll go wrap her presents," Greta said, eager to escape from the crushing feeling that something was wrong and she could not figure out what it was nor how to fix it.

The following day, Deanna's party was a success. All ten of the girls invited attended. The early summer sun was warm and pleasant, not too hot yet, allowing the celebration to be held in the backyard. Balloons and streamers decorated the fence above Lion King posters tacked onto every other picket. As each girl arrived, she received colored chalk to add African decorations and safari pictures on the blank boards of the fence. When everyone was present the organized games began. Greta led the girls in a number of old games that were new to Deanna's generation. The girls chanted, "a-tiskit, a-taskit, a green and yellow basket," as one girl dropped a letter and another picked it up to chase the first girl around the circle. Next, Greta taught them chants with accompanying hand clapping motions. That afternoon, many a ponytailed cat chased a giggling mouse in and out of an ever-changing maze of clasped hands. The afternoon overflowed with smiles and carefree, high-pitched laughter. Finally, the cake and ice cream were eaten and the presents opened. Just like Deanna, the girls excitedly and impatiently awaited the new Disney movie, which was soon to be released. And best of all, Mary observed no gaps in Greta's memory. Mary reassured herself that yesterday had been an isolated occurrence, an anomaly. Greta had been tired and focused on decorating the cake and had not really been attending to their conversation. At least, Mary tried to convince herself that was what had happened.

The exhilaration of the celebration and Greta's success as a game leader drove away her nervous foreboding of the night before. Over the next year, however, Greta had to search for misplaced items frequently. Her keyring being the worst culprit.

One day in October, Greta slumped dejectedly in her recliner with an uninteresting talk show blaring from the TV. Outside, the crisp autumn wind swirled red and brown leaves down the street, in and out of the lengthening shadows. Right about now, her friends in Clovis would be saying their goodbyes in the restaurant parking lot, the wind whipping their hair into wild mohawks. All week she had looked forward to spending time with her old colleagues. Instead, she was listening to celebrities she did not know discuss pop culture events she did not care about. Greta scowled at the TV as if it had caused her to miss the luncheon. She did not want to watch, but entering her bedroom or kitchen would be even worse. Tomorrow she would put away the piles of discarded clothing covering her bed and the disorganized mounds of junk, dumped from drawers, cluttering the kitchen counter. Tomorrow she would also find her keys. She had to. Where could they possibly be? There weren't many places left to look.

Finally, the long, disappointing day drew to a close. Greta entered her disheveled bedroom. A mountain of clothes, with all the pockets turned out, lay on the bed. She moved them to a chair. The pile reached to the top of the chair back. She unpinned the floral brooch from her blue blouse—the brand-new blouse she bought for today's luncheon—and lifted the lid to her jewelry box. Greta stared, stunned. Propped on top of her small collection of costume jewelry was the metal circle with her car and house keys. Why were her keys inside her jewelry box? And worse, how did they get there? She could not remember having her keys at any time today. She did not have them when she dressed for her outing and chose the pin. The last time she saw them or used them was yesterday morning when she dropped Deanna off at school. She was positive she had not touched them today. She either left them in a pant or jacket pocket or dropped them into a kitchen drawer when she got home yesterday. They had to be in a pocket or a drawer. But they weren't. They were in front of her, inside her jewelry box, mocking her.

The next day, when Deanna arrived after school, Greta bundled them into the car and headed to Walmart. They collected soap, shampoo, a new vinyl tablecloth with autumn leaves, and a few snacks in their shopping cart. Then, as Deanna maneuvered the cart toward the checkout stand, Greta said, as if by a sudden inspiration, "I wonder if they have a small basket or something that I can use to hold my keys?" They zig-zagged up and down the home office aisles. The shelves contained tape, envelopes, scissors, and other items unsuited for Greta's purpose.

Deanna lead her grandmother to the home decoration department. Two steps down the first aisle, the perfect piece caught Deanna's eye. She grabbed it off the shelf, spun around, and proudly held up for her grandmother's inspection and approval an eight-inch, black wrought-iron skeleton key with three hooks along the spine for holding other keys. They added the decoration, plus hardware to hang it, into their basket, hurried to the checkout stand, and headed home to begin their new project. Fortunately, neither the wall decoration nor Greta's keys were heavy, so without bothering to find studs, they attached the new key holder to the kitchen wall near the door into the garage. Entering the house and immediately turning to the left to hang up keys quickly became a habit for Greta, saving her from the frequent annoyance of searching for them.

Mail, however, replaced the problem of lost keys.

"Have you see my mail?" Greta asked with artificial nonchalance one Tuesday afternoon in February.

"Nope. Haven't seen it," Deanna answered as she

opened up her history book and dropped it on the kitchen table. She flipped pages until she found pictures of Native American villages. The best pictures were the tribal, ceremonial costumes. She examined the beaded fringe of the women's tunics and ignored the names, dates, and locations she was supposed to memorize.

An hour later Deanna yelled from the bathroom, "Grandma, I found your mail."

"Oh, did I take it in there?" Greta tried to trigger a memory of picking up her mail today and taking it with her into the restroom. No such memory existed. Anxiety bubbled up in her stomach and tension knotted her shoulders over the unrecallable event.

Deanna emerged and proudly offered her grandmother a couple letters and a magazine. "There was a pile of towels on the counter with the mail stuck right in the middle of it. I barely saw it. Just one corner of the magazine was sticking out." Greta's muscles relaxed. Her shoulders dropped several inches with relief. This memory was present. Earlier today she had washed a load of towels. She could picture herself on the couch folding and stacking the clean towels into a precarious turret. Tension ricocheted back, tightening Greta's neck and shoulders. That was where the memory ended. Did she stop in the middle to go get the mail? No. She'd gotten the mail when she finished lunch. Or was that lunch yesterday? Or last week? Why were recent events so hard to keep in chronological order? Memories were like naughty gnomes who delighted in randomly running around and reordering themselves just to confuse her.

Fitting each day's events together reminded Greta of Deanna's favorite preschool picture book, which had animal bodies on three interchangeable flaps. The top flap contained six different animal heads. The middle flap had a choice of six bodies in various outfits, and the bottom flap pictured the corresponding feet in silly shoes. Deanna loved creating a smiling lion's face on top of a tutu clad hippo with alligator feet in rain boots. The cardboard book was easier for Greta to visualize in her mind's eye than this morning's activities.

"Thank you, dear," Greta said with an affected air of indifference. She took the mischievous mail from Deanna. "Put those towels into the linen closet in your bathroom." With the letters in hand, Greta retreated to the front room and dropped onto the end of the couch, the same spot where she'd sat with the laundry earlier today. Tapping the top letter with her finger, she racked her brain trying to remember how the mail and towels had gotten combined. It fit together as poorly as the lion head, hippo body, and alligator feet.

8:30 a.m. Alone

The Wedding Day

Deanna emerged from her bedroom and wandered across the family room. Her long, brown hair hung wet and loose down her back, creating a dark spot of moisture on her old t-shirt. Deanna could not remember when she got this shirt nor where it came from. After innumerable washings, its inconsistently faded blue looked like a single-color tie dye. It had also lost its shape. For some reason, this shirt shrank in length while it expanded in width. It was proportioned to fit the oval torso of a Who from Whoville better than it fit Deanna. But, its comfortable worn cotton prevented it from ending up in the rag bag, even though it was in worse shape than many shirts that had preceded it to that inevitable fate.

Deanna paired the top with sweatpants from her coed wardrobe. As a freshman, she had envisioned herself displaying school spirit while sprinting late to class in logo sweats. Even though she had finished her four-year degree (in four and a half years) and completed a year of the teacher credentialing program, every letter was intact, spelling FRESNO STATE down the left leg of the bright red sweat pants. Clearly, she had not raced late to class very often.

Deanna scanned the empty family room. Santas of different sizes and styles greeted her from the mantel and decorative snowmen peeked out from the bookshelf, but there were no humans to be seen. "Hello. Anyone here?" she called. No answer. It was too early to get ready for the wedding—Deanna needed a diversion. She passed through the arched doorway into the formal living room and dining room at the front of the house. "Hello?" she tried again. Still, no answer.

It had felt like the wedding celebration had begun in earnest twelve hours ago, with people bustling in and out of every room. After the steak and wine rehearsal dinner, Deanna's friends and extended family had returned to the house to discuss plans for today over cake and coffee. This morning, only the dirty dessert plates stacked in the sink and disposable cups in a trash bag leaned against the kitchen island attested to the activity of the night before. "Where is everyone?" Deanna asked the silent air. She looped through the house and ended up back in her bedroom. Picking up one of her shoes for today, she twisted it around, admiring it from multiple angles. Deanna loved the scallop of golden bling around the open toe and top of the simple pump. The two-inch heel left her an inch shorter than Hank. Perfect. She fingered her dress through the plastic protector as it hung from the door jam on the outside of her closet. This was going to be a wonderful day once it got underway, but where was everyone now?

Deanna's mom and aunt were at the church arranging and rearranging candelabras, netting, and flowers. Early during the wedding planning Deanna had made the mistake of suggesting, "Let's have the florist set up the flowers and decorations at the church." Neither her mom nor her aunt trusted a florist with the placement of candlesticks and the scattering of flower petals, even if the florist did two or three weddings every weekend. They were appalled Deanna would even consider it.

Deanna's father, extended family, and close friends were at The English Garden preparing for the reception. For some reason, Mary and Dean had opted to set up the tables, chairs, and place-settings themselves instead of paying the caterers to do the work. Deanna's parents had given her an extensive wedding allowance, but then they'd decided to be frugal in various illogical areas.

This morning, as everyone completed the tasks that had been removed from the wedding budget, Deanna was left alone. With an audible sigh, she flopped down on her bed and glanced at the blue glow emitted from the numbers on her alarm clock. Nothing to do and no one to talk to for the next hour and a half. She felt lonely and a bit forlorn; everyone seemed more concerned about the wedding than the bride. Not that she wanted to decorate the church or reception venue, but she wanted company, others to share in her happy anticipation. Solitude made Deanna think of her grandmother. Perhaps Greta hadn't minded being single and raising a daughter on her own when she was young, but as she got older she craved company. She'd told Deanna so.

Thirteen Years Before

"Is that you, Deanna?" Greta called from her place on the worn recliner when she heard someone fumbling with a key at the front door. The key suddenly caught and the door flung open, lunging Deanna forward into the room. With two quick, large steps Deanna caught her balance. "It's me, Grandma," she yelled. She kicked the door shut with her left foot and a reverberating bang announced her presence. The gray tabby, aroused from his nap, sprang off Greta's lap and sauntered across the room to weave in and out between Deanna's legs. Deanna dropped her purple Jansport backpack on the floor and scratched the top of his head as he purred and postured to facilitate petting. Deanna trotted toward the kitchen anticipating her afternoon snack. Greta pushed herself up out of the chair and followed her granddaughter. Usually something tasty and of limited nutritional value lay on the table, anticipating Deanna's arrival. Something Mary refused to buy and Greta refused to eliminate. Today the basket containing condiments sat in the middle of the table and an old newspaper awaiting the recycling bin lay on the far end, but the table was devoid of anything edible. Deanna cocked her head and spun around toward her grandmother. "What's for snack?"

"Oreo cookies and milk. Didn't I put it out? Oh well, it's a good thing I didn't or the milk would be warm by now." Greta glanced at the clock over the stove. "You're almost an hour late! Was there a problem with the bus?" Greta retrieved the package of Oreos from her pantry, which was a floor-to-ceiling cupboard beyond the table.

"I know. I was talking to some girls and we missed the bus. I had to walk," Deanna grumbled, trying to sound inconvenienced, even though there was some intentionality in being so engrossed in their conversation that they did not see the other children boarding the large, yellow school buses nor hear the diesel motors revving to leave.

"You should have gone into the office and called me," Greta said, concerned. "I would have come and gotten you."

"I know but one of the girls—her name is Ashley—she only lives a few blocks away, so we walked together. You weren't worried were you?" Deanna pulled the half gallon of milk out of the fridge as she spoke.

Greta took some time to contemplate the casual question. "Honey, I wouldn't say that I worry--not about you, anyway--but I look forward to our afternoons together. This house is too quiet when it's just me and the kitty."

Deanna turned to look at her grandmother, surprise and concern emanating from her young face. "Oh Grandma, I'm sorry. I didn't think it mattered if I was a little late," Deanna apologized, then returned to pouring two glasses of milk and replacing the cardboard carton in the refrigerator.

Greta's face remained serious, even though her tone lightened. "It shouldn't matter. You need to have time with friends and a chance to be a girl. I'm just being a selfish old lady."

"No you aren't. I shouldn't have been so late."

"Don't you worry, dear. It's fine. It's just that I have never liked being alone and the older I get the less I like it." Greta set two small plates in front of their usual chairs and placed the open package of Oreos on the table. She sat down, waiting for Deanna to bring the milk.

Deanna slowly and carefully moved toward the table, carrying a full glass in each hand. "You aren't alone. You have Mom and Dad and me." Greta slid Deanna's chair out to facilitate the precarious motion of sitting down without spilling the brimming glasses. They moved like two well-rehearsed dancers. Deanna's bottom settled on the seat simultaneously with the glasses touching the table, one in front of each of them.

Greta nodded. "You're right. I do. But, this house seems so empty when you aren't over here to keep me company. For some reason, I have no motivation to do anything when I'm here by myself. You'd think I'd be used to being alone by now." Greta leaned in close, as if sharing a secret. Conspiratorially she whispered, "I may have spent most of my life alone, but I don't really like it."

Deanna, in her ten-year-old naive sincerity, wrapped her arms around her grandmother and squeezed her tight. Solemnly she promised, "I'll never be late again. You took care of me so now I'll take care of you." With a melancholy grin, Greta returned the hug, and feared Deanna's innocent comment might prove to be prophetic.

Greta and Deanna dunked their Oreos into the cold milk. They were dunkers, not separate-and-lickers. Between bites, they chatted about the small things that were big in the world of fifth grade. Greta learned that three boys, two named Matt and one named Justin, did the best and most dangerous tricks on their skateboards, and that yo-yos were making a comeback. Deanna informed her grandmother she could no longer include Nancy Drew books on her reading log. Greta's mouth dropped open in dismay as she questioned the teacher's sanity. "What could possibly be better for you to read?"

Deanna chomped her cookies and continued to mull over the problem of her grandmother's solitude. An idea came to her. A really good idea. It was so good Deanna bounced up and down on the squeaky chrome chair. "Grandma," Deanna spouted, "I know what you should do! You should call your friends, the other helpers at the school where you worked, and plan a party. You can go somewhere with them and I'll walk home with Ashley that day. That way, you won't have to be alone while you wait for me."

"Oh, don't worry about me, dear. Besides, I don't know where their phone numbers are."

"I do." Deanna jumped up, ran over, and pulled open to the draw next to the silverware. Inside, under a few loose papers and the local yellow pages, was a five-by-seven address book. "I only know Mrs. Kim and Mrs. Smith," Deanna said. "Aren't there two other ladies who go to lunch with you guys?"

"Yes. Pam Goodly and Janet Burnett. We worked together for years in the school office. I do miss them, but I don't get together with them anymore."

"I thought you guys went to lunch together every month?"

"They go. I haven't joined them in a long time. I usually don't feel like going out. Plus, they all live in Clovis and I don't like to drive that far."

Deanna refused to be dissuaded. If her grandmother was lonely then getting together with friends would fix the problem. The answer was too obvious to ignore.

"I have the perfect solution. Have them come here." Deanna grabbed her grandmother's personal phone book out of the drawer, dropped it onto the counter, and slammed the drawer shut, all in one excited movement. The cover of the small hardback book had originally displayed kittens playing with a ball of yarn, but now it was too faded to distinguish what type of animal the furry creatures were. "I can call them for you. I'll see if they can come next week so I can walk home with Ashley again." Deanna eagerly reached for the phone, proud of her brilliant solution.

Greta pounded her fist on the table. "Deanna, no! You put that down right now!"

Deanna startled and dropped the phone like a child caught with her hand in the cookie jar. With a waver in her voice she asked, "Why?"

Softening her expression and tone, Greta retracted her misplaced anger. "Tell you what. The next time they schedule lunch I'll go. But, I'm not going to call them and schedule anything!" Greta raised her eyebrows and gave Deanna a penetrating look of finality.

Deanna remained confused by her grandmother's refusal to initiate a lunch date with former coworkers, but she was satisfied that her grandma would have an outing with friends soon. Which also meant Deanna would have another opportunity to walk home with Ashley.

The afternoon passed like they all did. Deanna did homework and watched television, while Greta puttered in the same room as her granddaughter. Sitting at the kitchen table, Greta sewed a button on a blouse while Deanna read about the ancient civilization of Mesopotamia, then multiplied and divided fractions. After homework, they moved to the front room, where Greta dusted and rearranged the mantle as Deanna sprawled on the faded, floral couch and watched cartoons.

As evening approached, the phone rang. Greta made no effort to answer it. She remained in the recliner with her feet elevated. Deanna sat up brightly. "Do you want me to get that?"

Greta shook her head. "No. Let the machine pick it up."

"But it's probably Mom or Dad telling us they're home.

It might be time for dinner."

"They can leave a message easier than we can go and pick up the phone," Greta insisted. Deanna looked back and forth between her grandmother's stationary body and the jangling telephone, as if she was a spectator at a tennis match. After three more rings and a couple loud clicks, Greta's recorded voice erupted from the answering machine. In the staccato cadence of someone uncomfortable being recorded, Greta said, "You have reached the Miller household. Please leave a message. *Buzzzzzzz.*"

"Mom, Deanna, are you there? Well, Dean and I are home and we're starting dinner. It'll be ready about six. Come over whenever you get this message." The phone clicked off. Deanna jumped up from the couch and grabbed her backpack. Greta pushed herself out of the cushy recliner and shuffled toward the TV, reaching for the on/off button. But before she touched anything, the black rim surrounding the picture grew, widening until the entire screen turned dark. Greta shrugged her shoulders in feigned confusion. Deanna, with the black remote in hand, snickered behind her grandmother. Together they walked to Deanna's house.

Twenty-three years before

A few weeks before Deanna's birth, Greta retired after more than thirty years as the school secretary. She entered the school office on her last day to find multicolored crepe paper streamers and helium balloons filling the small work space. Her office coworkers, the principal, teachers, and parents-- many of whom had also been students under her reign-- jumped out of the tightly packed corners and yelled "surprise." The colorful decorations and successful surprise could not overcome the gloomy atmosphere. It felt more like a wake than a party. Guests embraced Greta and dabbed their eyes, lamenting the loss of Mrs. Miller's encouraging smile and efficient handling of the front desk. No one knew how the school was going to be able to survive without her.

Greta sought to maintain an appropriately stony exterior but failed to contain the gleeful sparkle in her eyes whenever she heard the words "your last day." She had no misgivings or regrets about leaving. This was the chapter of life she had been longing for. She was about to become a grandmother, and she planned to be involved daily in her grandchild's life. In order to carry out her plan, she had listed her house in Clovis with a realtor and put money down on a lot in the housing development where her daughter and son-in-law lived.

Three days after Deanna's birth, Greta waited in Dean and Mary's formal living room, perusing a magazine. Every minute or two she went to the front window and pushed the blue broadcloth curtain aside to peer out, impatiently anticipating her granddaughter's arrival. Finally, she heard a car pull into the driveway. Greta rushed to the front door and stood at attention as if she were a noble guard at the gate of a great castle, honoring the triumphant arrival of the long-awaited princess. The long-awaited princess part was accurate.

Dean was only half way through the door when Greta snatched the car seat from his arms and set it on the couch. She extracted Deanna from the buckles and straps. Lovingly, she rocked and cooed the sleeping infant. Dean flopped down in the chair closest to the front door and rubbed a crook in his neck. The extra bed in the birthing center had been far from comfortable. Mary gingerly waddled through the front room and into the family room, keeping pressure on the incision site of her C-section with one hand.

"I have turkey sandwiches, potato chips, and iced tea for you on the breakfast counter," Greta said as she gently loosened the pink flannel receiving blanket to examine Deanna's delicate hands and fingers. Dean reluctantly got out of the soft chair and headed to the hard oak bar stool. Mary slowly and gently eased herself onto the other stool, like a swimmer entering frigid water. "Did you notice the empty lot two doors over sold?" Greta asked between clucks and coos. They nodded without much interest and began eating. "Don't you want to know who your new neighbor is going to be?" Greta questioned.

Dean swallowed and answered, "I'm sure they'll be around watching the construction, so we'll get to meet them soon enough."

"I wonder who would buy that lot," Mary added between bites. "Because of the bend in the road the backyard will be a tiny triangle. I can't imagine anyone with kids would want to live there. Plus, I think only the smallest model fits."

"Your new neighbor is widowed with one grown daughter, so a small house and yard is perfect. You've met her before," Greta said. Her eyes twinkled as she struggled to hold in her mirth.

"Oh, is it someone you know?" Mary asked.

Greta laughed out loud. "I know her very well, because...she's me." Mary and Dean froze mid-chew. Only their enlarged eyes showed evidence of life inside the two human statues. "I sold my house and I'm moving to be closer to my granddaughter." Greta directed her attention to the infant in her arms. In a high falsetto she chirped, "We're going to be the best of friends. I'll come see you every day." Dead silence. Greta addressed Dean and Mary again. "Don't worry, I won't need to live here during the construction. I'll be able to stay where I am as a renter for the next four months while they build my new home." Greta reveled in the dumbfounded silence her announcement evoked.

Usually Dean enjoyed his fun, self-confident mother-in-law, and he admired the close relationship she shared with Mary; however, one hundred feet away was a little too close.

Thirteen Years Before

Deanna was quiet during dinner after the disagreement with her grandmother. She twirled her fork in her mashed potatoes, creating miniature mountains with high peaks and dangerous crevasses. They were her favorite food, but not a forkful of potatoes went into her frowning mouth. Mary waited uncomfortably throughout the evening, hoping Deanna would divulge her preoccupation. Finally, as Mary put her daughter to bed, they had the opportunity to talk alone.

"What's bothering you tonight, honey?"

"I'm worried about Grandma. She seems lonely but she doesn't want to go out and be around her friends. Today, she got mad when I tried to get her to call and talk to them. I don't get it." Concern shown in Deanna's eyes. Mary understood it. Withdrawing from social interactions, and especially phone conversations, seemed to be Greta's coping mechanism for her occasional forgetfulness. Perhaps more accurately, her lack of coping. Mary kissed Deanna's forehead and pulled up the comforter, tucking it in around Deanna's sides, pinning her arms down underneath. "Well, if Grandma seems lonely, then we'll have to spend some extra time with her doing fun things. Why don't you think about something special we can do? In the morning you can tell me what you've picked and we'll figure out when we can schedule it."

Deanna nodded, satisfied. Reassured that they could provide Greta with the social interaction she needed, Deanna closed her heavy eyes.

Mary sat on the edge of Deanna's bed for several minutes as her daughter meandered into unconsciousness. Then, Mary gently kissed Deanna's cheek and retreated to her own bedroom to take over fretting about Greta.

Deanna had just learned to smile and coo when Mary's maternity leave came to an end. On the first day of the fall semester. Mary wiped her eyes and kissed her baby girl before handing her over to Greta. Mary must have called her mother ten times that first day. Even as Deanna grew and Mary's new-mom anxiety shrank, the habit of multiple daily phone calls continued. Mary would call between classes and offer to pick up items from the store on her way home, or request her mom purchase something if Mary was running behind. Sometimes Mary could not bear to read another student paper without a break, so she would pick up the phone and enquire about Greta's day. Lately, Mary noticed, many calls to her mom went unanswered even though she knew her mother was at home. When Greta did pick up the phone, the conversation was short. Greta seemed to need to use the restroom within minutes of answering the phone, or the cat's water was empty, or the laundry was waiting, or some other trivial task was suddenly urgent.

The telephone was only one symptom. Several times in the past month Greta had adamantly insisted a recent conversation never took place. Just yesterday, Greta asked Mary twice what day of the week it was during a five-minute conversation. Greta was just as surprised that it was Tuesday the second time as she was the first.

Mary started asking co-workers with aging parents if Greta's behavior was typical. Unfortunately, the families battling Alzheimer's concurred while the others could not relate. News stories and magazine articles about dementia taunted Mary. Her hands grabbed the page and her eyes focused on the text, compelled to read, even as her stomach fought and churned in dissent. Each story put another chink in her fragile shield of denial. Mary attempted to avoid comparing her mother to the subjects of the articles, but the parallels were becoming un-ignorable. Even her ten-year-old daughter was noticing symptoms.

Mary hesitated to initiate a conversation with her mother about the increasing forgetfulness because she assumed Greta was unaware. Greta, on the other hand, thought she was successfully hiding her memory lapses from her daughter. Following phone conversations was becoming difficult, so Greta avoided the telephone. Remembering appointments was nearly impossible, so Greta turned down invitations for future events or activities. If she could dodge situations that were hard for her to remember then, hopefully, others would not notice how many things she was forgetting.

Some days Greta's mind stayed sharp. Her keys were hanging conveniently on their hook when she needed to go out. Her mail was waiting on the corner of the kitchen counter to be sorted while Deanna started homework. After several consecutive days with no lost items, Greta reassured herself that her memory was not all that bad; certainly not bad enough to merit any real concern.

On Wednesday morning, Mary popped into Greta's house before work, as she did most days. Greta was in the compact kitchen, putting a mug of water into the microwave to brew her morning tea. Mary lifted the shades, letting in the warm sun. "What are your plans for today Mom?" she asked.

"Oh nothing much. I'll just drink tea and read the paper until Deanna gets home this afternoon. What's on your calendar for today?"

"I have a couple meetings after my classes so I won't be home until fairly late. If it's really late I'll pick up Chinese takeout for dinner. If the meetings don't go as long as I'm expecting, I'll stop at the grocery store and get something to make. Either way, I need to stop somewhere because I'm out of everything. There is nothing we can eat for dinner in my fridge."

"Would you like me to go to the store for you?" Greta asked.

"Um, well...no. I don't think so. If my meetings run long I'm not going to want to cook and if they're short I'll have time to stop myself. Thanks for offering, though."

The buzzer on the microwave sounded. Greta removed the hot cup and set it on the counter.

"Ok, Mom. I've got to go. I'll see you tonight."

"Bye, dear," Greta called as Mary rushed off. Greta opened the cupboard above the microwave and retrieved a tea bag. She submerged it into the steaming water as she heard the front door shut behind her daughter. With steeping tea in hand, Greta crossed the kitchen and looked into the sugar bowl on the center of the table. It was empty. Setting down her mug she retraced her steps and opened the tea cabinet. On the righthand side of the lowest shelf sat a transparent, square, twelve-cup Rubbermaid canister. It held nothing but air and a few irretrievable sugar granules stuck in the corners. An orange sticky note adhered on top read "Out of sugar. Buy sugar" in Greta's loopy cursive. Turning around to glare at the cup of unsweetened tea on the table, Greta made a decision. She would go to the store and buy sugar and perhaps some meat and vegetables for dinner as well. Ignoring the rejected beverage, she started out the kitchen door into the garage. Realizing she should use the restroom before leaving, she turned around, and proceeded down the hallway to the door at the end which opened into the guest bathroom, or as Greta usually referred to it, Deanna's bathroom.

After emptying her bladder, Greta yanked the last few squares of toilet paper off the cardboard roll. She finished, washed her hands, and opened the cabinet under the sink to replace the empty toilet paper. There was none. Greta made the quick left from the hall bath into the master bedroom. She passed through the tidy, doily-filled master bedroom, heading to the door at the far end where she spotted another empty brown tube on the toilet paper holder. Inside the linen closet, on the floor, sat an unopened shampoo bottle, cleansers and sponges, a plunger, and nothing else; not a single roll of toilet paper. She was totally out. Even if she was not planning to go to the store before, she had no choice now. As she crossed the kitchen on her way to the car, Greta briefly considered stopping and writing down the needed items, but there were only two essentials, sugar and toilet paper, and picking up something for dinner was optional. Surely, she could remember her short shopping list.

Greta drove the five blocks to Town and Country Market, following her usual route. A large Safeway had opened nearby the previous year, but their shelving system was confusing. Nothing was placed where Greta could find it and the brands they carried were packaged differently, which had caused her to mistakenly buy the wrong item a few times. Greta preferred the friendly reception and familiar aisles of the smaller store. Turning into the parking lot, Greta pulled into a spot three spaces from the front door-- another benefit of shopping here. Entering the store, she grabbed a shopping cart and headed to the meat counter at the back to find something for dinner. Even if Mary did not want to make it tonight, it would keep for a few days. The butcher was placing packages of thick, lean pork chops into the chilled display. They were a lovely, moist and tender pink. Greta's mouth watered as she imagined eating them with potatoes and peas. She grabbed a package with four large chops. Next, she collected six russet potatoes, and a can of sweet young peas. Then she looked around. There was something else she'd come for. She was sure of it. The supplies in her cart were for dinner. Those were for Mary. There was also something she needed for herself. What could it be? She tried to remember but a dull, insistent pressure pushed on the top of her head, making it hard to think. She wondered if she drank any tea this morning. That would explain the headache. Perhaps she came for tea bags. She must be out of tea, why else would she skip her usual morning dose of caffeine?

Tea was in aisle four, one row to her left. Greta exited canned goods and twisted her basket around to made the sharp 180-degree turn to head up the beverage aisle. The endcap caught her eye. Fruit cocktail was on special at two cans for a dollar. One of Deanna's favorite snacks was fruit cocktail in Jell-O with a dollop of cool whip on top. Greta grabbed two cans of fruit cocktail and added them into her basket. The advertisement read "maximum quantity four cans." It must be an especially good price if they are limiting shoppers to four cans, so Greta took two more.

Tea was halfway down the aisle on the left. Greta found Lipton and placed the twenty-four count yellow box into her cart. Heading toward the front of the store to check out, Greta smiled, confident she had what she needed, and anticipating the succulent pork chops for dinner.

At the register she handed Sheila, the sales clerk, a ten-dollar bill to pay for her purchases. Sheila pointed toward Greta's wallet. "I need another ten. It's seventeen eighty-four." Greta stared at Sheila in wide-eyed disbelief. After ringing up Greta's purchases accurately for the past ten years, had Sheila suddenly become dishonest? Greta attempted to calculate an estimate of her purchases, but the mental concentration made the pressure inside her head increase to a bounding throb. It seemed unlikely Sheila was trying to cheat her, but it was hard to fathom that dinner for four people plus some tea and canned fruit—sale canned fruit at that—could add up to almost twenty dollars. Slowly, Greta removed another ten from her wallet and held it out, her fingers clinging to the bill in distrust. Sheila pulled on the other end. For several seconds, Mr. Hamilton's face was the rope in a tug-of-war. Reluctantly, Greta released her end. She received her change, picked up her bag, and left with her head pounding, ignoring Sheila's well wishes.

Greta needed to get home and drink some tea. Tea would relieve her headache. Then, she could study the sales receipt and determine if Sheila was still as honest as she used to be.

Immediately after entering her house, Greta put a cup of water into the microwave and removed the crinkly plastic wrapper from the Lipton box. She took out a tea bag to use and opened the cupboard above the microwave to put the rest away. Greta stared. Two boxes of tea bags filled the middle shelf already. She lifted them up. One was unopened and the other was nearly full. Greta attempted to squeeze the new box into the tight space above the existing boxes. It did not fit. With the new carton of tea bags in her hand, Greta turned around, and focused on the pantry. If she stored it there, would she remember where it was? Her attention was captured by a strong, full cup of tea sitting alone on the table. Greta's concern switched from Sheila's honesty to the unexplainable mysteries she was discovering in her own kitchen. Greta tossed the new, extra box of tea bags aside onto the counter. Deliberately and warily Greta scooted across her kitchen in a slight crouch, like a predator moving into position to capture its prey. At the table, she peered into the cold, full mug. Reversing roles, she carefully reached around the tea, avoiding it as if it were the sleeping predator and she the prey, dangerously close. Just beyond the menacing cup waited the blue willow patterned sugar bowl. Slowly, stealthily, Greta stretched her arm out, wrapped her middle and index fingers around the handle, then in one quick movement, which sent the sugar spoon clattering around in circles, rescued the bowl and escaped to the other side of the kitchen. Greta placed the piece of china down safely on the counter. In its new location, the ceramic bottom was clearly visible. Not a speck of sugar was inside. Greta glowered at the ungrateful crockery which seemed to be part of the conspiracy against her this morning.

Opening the tea cupboard again, Greta forced in the additional box, compressing it to fit in the shallow space available between the shelves. Next to the smashed Lipton boxes was an empty, re-sealable container for sugar. The note affixed to it prominently declared, in Greta's own writing, it was empty. Greta slammed the cupboard door shut. Yanking open the draw next to the sink, she dug through miscellaneous items and found a pad of sticky notes. She wrote "GET SUGAR" in large capitals and adhered the yellow square to the outside of the tea cabinet. She would surely see it there. Then, she continued to rummage through the back of the junk drawer until she found two wrinkled and discolored sugar packets from McDonald's. At least her tea would be the way she liked it. She mixed the sugar into her fresh tea and defiantly sat down at the table, boldly confronting the stale drink, holding a hot mug in her hands.

After a few soothing sips, Greta was ready to put away the other groceries. She deposited the meat and potatoes, still inside the store bag, into her refrigerator. Greta considered writing a note reminding her to bring the dinner items to Mary's house in the afternoon, but she decided the full, white plastic, Town and Country bag in her nearly empty refrigerator was an adequate reminder. Leaving the can of peas on the counter, Greta pulled open the pantry door to put away the fruit cocktail. Eight identical green labels on eight cans of fruit cocktail confronted her, lined up in military formation on the center of the middle shelf. Greta angrily glared at them, as if they were naughty children she could intimidate into acceptable behavior. Then, Greta sighed in defeat, her shoulders drooping in surrender. Greta added four new troops to the small battalion of tin cans gloating over winning the battle against her memory.

With nothing to do but wait for Deanna to arrive after school, Greta dropped into a chair at the kitchen table and finished her tea. She picked up the newspaper and scanned headlines, without giving her full attention to the current events of the world.

When her teacup was empty, Greta was headache free, less suspicious of the sales clerk, and frustrated but no longer defeated by her disastrous morning. She rehearsed in her mind how to tell Deanna about the trip to the store, maximizing the humor and minimizing her incompetence. A few minutes later, Greta rose to go to the restroom. As she entered the bathroom at the end of the hall, the empty, brown, cardboard cylinder on the toilet paper holder caught her eye. She immediately turned, entered her bedroom, and proceeded to the master bath where she saw an identical empty toilet paper roll. She was going to have to talk to Deanna about this. That child knew better than to use up the toilet paper and not replace it. An elusive image hid in the corner of Greta's consciousness. She vaguely remembered finishing a roll and not finding more to replace it. Greta leaned against the doorframe of the master bathroom, struggling to construct a concrete memory from the distorted, swirling tendrils of vague images. Did she leave the bathrooms without paper? No. That memory was so hazy it must be ancient. It could not be her fault; she would never leave both bathrooms without toilet tissue.

Brrrrring........Brrrrring. Greta grabbed the telephone beside her bed. "Hello?"

"Mom, I was getting some students' papers out of my trunk and I found the grocery bag with sugar and toilet paper. I bought it yesterday like you asked, but I forgot to bring it over. I'm sorry. Are you totally out or will you be ok until I get home?"

"I'm totally out of both. In fact, I just walked into the bathroom and fortunately I looked before using the toilet or I would be in real trouble right now."

"Well, I'm glad you noticed in time. Run over to my house and use our bathroom. You can take a couple rolls back with you. We've got extra. You've got your key to our house, don't you?"

"Of course, it's on my key ring. I'm going to go right now. I'll talk to you later."

"Ok. Sorry Mom."

"It's ok, Honey. The timing of your call was perfect. Bye."

Greta hung up and dashed over to her daughter's house. After using the restroom, she brought back two toilet paper rolls to equip her bathrooms. She remembered everything she needed to do. Greta felt better than she had felt all day. Her confusion this morning was probably related to caffeine withdrawal. The problem was not her memory; it was Mary's. Mary forgot to give her the new toilet paper. Mary failed to refill the empty sugar container. Mary worked too hard. Mary's mind was so full of school meetings and students' progress that everyday things like stocking the houses with sundries sometimes got skipped. Greta sighed with relief; Mary was the culprit for today's troubles.

After hanging up with her mother, Mary propped her elbows on the desk, supporting her chin in her hands. When

Deanna had expressed concern about Greta, Mary had considered scheduling a doctor's appointment. But after today's conversation with her mom, it seemed unnecessary, or at least premature. Her mother was doing better lately. If today was typical, then Greta did not need to have a doctor evaluate her memory.

10:00 a.m. Bad News

Thirteen Years Before

Two days later, on Friday, Mary waited in her office for nonexistent students to utilize her office hour. Soft rock emanating from a small, black radio filled the small room. Lecture notes awaiting review laid open on the desk. Mary ignored them. Instead, she leaned back in her desk chair, staring up at the angle where the ceiling and wall intersected. Her arms crossed over her white blouse and her gray slacks crossed at the ankles. Mary contemplated what to do about her mother. Over the past year, Dean frequently suggested Mary call their doctor to discuss Greta's forgetfulness. Mary knew a problem existed but she had resisted contacting their physician. What could the doctor do anyway? Calling now seemed hasty. Mary did not want to prematurely alarm her mother. And at this stage, Greta was sure to resist any discussion and refuse medical intervention.

This past week Greta had been sharp. Her memory seemed to be improving. Perhaps there had been an undiagnosed medical issue that was resolving on its own. There was no reason to expect it to return. Involving the doctor now, when Greta showed signs of improvement, was unnecessary. As Mary justified postponing notification of their doctor, a revelation hit her, as if someone had flipped on a light in a dark room. Maybe the doctor should evaluate Greta at her best rather than at her worst. Mary put her hands behind her head and leaned back as far as her ergonomically designed desk chair allowed. She swiveled the seat a few inches to the right, then back to the left, in a peaceful, rhythmic motion as her decision to call the doctor waxed and waned. Anyone walking past her open office door would have thought she was relaxed and carefree rather than embroiled in an internal emotional battle. Finally, Mary made a decision. Sitting up straight and slapping her palms on her desk, Mary deemed this was the best time to contact the doctor, appease her husband, and definitively identify what was happening to her mother's memory.

Mary's resolve held strong through the rest of the day, but not quite strong enough to place the call. That night in bed she informed Dean. "No one came to my office today so I had plenty of time to think. I've decided to call Dr. Gonzalez on Monday and schedule an appointment for Mom." Without lifting his face from his book, Dean responded with a droll, "Finally." In his peripheral vision, Dean saw Mary's face pucker in annoyance. Leaning over and giving her a reassuring kiss on the cheek, Dean said, "You're doing the right thing." However, the weekend forced Mary to wait through two long days of flavorless food and restless sleep before making the call.

Monday afternoon, after her classes, Mary sat alone in her office and stared at the telephone. She picked up the receiver and raised it to her ear in slow motion. With trembling fingers, she pushed the buttons on the base of the phone. She cleared her throat, attempting to loosen the swollen lump lodged there. A curt receptionist answered. All morning Mary had silently rehearsed describing her mother's forgetfulness and requesting an appointment, but when actually talking to a person, Mary's prepared script flew out of her brain, causing her to ramble and stumble. She sounded like one of her students, inserting "um," "like," and "y'know" into every sentence. The information Mary attempted to convey did not coincide with the standard scheduling form. After several unproductive minutes the receptionist sighed rudely and asked again, "Has she had any fever, vomiting, or diarrhea in the past twenty-four hours?" Now, Mary was irritated. With no attempt to hide her emotions, Mary scolded, "No. I've already told you, she is fine!" Then, Mary repeated a tortuous description of her mother's forgetfulness. The exasperated receptionist rolled her eyes and interrupted, "I don't know what kind of appointment you need if she is not sick, is not scheduling a follow up, and is not due for a physical. We don't have any other type of appointments! If you want to talk to the doctor about your concerns, whatever they are," she added in a snarky aside, "you can leave him a voicemail, but there's no guarantee he'll call you back." Without waiting for another convoluted response, the receptionist hit the transfer button, sending Mary's call to Dr. Gonzalez's voicemail, and returned to the tall stack of charts on her desk. Mary left a long, incoherent message during which her voice cracked and she dissolved into loud sniffing several times.

The next day at twelve forty, Dr. Gonzalez shook hands with his last patient for the morning. He ambled out into the front office, removing his lab coat and folding up his shirt cuffs. On the corner of the receptionist's desk, away from the mass of files and papers, he placed a prescription slip. The young woman swiveled her chair around, flashed a saccharine sweet smile, folded her salon manicured hands in her lap, and awaited his instructions with pristine interest. Greta's name and the phone number of a geriatric care clinic were scribbled on the back side of the paper. "Schedule a cognitive work up for this patient. Take the first thing they have available then bring the appointment to me. I'll be in my office on the phone with her daughter. Even though her daughter called me yesterday, I have a feeling I'll have to persuade her to agree to the work up. Hold everything else. I don't want to be interrupted and this might take a while." The young woman's head and dangling earrings bobbed in agreement. Her face furrowed at the gravity of the situation.

As soon as the doctor's office door clicked shut, the receptionist slumped in her seat and grabbed the slip of paper. Seeing the name, she let out an exasperated grunt and complained out loud, "What a waste of time! I can't believe he's calling that crazy lady back. She wanted an urgent appointment for this woman who isn't sick. And, the appointment has to be kept a big secret."

But the doctor, based on experience and training, had correctly interpreted Mary's confusing message and sympathized with her ambivalence about seeking medical help. A full twenty minutes elapsed before Dr. Gonzalez left his office to get lunch and Mary accepted the referral to take her mother to a geriatric and cognitive care specialty clinic. The earliest diagnostic appointment was eight weeks away, which meant Mary had eight weeks to fret and second-guess her decision.

The week of the appointment eventually arrived. Mary cautiously lifted her office phone off the cradle and slowly punched in the clinic number, prepared to cancel the appointment. All older people get forgetful. Her mother was no different than anyone else her age. "Geriatrics and dementia care, how may I help you?" the peppy female voice of someone in her twenties asked. Even though Mary had initiated the call, she startled at the voice and reflexively slammed down the receiver. Her heart raced and her palms sweated, like a junior high school girl calling a boy for the first time. She longed to cancel the appointment, but what would she tell Dean? Last night she'd broached the subject with him. She'd suggested postponing the appointment. Perhaps they were rushing into this. It might be better to wait until her mom's memory became problematic. Dean slid his reading glasses down to the tip of his straight, thin nose and turned to Mary. With a look of incredulity, he stated, "I can't imagine what level of confusion you consider 'problematic.'"

Mary scowled at the phone in indecision. The desk clock ticked slowly and her heart pounded rapidly in a dysrhythmic battle for control. Finally, she pushed the phone to the back of her desk, got up, and walked out of her office, slamming the door behind her. She would keep the appointment. After all, the doctor could just as easily say Greta had nothing wrong with her, outside of normal aging. The approaching appointment had ruined Mary's sleep and appetite for weeks already. Deferring it would force her to go through this miserable anticipation again. Keeping the appointment was the best of bad options.

As hard as it was to keep the appointment, informing Greta was even harder. Mary needed to give her mom enough prior notice to be prepared, but not enough time to concoct reasons to skip the evaluation. The ideal date to inform Greta had come and gone two days ago. Today was Wednesday and the appointment was scheduled for Friday afternoon. Today was the last possible day to tell Greta. It could be put off no longer.

"Mom, I made a doctor's appointment for you on Friday. I don't have any classes, so I can take you." It was early evening. Greta and Mary were in their usual spots. Mary prepared dinner at the kitchen island while Greta watched from her comfortable, padded stool at the breakfast bar on the other side of the island, across the sink. The empty family room opened up behind them.

"I'm feeling fine. Why do I need to go to the doctor?" Greta asked. After a pause during which suspicion sprouted, she added, "Plus, I can go by myself."

"The appointment is in Fresno and I don't like for you to drive that far," Mary said, evading the real question. She cut and rinsed broccoli crowns with focused precision, keeping her hands and eyes directed into the sink.

Greta waited for further explanation. None came.

"Why Fresno?" Greta watched her daughter intently, wariness growing as Mary continued to wash the same piece of broccoli. "Why aren't I seeing Dr. Gonzalez?"

"I spoke to Dr. Gonzalez and he suggested you go to Fresno." Mary turned to the stove, putting her back toward her mother. She dropped the well-scrubbed broccoli into a large frying pan along with the other unwashed flowerets. Her spine tingled with the prickly sensation of being watched. "Should I steam or sauté the vegetables?" Mary asked lightly, in an obvious attempt to avoid discussing the scheduled appointment.

"Sautéed tastes better unless you're on a health kick again. Now," Greta leaned forward, elbows on the tile, settling her chin on clasped hands, "tell me why am I going to the doctor?"

Greta's direct communication style had not changed over the years. She was still Mary's mother and she continued to speak to her daughter with parental authority when necessary. Realizing half-truths and evasions were not going to be possible, Mary took a deep breath and turned around, squaring off with her mother. She attempted to use her talk-reasonably-to-a-student-who-is-not-being-reasonable voice, but her mother's insistence drew out the insecurity of a little girl, and Mary's voice sounded nervous rather than certain. Mary had rehearsed this speech in her mind all day. It was like reciting a piece of prose. "Mom, you frequently complain about losing things, like your keys or the mail. You've told me your memory is not what it used to be, and—"

"I am seventy, you know," Greta interrupted.

Mary nodded, validating the comment. "Yes, you are seventy, and it's very possible there is nothing wrong. If they tell us this is normal for your age then all we've done is waste an afternoon." Mary returned to her memorized lines, direct quotes from Dr. Gonzalez' argument to persuade Mary into scheduling the appointment. "But, maybe there is something medically going on. There are several treatable medical conditions that can affect memory. Many of them are reversible as long as they are caught early. If this is a correctable medical problem you need to be evaluated in order to begin the proper treatment, and the sooner treatment begins the better the results. Even if it is not a treatable medical issue, a gerontologist can give suggestions for accommodations to minimize problems. " Mary was facing her mother, but focusing on the script in her mind's eye. At the conclusion of her speech, her vision shifted and the image of her mother's face appeared. Greta's pursed lips and contemplative expression prompted Mary to ask, "Don't you want to fix this if we can?"

Greta hated to acknowledge her periodic confusion. She had been trying her hardest to hide it. However, she could not refute the merit of Mary's concise and coherent argument, and the possibility of improving her memory was so appealing it made her almost giddy. Greta nodded, surprisingly quickly and vigorously, and said, "Yes, it would be nice not to lose and forget things. If there is a treatment that can help, I'm willing to try it. And, I'll let you take me because I don't like to drive in Fresno anymore. I don't know if it's my eyes or they have changed how they make maps, but I seem to get lost every time I go there. Plus, the traffic is getting terrible."

Mary smiled at her mother with relief. She reached across the island and grabbed Greta's hand, squeezing the thin, aged skin. "We'll see what they say." Mary was stunned at how quickly and easily Greta had conceded to the appointment. She remained oblivious to Greta's level of awareness and concern over her memory.

Time accelerated over the next day and a half. Friday rushed forward, shocking Mary and Greta with its rapid appearance. Mary backed her car out of the garage, drove a hundred feet, and pulled into her mother's driveway. Prepared and waiting in the car was a Ziplock bag with

Greta's medications—calcium and Fosamax—and a paper grocery bag with a change of clothes, a hairbrush, and a toothbrush and toothpaste. The evaluation was scheduled in two parts. First, a gerontologist would perform a medical assessment on Greta's cognition. Then, a therapist would evaluate Greta's ability to perform activities of daily living, such as grooming and dressing herself. "Understanding your mother's current functional level as well as her cognitive abilities will be important in developing a comprehensive plan of care," the gerontologic nurse specialist had informed Mary two weeks ago during a pre-visit phone interview. The call was designed to ensure Mary and Greta were prepared for the clinic visit, but it was that conversation which had prompted Mary to consider cancelling the appointment. Why did medical professionals make everything sound so sterile and distant? This was Mary's mom, not some theory on dark matter millions of light years away.

While the knot in her stomach gnawed and churned, Mary put on a forced smile, revealing her teeth but leaving her eyes dull. She opened her mother's front door and stepped inside. Greta sat idly and stiffly on the worn, print couch. Dressed in her best khaki slacks with a blue print top, Greta waited, maintaining perfect posture, like a child under strict orders to act properly in a hard wooden pew at church. "Hi, Mom. It's me. I'm going to make us an early lunch because this afternoon is your doctor's appointment, remember?"

"Of course I remember," she answered testily. Greta stood up and smoothed her pants, ensuring no wrinkles developed in the nicely pressed outfit. Marching into the kitchen, Greta grumbled, "I'm still not sure why I have to go to a doctor in Fresno. How will they know what's wrong with me when they have never met me before? For all they know my memory has been exactly like this my whole life."

Greta vacillated between being relieved and terrified of the approaching appointment. What if the doctor did find a problem with her memory? What then? She tried to reassure herself that knowing she was losing her memory would allow her to make the best use of her remaining productive years. But if they told her she would never get better, how would she motivate herself to try to remember things? A diagnosis of Alzheimer's, condemning her to progressive worsening symptoms, would be utterly depressing.

The Wedding Day

Ashley was the first of the bridesmaids to arrive. She opened the front door and peeked her head in, calling "Hello." Deanna rushed to the door, eager to welcome her friend and begin preparations for the day. "Hey, hey little bride. I brought something to ease the pain at your premature loss of freedom." Ashley held up a heavy brown paper bag from Bevmo. The movement caused glass to clink.

"I think you're the one who needs that to drown your sorrows that I got Hank and you have to put on a brave face and pretend that you aren't jealous."

"As if!" Ashley exclaimed with an exaggerated roll of her brown eyes and flick of her platinum dyed hair. "The only loss I'm feeling is the loss of my designated driver. I wonder if there's any other girl at Fresno State who doesn't over-indulge on the weekends. I'm going to have to put up a notice at the student union. You're going to be hard to replace, my friend." They hugged and laughed. The two had always been polar opposites, yet they enjoyed and even admired each other. But, they had no desire to trade lifestyles.

Within a few minutes the other girls arrived. Instead of pressing their dresses and beginning their make up as the unofficial schedule for the day dictated, they plopped down on the seldom-used brown leather couches in the front room. Delicate white lights twinkled on the Christmas tree framed by the picture window. Gray fog hovered outside. The girls peppered Deanna with questions about her romance. The stories had all been told before, but repeating them seemed like the appropriate way to begin the day and create a sappy, romantic mood.

"How did you know he was the one?" Brittany asked dreamily, sounding like a cheesy Disney special for 'tween girls.

"You've heard this before. You've even seen the pictures of when we got engaged," Deanna said. Hopeful enthusiasm and a twinkle in her eyes demonstrated her desire to repeat the story.

"Your engagement pictures were the worst ever!" Ashley exclaimed. "I expected Hank to do something over the top and instead he popped the question in a bait shop."

"It wasn't a bait shop. It was a small, run-down coffee shop," Deanna corrected with a smirk in her voice.

"Oh, good choice for the girl who hates coffee."

"Yeah, it was kinda a bad outing all around for Hank," Deanna confirmed with a chuckle. "He didn't want to propose on Christmas or New Year's Eve because he thought that was too cliché and I would be expecting it. He wanted me to be surprised."

"Then he succeeded," Ashley said, "Since no girl expects to admire her diamond against a backdrop of fish scales."

"There were no fish scales," Deanna said, then paused. "Well, not very many, at least." Deanna had enjoyed teasing Hank about that day for the past year. "He'd planned to propose on the beach, but it was too windy."

Ashley nodded. In sarcastic seriousness, she said, "Yeah, wind would put a damper on the joyful moment. Fish odor is so much more romantic."

Deanna raised her hand and pantomimed a slap to her friend's cheek. "His friend, Dave, is a grad student at SF State. He told Hank San Francisco is crisp, clear, and beautiful in January. But, when we got there it was damp, cold, and miserable. We walked out to look at the ocean, and Hank realized it wasn't safe to propose. He was afraid the wind would rip the ring from his hand and bury it in the sand or fling it out into the cold, violet waves. He didn't know what to do. Within minutes I was frozen, so we went looking for hot chocolate." Deanna spread out her hands indicating the obvious correlation. "Hence, the tacky coffee shop."

"I'm sure I saw a sign advertising bait for sale," Ashley insisted.

Deanna snickered. "I think they did sell bait, but I can assure you, we only bought hot chocolate."

After a short pause Brittany gave Deanna a playful shove and demanded, "Keep going. I want to hear the rest."

"Oh, okay. Well, Dave was following us with a camera. Hank was afraid I would either get suspicious or frightened if I noticed paparazzi trailing us, so as soon as we were inside and protected from the wind, he dropped to one knee and proposed."

"The story is only slightly more romantic than the pictures," Jenna grumbled.

Brittany sighed, "Tell us the good parts, Deanna. I want to hear how you fell in love."

"Really? Are you sure you want to hear this again?" Deanna asked, eager to be persuaded.

"Yes!" they all answered at once.

"Ok. I kinda want to hear it again too." Snuggling down into the soft leather, Deanna prepared to enjoy a happy reminiscence. "Well, you all know that Hank and I met my sophomore year. We were attracted to each other from the very beginning but Hank was my TA so there was nothing more than a little flirtation until the end of the fall semester. Over Christmas break, we spent nearly every minute together. By spring semester, I was head over heels."

"You were beyond head over heels. You were simpering and obsessed," Ashley interjected.

"Yeah, I kinda was," Deanna purred in agreement. A warm rush of attraction bubbled up in her abdomen, spreading through her trunk, and tingling out to her extremities at the memory of her early relationship with

Hank. "I failed my biology class that spring because all I could do was daydream about Hank," Deanna confessed. Grimacing, she continued. "That was the first real fight we had. Hank couldn't understand how I failed a class."

"Oh it's easy. I've failed lots," Ashley said with a dismissive flip of her bright red, professionally manicured nails.

Deanna laughed with her friends. "Things got pretty serious pretty fast. In fact, I knew I wanted to marry Hank within a few weeks. I was way too young to get married and I still had a lot school ahead of me at that point, but I knew."

Deanna paused and glanced around at her friends. She wanted to edit out the next chapter of her story. But, these were her closest friends. They were the ones who pulled her through that miserable year. They deserved to hear the unabridged version of that episode, just not today.

Even now, when Deanna and Hank were about to pledge marriage vows to each other, she struggled to talk about it. The joy dropped out of Deanna's voice and her stomach lurched as if she had rounded the summit and dropped into the first steep slope of a roller coaster. With forced effort she continued, "Unfortunately, Hank couldn't find a job here so he moved to Oregon where his mom lives." Condensing the next year into one short, painful sentence, Deanna said, "That was a rough year for us."

"Yeah, and you pined away, which made you very boring company on Friday nights," Ashley said.

"What do you mean? I hung out with you more while Hank was gone than I did before."

"Exactly. You hung out with me because you couldn't hang out with Hank. You were pretty pathetic when you weren't with him. I wanted to find some hanky-panky and all you wanted was your Hanky back. So, like a good friend," Ashley gently patted Deanna's knee like a parent soothing a distraught child, "I listened to your sob stories, then I went out late, after you had gone home to mope."

"Why did Hank leave?" Brittany asked in a soft voice.

"I don't think you've ever told us the whole story."

Deanna sighed with reluctance, but continued. "At the time I didn't understand it myself," she admitted. "Hank was having trouble finding a job. He was working part-time for Fresno State in the graduate department reading masters' theses and also doing some substitute teaching. His mom lives in Oregon. She had just gone through another messy divorce and she invited him to come live with her. His mom has a friend who's a principal at a middle school. An English position was opening up, his mom told him about it, he put in an application, and they offered him the job. Credentialing is different up there so he was able to get a teaching contract because of his master's degree. So," Deanna heaved a dark sigh, "my junior year he was in Oregon."

"I thought he didn't get along with his mom," Jenna commented. "Didn't he move to Fresno with his dad when his parents divorced because he didn't want to live with her? Why would he go to Oregon to be around a woman he doesn't like when the love of his life was waiting in California?"

Deanna acknowledged the truth of Jenna's comment with a nod and crooked smile. The same questions had plagued Deanna at the time of Hank's relocation. "Back then, it didn't make sense to me either. I had trouble believing him when he tried to explain it." Deanna paused, trying to remember Hank's faulty logic and phrase it in reasonable words. "Basically, he was afraid I was too young to be sure about my feelings for him. He was right that I was young. I was only nineteen when we started dating. I turned twenty the summer he left. He thought time apart would help me determine if I really loved him or just loved having a serious boyfriend."

"That was so wrong of him," one of the girls interjected.

Deanna agreed. "Yeah, I was pretty hurt at the time. I finally understand his motives, but I still don't agree with him. Even though he loved me, he wanted to give me time and space to be sure about my feelings for him. He believed the only way I could be objective about what I wanted for my future, and our future, was to have some distance. He told me I was free to date other people if I wanted to, even though he vowed he wouldn't. That left me really confused and scared about our future together. For some reason, he thought physical separation would give us a 'clearer perspective for defining our relationship,'" Deanna said in a deep, masculine voice, mimicking Hank. "One of those stupid things that only makes sense in sappy poems and country songs. I guess he was afraid I was settling for the first guy who fell in love with me. He's always been one to overthink everything."

"He's not as smart as he thinks he is," Ashley said. Deanna laughed in agreement.

"Didn't you guys break up for a while when he was in Oregon?" Brittany asked cautiously. "Please tell us what really happened. What caused your breakup?"

"His selfish, meddling mother," Deanna answered emphatically.

"Ok. Not feeling the love there," Ashley stated. "Do we need to keep the two of you in separate rooms today? Do you guys have trouble playing nice together?"

"If you and his mom get into a girl fight, we can't let her pull your hair. You're spending too much money having it professionally done today," Brittany added and giggled. All of the girls piled on, making outrageous speculations about what might happen between Deanna and her soon-to-be mother-in-law on this special day. Deanna smiled weakly, tolerating their teasing, even though she found little humor in their comments. After a few minutes Jenna stopped joking and asked, "Why would his mom interfere between you two, anyway? Most moms want their sons to settle down with a sweet, young thing like you."

Deanna shrugged. "I haven't decided if she was bored and wanted some drama in her life or if she was trying to get Hank to stay in Oregon with her. Either way, the bottom-line answer is: she's a bitch," Deanna stated unequivocally.

"Woohoo. Well put my friend," Ashley said, raising her right hand and initiating a high five.

"Come on Deanna, tell us what she did. You've never really told us the whole story," pleaded Jenna.

"Honestly, it was just miscommunication. I was confused and suspicious about him leaving in the first place, so when I couldn't get ahold of him one night I jumped to all the wrong conclusions. I thought he was seeing someone else."

Leaning in, Ashley probed for previously withheld information. "What would make you think that?"

Deanna sighed, reluctant to recount that painful year. Even now, she felt her mouth go dry and her chest tighten. Her breathing required forced, intentional effort.

"Please tell us."

Deanna scrutinized their faces. Eyes large and attentive, they were eager for information. They cared about her and wanted to know out of a desire to share in her life, not to gloat over her pain. Unfortunately, they didn't realize thinking about that year still made her heart ache and her stomach roil.

"Okay, okay." Wiping her slick palms on her sweatpants she began, "Well, for the first couple of months after Hank moved we talked every day. We texted whenever we had a few minutes and had long conversations late into the night several times a week. I was still upset, but I was starting to believe that he wanted us to be together in the long run. Finally, I accepted that the main reason he left was he needed the job, and somehow in his warped view of things, he convinced himself that time apart could actually strengthen our relationship. I didn't agree, but I came to the conclusion that he believed it. Then," Deanna swallowed in an attempt to moisten her sticky, dry mouth. She pressed her hands flat on the top of her thighs to stabilize their tremor. "One night he didn't answer his cell phone, so I called the apartment where he and his mom lived. She answered and acted confused and guilty when I asked if Hank was there. After several lame beginnings to poor alibis she said, 'He's with Kathy. I don't know what he wants me to tell you,' and she hung up."

"She blurted out he was with someone else and hung up! That woman is cruel. I might decide to have a cat fight with her today if you don't," Ashley exclaimed.

In a gentle, sympathetic voice Jenna said, "I'm so sorry. I didn't know he went out with someone else. No wonder you didn't want to talk about it."

"No, no. It's not what you think." Deanna reared up defensively. "He was faithful to me the whole time. I told you. It was a miscommunication."

"Don't defame the honorable Hank," Ashley scolded and shoved Jenna. "If you do, we won't get the rest of the story."

"I guess I can't really blame you for thinking that," Deanna continued with a dejected tilt of her head. "I jumped to the same conclusion and thought he was dating this Kathy. For the next few days I didn't answer or return his calls or texts. He knew I was avoiding him. The only reason he could imagine for my behavior was he assumed I must be having doubts about our relationship. He didn't want to pressure me so he started calling less. Because he called less, I became convinced he was seeing Kathy. When we did talk it was short and awkward. Pretty soon our communication deteriorated into a newsy, impersonal text or email once a week or so. We each feared the other wanted out of the relationship, so we drew back to protect ourselves. I guess we were both too proud to bring the subject up. We felt like the other one owed it to us to be honest and straightforward. The deceiver should confess not the deceived." Deanna stopped. Even though more than two years and many sincere apologies had elapsed, a lump formed in her throat and tears threatened to follow.

"So who's Kathy?" Jenna asked, laying a sympathetic hand on Deanna's knee.

The tremble in Deanna's voice hardened into anger. "His boss. She was the principal at the school and they were having some sort of parents' night. His mom swears she didn't lie. She claims she expected me to know who Kathy was. So while I was falling apart and nearly dying of a broken heart, Hank was talking to parents about how to get their kids to read and what kinds of books are appropriate for tweens and young teens. He said Kathy was standing in the back the whole time, with her doughy arms crossed over her double-wide body, and a sour expression on her wrinkly, middle-aged face. Not exactly a hot date."

"Oh, his mom really is low!"

"Let's just say we don't ever plan to live anywhere near her. I can put up with her shallow, selfish, maliciousness for a short visit once a year maybe, but not any more than that. And considering the fact that when Hank lived with her she succeeded in breaking us up for a while, he agrees with me."

Thirteen Years Before

At eleven-thirty, nearly an hour before Greta's usual lunch time, Mary placed two sandwiches on the table. For the next fifteen minutes, she and Greta picked at the lettuce and cheese and pretended to eat in uncomfortable silence. Finally, Mary dumped the food from the nearly full plates into the trash. "Ready to go?" Mary asked with fake, stilted cheerfulness. Greta nodded impassively and followed her daughter out the front door.

Inside Mary's car, Greta perched stiff and erect on the brown leather upholstery of the passenger seat. She grabbed the seat belt and stretched it across her body, securing it with an ominous click. Mary turned the ignition on, and put the car into reverse. They backed out of the driveway and headed toward Fresno and Greta's medical evaluation. Greta remained upright, tense and rigid. Her neck was extended to its fullest and her eyes peered straight ahead through the windshield. She could have balanced a book on top of her head.

"Turn right." Greta pointed.

"I know, Mom."

"Another right at the end of the block."

"Yeah, I know. I live here." This was new and irritating behavior.

"Ok. Now take this street to the stop sign, where you'll make a left. That's the main road. Take it all the way to the freeway entrance."

"Mom, why are you telling me how to get to the freeway?"

"Just making sure." Greta leaned back and visibly relaxed, settling into the upholstery.

As they drove to Fresno, Mary or Greta periodically interrupted the silence with comments about the weather, weekend plans, or what they should have for dinner. They awkwardly and judiciously avoided the topic of the appointment. The forty-five-minute drive crept by slowly, leaving a wake of fatigue.

They entered the geriatric specialty clinic ten minutes before Greta's scheduled appointment. An indifferent receptionist, sheltered from clients' concerns behind a sliding glass window, checked Greta in. Mary and Greta took two padded but uncomfortable seats in the mauve carpeted waiting room. The walls were covered in textured wallpaper with subtle blue and rose vertical lines. A large grape vine wreath with silk flowers adorned the center of the wall, and television sets were mounted in the corners on either side. The room attempted to be homey and relaxing but felt stiff and forced. It reminded Mary of a slightly outdated formal living room. With nothing else to do, Greta stared at the seventies sitcom rerun on the television. Mary picked up a *Woman's Day* magazine displaying a large arrangement of spring flowers on the cover. It was currently November. She flipped the page every ten or fifteen seconds without focusing on a single picture or reading an article. Twenty-five long minutes crept by. Finally, a perky young medical assistant with a ponytail and a name badge that read "Hi, my name is Kourtnee" called Greta's name. Could the generation of misspelled names really be adults already, Mary wondered? Kourtnee chatted and led an unresponsive Mary and Greta into a small, square room with two metal-framed chairs, a stool on wheels, and an exam table. Greta and Mary sat on the chairs. Greta was not about to seat herself on the crinkly paper top of the portentous exam table. After a few more minutes that had the prolonged quality of watching a disaster occurring in slow-motion, a petite, Asian, female doctor in her thirties entered the room with a file tucked under her arm. She sat down on the stool, rolled near Greta, and began a comfortable, easy-going conversation about Greta's life and health history as she opened and skimmed the chart.

"It looks like you don't have any major medical problems, which is wonderful. Most people your age aren't so lucky." Looking up from the brown, tagboard file she asked, "Have you always lived here in the San Joaquin valley?"

Greta nodded. "Yes. Always."

Panic hit Mary like a blast of frigid air. "Mom, you grew up in Nevada. You know that."

Greta shot her daughter a disapproving glare. Turning to the doctor she said, "Can you repeat the question? My daughter distracted me."

Calm and relaxed, the doctor responded, "Of course. I asked where you're from."

Greta relaxed with relief. She knew the answer to this question. "I grew up in Sparks, Nevada. I moved to Clovis in 1947 after I got married. What else do you need to know?"

The doctor smiled reassuringly. "I just want to get to know you. Your chart says you're widowed. I'm so sorry. I bet he was a nice man."

"Yes, he was wonderful. He's been gone a long time but I still miss him."

"People from my generation have a lot to learn from

your generation about how to be happy in a marriage."

Mary glanced at the doctor's left hand. No wedding ring. She wondered if the doctor was divorced or never married. The doctor continued to engage Greta in irrelevant small talk for a few more minutes before directing the conversation to the purpose of the visit.

"I understand you and your daughter are concerned that your memory is not as good as you would like it to be." The friendly and complimentary preamble seemed to work. Without defensiveness or denial, Greta said, "I seem to lose things all the time and when I find them I cannot, for the life of me, figure out how they got there. Is this normal for my age? It's really starting to worry me."

"I can imagine that is very frustrating, and I would think it's scary sometimes as well. I'm afraid I can't tell you if it's normal or not until we do some testing. There are several medical problems that can interfere with your memory. Some can be reversed but, unfortunately, some cannot. We need to find out what is causing your memory lapses so we can determine the best treatment. I'm going to order lab work and schedule a CT scan of your head." The doctor wrote in Greta's chart as she spoke. "Right now, I would like to do a simple screening test to help me decide which other tests we should do." She looked up from the chart and into Greta's guarded eyes. "Is that okay with you?"

Greta pinched her lips and considered the doctor's request. She liked the idea that some memory problems could be corrected, but she hesitated to consent to the proposed tests.

The ensuing silence made Mary uncomfortable. She tapped her right foot and examined her short, clean fingernails in order to remain silent. Finally, Greta nodded and said, "Alright. You may do your tests." Mary exhaled and followed with a long refreshing inhalation. She hadn't realized she was holding her breath. The doctor, who maintained a calm, content expression throughout her conversation with Greta and the prolonged pauses, continued in her soothing voice, "Very good. The way this works is I will tell you three words. Then, I will ask you to do a task. I want you to remember the three words and repeat them back to me after you have completed the task. Do you have any questions?"

"No questions other than why we need to do this at all," Greta mumbled.

The physician nodded, her black bob swaying, as she seriously considered Greta's comment. "This is a simple screening tool that will let us know if we should do more tests. It will not, by itself, tell us what is going on inside the memory centers of your brain. Many things can damage the nerve cells or interfere with the connections between nerve endings, making it difficult to retrieve information on demand. This test cannot tell us exactly what is going on with your memory, only if we should pursue further testing." Greta remained silent and frowned suspiciously.

The doctor continued, "I want you to repeat these three words: baby, mountain, exercise."

Greta dutifully repeated, "Baby, mountain, exercise."

"Now remember those three words."

"Okay. Baby, mountain, exercise." Greta repeated the words again for good measure. She continued to silently repeat the words in her head as the doctor gave more directions. "What was that? I'm sorry. I wasn't listening," Greta said when the doctor finished and looked at her expectantly.

The gerontologist repeated in an unrushed, non-condemning voice, "Take this paper and pencil and I want you to draw a clock. Put the numbers on the face of the clock, and put the hands on the clock showing two o'clock. When you are done drawing the clock I will have you repeat back the three words."

"Baby, mountain, exercise," Greta repeated inside her head.

Taking the offered pencil in her right hand and settling the clipboard on her knees, Greta proceeded to draw a circle in order to make a clock. *Baby, mountain, exercise*, she silently reminded herself. She put the number one at the top of the circle and went around clockwise, writing consecutive numbers just inside the circle as she continued her silent mantra, *Baby, mountain, exercise*. Greta completed the ring of numbers with the numeral fifteen. That was not right. Fifteen was not on a clock. She looked up at the doctor. "I did this wrong. There should only be twelve."

"You may erase anything you want. Or if it's easier we can flip the paper over and you can start again on the other side." Greta opted to start over. She continued to repeat the trio of words to herself but pictured a clock face in her mind before writing any numbers. She realized her mistake; twelve should be at the top, and six at the bottom, three to the right and nine to the left. Now this is what a clock looks like. She filled in the missing numbers in the correct spots. "What time did you say?"

"Two o'clock" Mary blurted out before the doctor could stop her.

Greta proudly drew a clock hand pointing to the number two as she recited, this time audibly, "baby, mountain, exercise." She sighed, smiled, and relaxed into her metal chair as if it was an overstuffed La-Z-Boy.

"A clock should have two hands, Mom," Mary said. The gerontologist gave Mary a disapproving look and a quick shake of her head. Then in a soothing voice, spoke to Greta. "Are you finished?" Greta regarded the clock with frustration. She had remembered the words; her memory was fine—who cared about the stupid clock. Two hands. Mary said two hands. Yes, clocks have two hands. Greta drew another shorter arrow on top of the existing one, making two hands on the clock, both pointing at the two. There. She did it. She remembered the words and she drew the clock. Nothing was wrong with her mind.

Mary leaned toward her mother, right hand raised, index finger extended, ready to point out her mother's silly mistake. She wanted her mom to notice the error. The doctor snatched the clipboard off Greta's lap, preventing Mary from interfering further with the test. "Was that difficult?" she asked.

"Piece of cake," Greta lied.

The doctor shook hands with Greta and excused herself from the room. She pointedly made eye contact with Mary. With a quick jerk of her head, the doctor indicated a clandestine hallway meeting was in order. "I'll check where we go next," Mary told her mother and followed the doctor out. In the cluttered hall, next to the exam room door, a stainless-steel toolbox the size of a bathroom counter was pushed against the wall. Mary tried to prevent her mind from imagining the ghastly implements concealed in the drawers. The top doubled as a desk for the doctor. Scribbling on a prescription pad, the doctor ordered labs and tests. She ripped off the small, awful slip of paper, and handed it to Mary. Then, in a hushed voice, the doctor informed Mary that Greta demonstrated signs of early dementia. Blood work and CT results were required to confirm her suspicions. In a louder voice, meant to carry through the partially opened exam room door, the doctor said, "It was nice to meet you and your dear mother. Here's the order slip for the labs I would like to get. She is scheduled for a few more tests today. If you go back to the main desk, they'll tell you where to go next."

Mary remained fixed in place. The flimsy piece of paper hung from her trembling fingers as the gray suit and low-heeled pumps retreated down the hallway, abandoning her. She had never felt so alone in her life.

11:00 a.m. Telling Secrets

The Wedding Day

The hairdresser arrived promptly at 11 o'clock. She pulled an array of equipment and products out of her wheeled case and transformed the kitchen bar into a beauty parlor. Curling irons and flat irons of various sizes and widths created a long row of parallel line segments on top of the beige tile. It could have been a reality based geometry class. The hair styling equipment was bookcased by bottles and cans. One end of the counter looked like a miniature skyline with small, squat bottles of hair products interspersed with towering skyscrapers of aerosol spray. The opposite end had enough facial products to stock a department store. Deanna and her bridesmaids came running across the family room, giggling like fifth grade girls who had just discovered the wonder of boys. Even though the girls had been together for the last hour, they had not begun to primp or prepare for the event.

Ashley grabbed a large brown paper bag from under the bar, held it up high, and declared, "Time for margaritas, girls." Of Deanna's various high school friends, Ashley was the only one who ever got Deanna into trouble. Ashley was happy-go-lucky and extroverted, with a mocking disdain for rules. Diligence and work hard were not in her repertoire. Perhaps that's why after three years of community college and two and a half years at Fresno State, Ashley had not yet obtained a bachelor's degree. "Do you have a blender, Mrs. Nilsson?" she asked innocently, batting her unnaturally long, black eyelashes, sounding much too young to be holding a bottle of tequila.

"I'll make them," Mary said with incontrovertible authority. She was reluctant to condone drinking in the morning, but absolutely refused to let Ashley have control of measuring the alcohol. With one final bat of her lashes and an insincere grin, Ashley handed over the bag of margarita ingredients.

Mary set the bottles and glasses on the counter by the stove and retrieved the step stool from the laundry room. Even on the top step, she had to stretch to reach the blender, which was at the back of the top shelf. Clearly margaritas were a rarity in this house. Mary filled the blender with ice, poured in the margarita mix, and added a scant splash of tequila. She was not about to have intoxicated bridesmaids ruining the wedding. Mary blended the ingredients and poured the mixture into wide brimmed glasses, also supplied by Ashley, then distributed the drinks to the five girls. She intentionally avoided offering one to the beautician. A tipsy hairdresser could wreak more havoc on a wedding than an inebriated bridesmaid.

Ashley took a sip of her drink. Shuddering in disgust, she pinched her eyes shut and clamped her jaw, forcing a swallow. "Mama Mary, what have you done! You made these virgin. This is a wedding, remember? No virginity today, not even for your generation."

"There is plenty enough alcohol for *before* the wedding,"

stated Mary in a tone that refused discussion or compromise. After thirty plus years of teaching college students, Mary had perfected the no-I-will-not-change-your-grade tone and demeanor.

"Ok, we'll just have twice as many," responded Ashley with an abrupt one-hundred-and-eighty-degree twist to saccharine sweetness. Mary hoped, but doubted, Ashley was teasing.

The beautician got underway and Mary left, heading to her bedroom to begin her own toilette and to check on a very nervous father-of-the-bride. As Mary dressed, she frequently migrated back to the kitchen to keep tabs on how many margaritas were being consumed. As it turned out, Ashley's threat never materialized. The girls nursed their one, weak margarita until the ice began to melt and the ingredients separated. They put far more effort into doing each other's makeup and ogling the evolving hairdos than they did into drinking. Mary could not help but picture them as sixteen-year-old girls in this same setting, minus the alcohol, getting ready for homecoming or Sadie Hawkins. The girls seemed to be feeling like teenagers as well as they reminisced about the bygone days of high school. Ashley, Brittany, and Deanna had been friends since grade school, but Jenna and Katie were college roommates. Even though the girls represented three different high schools, they shared the same stories about cute boys who didn't notice them and mean girls who did. With time, the stories shifted from universal experiences to each girl divulging closely held secrets, just like junior high girls playing truth-or-dare at a slumber party, but without any dares. Ashley leaned in, dropped her voice, peered at Deanna, and in a conspiratorial whisper urged, "Tell us about...."

Mary left quickly. She had a long list of details she was already nervous about today. If she added fretting over Deanna's deep, dark secrets onto that list, it just might push her over the edge. What was it about those bar stools, anyway? They seemed to have a magic about them that loosened the tongue and brought forth streams of longings or long-concealed pains. In second grade, Deanna had lamented, while perched on a bar stool, that she was the only student who had not lost any teeth. A decade later, from the same roost, a tear-stained, teenage face had told Mary how Mike Murphy had publicly and cruelly accused Deanna of being a stalker. Then Deanna had confessed, beginning to laugh through her tears, that she had walked past his house at least ten times the day before. Even Greta, sitting on a bar stool as early Alzheimer's decreased her inhibitions, had disclosed a story which she'd withheld for decades. A story which explained some peculiarities and inconsistencies in her life.

Thirteen Years Before

It was an ordinary evening. Mary washed dinner dishes and Greta relaxed at the kitchen bar, across from the sink. The TV in the family room behind them blared current events to no one. Dean was hidden away in his small office next to the master bedroom, reviewing balance sheets for a meeting at work the next day. Deanna lounged on her bed and talked on speaker phone as she painted her nails dark blue. She knew her mother would insist she remove the depressing color in the morning, but tonight, encouraged by a friend, she felt bold and defiant.

"It's nice when I have a shorter day and can come home early to make a real dinner. Did you like the roast?" Mary asked her mom, speaking loudly to overpower the dramatic MC of the prime-time news special.

"It was delicious. You certainly did not learn to cook from me. I served you more TV dinners than any self-respecting mother should admit to." Greta sighed, remembering the long years of working and raising a daughter on her own.

"I liked your cooking. No one was very health conscious back then. I'm sure everything was high in sodium and fat. That's why it tasted so good."

"You should have tasted my mom's cooking. She was an excellent cook, but I didn't take after her." Greta slapped the counter and vehemently declared, "I was determined I would never be like her!" Mary jumped, startled by the unexpected noise and animosity. Greta's squinting hazel eyes appeared black, and her lips puckered in a bitter scowl. Mary's flippant, placating response retreated deep into her chest rather than emerging from her mouth. In the past, Greta had remained very closed about her family. Whenever Mary asked for stories, Greta responded, "There's nothing to tell." Mary always suspected the evasiveness existed precisely because there was a lot to tell, and it was intentionally being withheld. Most young widows with a small child would have moved close to family, but whatever kept Greta in California and away from her parents had remained a well-kept secret.

"Why was that, Mom?" Mary prompted gently, sensing a rare opportunity to encourage her mother's self-disclosure.

"Well she wasn't really a bad person when I was little, but I could never forgive her for the incident with Brian Wells." Mary knew about Greta's high school boyfriend, Brian Wells. It was practically a girl-next-door story. The two families had been close friends, and Brian and Greta had known each other and played together from infancy. As they got older, their feelings for each other had matured. In high school, to the delight of both families, they'd dated, and everyone had considered them quite serious. World War II had recently ended. There was no more draft, and no reason to prevent Greta and Brian from getting married after graduation. It seemed to be the perfect plan, accepted by everyone. Everyone except Greta. She broke up with Brian shortly before graduation, about the same time their parents were anticipating an engagement announcement. Both families, as well as Brian, were shocked and devastated. In the past, whenever Mary asked Greta for details, she received the caution, "Don't get married to please other people. Wait for the right one." Mary had taken her mother's advice to heart, which was why she had been thirty-five before she married.

Mary resumed scrubbing a pot, trying to not look overly eager to hear her mother's story. In the past, Greta had clammed up as soon as Mary began probing about family, or especially, about Brian Wells. Hoping to encourage her mom to expand upon that well-guarded life event, Mary asked, "Why did you break up with Brian?"

"Because I had to!" Great crossed her arms, glowering at the memory. "I was having doubts before, but there was no way I was going to marry him after that night. To get home, I ran over a mile, in the dark, with my dress ripped open. I had to hold the pieces together to prevent it from falling off entirely." Greta clutched at the front of her blue and green print shirt, gripping the pieces of the dreadful memory. "Even before that night I didn't really want to marry him. I was looking for the right time and way to let him down easy, especially since our families were so close. I knew everyone would be disappointed. But what else could I do? I wasn't going to get married just because other people thought I should. After that night, however, I simply refused to ever talk to him again."

Mary froze, unable to respond. Her knuckles turned white, gripping the fry pan and pressing it with all her weight against the porcelain bottom of the sink. Her mouth and eyes gaped open. Fortunately, Greta continued without prompting. "I told him 'no' but he was going to force me. He said I was the only one who had these crazy old-fashioned morals." Greta looked at her daughter with the hungry, pleading eyes of an insecure child seeking approval. Fifty years after the trauma she still sought affirmation that she had done the right thing. "I said 'no' because I wasn't in love. I liked him, but I didn't love him, and I didn't want to spend the rest of my life with him." Her voice switched from angry to imploring, "What's wrong with old-fashioned morals like that? I guess since he couldn't seduce me, he tried to force me into making love, expecting I would feel obligated to marry him. Girls didn't sleep around back then. If you slept with a boy, you married him."

Stiff movement returned to Mary's body and breathy sound to her vocal chords. "What happened when you got home?" she squeaked out. Mary surfaced the pan from the soapy water, dumped it aside, and supported her weight against the tiled bar, abhorring and absorbing every detail.

"My mom told me I needed to call and apologize. She wanted *me* to apologize to *him*! I couldn't believe it. She saw my dress and my hair and how upset I was and she still thought I was the one who was wrong. My sister, Sarah, came in. She could tell what happened just by looking at me. Then, they proceeded to lecture me. Can you believe it! Both of them were mad at *me*. I heard my mom talking on the phone to his mom several times over the next few weeks and she kept saying things like 'I can't imagine what has changed Greta's mind.' That was a lie; she knew exactly what changed my mind. Mom told me I needed to get over it and take him back. 'I'd never find such a nice boy again,'" Greta quoted in a high-pitched imitation of her mother's voice. "She said 'that is the way it is for women.' After she said that I could never look at my dad the same way again. Do you think Dad forced Mom into lovemaking when she didn't want to?" Greta's eyes glistened and pleaded for answers from her daughter's bewildered face. A single shimmering line slipped down Greta's cheek.

Greta's words ceased and her tears increased. She brought her hands up, pressing clenched fists against her trembling mouth. Crying escalated to sobbing. Her shoulders bobbed. Muffled wails escaped between her clenched fingers. Mary shook herself out of a petrified state of shock and scurried around the counter, wiping her still wet hands on her jeans. She wrapped her distraught mother in a reassuring embrace.

They say with Alzheimer's there is a role reversal. The child becomes the parent as the parent regresses into a child, but Mary never expected such an instant, complete switch this early in the disease process. "You aren't mad that I kept you so far away from your grandparents, are you? I tried to pretend everything was fine. We spent Christmas with them almost every year when you were small. I really tried," Greta pleaded, then resumed bawling. Mary was shocked by the story as well as her mother's insecure, child-like outburst. *The 36-Hour Day*, along with the medical resources Mary had read, told her to expect this. Still, expecting it and experiencing it were worlds apart. Mary held her mother tightly. Slowly and rhythmically they swayed back and forth. Mary patted the heaving back. Mary's maternal instincts took over--a mother's heart comforting a hurting child. "Shhh, it's okay. It's okay. You did the right thing."

Greta pulled her head back, looking beseechingly into her daughter's eyes, "I did?"

"Yes, you did."

"Oh, I'm so glad. I thought so, but they were all so mad at me."

"Shhh. It's okay." Mary pushed Greta's head back down to rest on her shoulder. "They were wrong and you were right."

"My sister said I let him go too far before making him stop. She said it was my own fault that he tried to force me."

"She was wrong."

"Your dad said I was right."

This time Mary tipped her head back to scrutinize her mother's face. "You told Dad?"

"Of course I did! I wasn't going to marry him unless he knew and agreed with me. He said he would never force me like that. That's why I married him. He understood."

"He was a good man."

"Yes, he was."

Even after the tears subsided, Mary and Greta clung to each other and rocked back and forth. Neither one spoke. A deep male voice rumbled from the television, exposing the true story behind recent events, but the noise was drowned out by important thoughts as each woman newly processed an old event.

Mary was at the kitchen table hunched over a stack of essays, red pen in hand. The phone rang, interrupting her work and saving a student from a deserved deduction. She placed the pen on the paper, strategically marking the line where she'd stopped reading, and crossed into the adjoining family room to pick up the phone.

"Hello?"

"Good afternoon, Mary. This is Dr. Gonzalez." Mary's hand trembled. She nearly dropped the receiver. Quickly, she returned to her chair for fear her legs would betray her. One week had passed since Greta's appointment at the geriatric specialty clinic. "I have Greta's test results." Mary could barely hear him over the fast, bounding pulse echoing in her ears. "All of Greta's tests came back negative, which means we have ruled out stroke activity, carotid artery sclerosis, endocrine and regulatory imbalances such as diabetes, renal, or pituitary diseases...." Mary took deep breaths, forcing her heart rate down, closer to normal. She concentrated, trying to glean some meaning out of Dr. Gonzalez's words. Was this good or bad news? The doctor's cold, professional voice continued, "The only likely possibility left is dementia." Mary's stomach constricted in a sudden, intense spasm, as if the doctor had landed a powerful right hook into her gut, making vomiting a very real possibility. Mary did not know some of the terms Dr. Gonzalez had used earlier, but she knew the word dementia. Dementia was bad. Very bad. It was the worst word he could say.

Doctor Gonzalez continued, unaware of Mary's precarious battle with nausea. "Given her age and excellent overall health, Alzheimer's is the most likely type, although specifying a type does not change the treatment or prognosis." At the word "Alzheimer's," the pain radiated from Mary's gut up into her chest. Mary had to force herself to inhale, fighting the crushing pressure that was trying to prevent air from entering her lungs.

There was an uncomfortable pause as the doctor waited for a response that Mary was incapable of making. Finally, with an impassive, sterile voice, he resumed spewing medical jargon. "We have some new psychotropic medications I want to start her on. They have shown promising results in retarding the cognitive deterioration associated with dementia. The earlier in the progressive course they are initiated the better the results. So, if she starts them now she should remain at a level of mild impairment for many years." Mary listened to the syllables the physician uttered but did not perform the mental gymnastics required to associate meaning with the words he spouted. Her brain persisted in trying to find different and preferable definitions for "dementia" and "Alzheimer's." Another long, silent gap in their conversation ensued. Finally, Mary forced enough air through her vocal cords to whisper, "I'm not sure why I'm so shocked. This has been my fear for the last two years."

Dr. Gonzalez leaned back in his office chair. Mary's fragile voice pulled him out of Greta's open medical chart and into the human struggle he was diagnosing. Raking a hand through his thinning dark hair, he switched to a comforting tone, as someone well acquainted with the family. "Mary, I'm sorry for this bad news. I know it's not what you were hoping to hear, but it's not the worst diagnosis possible. She is not going to die any time soon and with new medications we can keep her at this level of functioning for quite some time. I'll call the pharmacy and place the order. The prescription should be ready for you to pick up later today. While dementia is not reversible, we can slow down its progress. Greta still has many good years ahead of her." Mary tried to wrap her brain around what the doctor had just said. That sounded like good news, or at least, not more bad news.

Mary immediately called her husband to pass on the disappointing, but expected results. While speaking to the doctor, Mary had remained composed. As soon as Dean's soft-spoken voice flowed through the receiver, tears poured out of Mary's eyes and rolled down her cheeks. Her voice cracked as it squeezed around the lump clogging her throat. To her surprise, Mary recited the parts of her conversation with the physician that she had been unable to comprehend at the time. Dean listened and murmured sympathetically. He offered to pick up the Aracept from the pharmacy and suggested they bring the new medication to Greta together. He was not sure Mary would listen attentively to the dosing directions from the pharmacist and he was quite sure she could not explain the need for dementia medication to her mother.

Later in the afternoon, Mary and Dean spent half an hour convincing Greta that taking medication to help her memory was a good thing rather than a bad thing. The next hurdle to tackle was explaining the situation to Deanna. As usual, after dinner and an uneventful evening, Mary walked Greta home. Mary made sure her mother got safely inside, then she rushed back to her own house.

Deanna sat at the kitchen bar, swinging her bare feet from the high stool and doodling on, rather than completing, a science worksheet. Dean waited on the family room couch with an open book in his lap. He had been reading the same page since Mary left with Greta. For all he had gotten out of the passage, it might as well have been written in ancient hieroglyphics. He looked as stiff as his starched white shirt and pressed gray slacks.

Mary returned, went to the dishwasher, opened it, and began unloading. She put a Tupperware bowl on a shelf inside the kitchen island. Then, she took its lid out of the dishwasher and placed it inside the island with its base. Next, she removed a few plates and stacked them on the beige tiles of the island. They belonged in the cabinet behind her, but she was not about to turn around, putting her back toward her daughter and husband. Dean set his book aside and joined Deanna at the breakfast bar. Mary closed the nearly full dishwasher and leaned onto the counter opposite her husband and daughter. She attempted to strike a casual pose, with her weight on one leg and elbows on the countertop. The artificially relaxed stance felt awkward and looked as stiff and unnatural as a posed Barbie doll. Every one of Mary's muscles was taut and her intense gaze belied her indifferent posture. As they had decided, Dean initiated the conversation with Deanna.

"Honey, you knew that Mom took Grandma to the doctor, right?"

"Yeah. Grandma told me she was going but she didn't know why Mom made an appointment in Fresno. Grandma doesn't really like going that far anymore if she doesn't have to." Since her parents were hovering, Deanna read the first question and filled in the blank on the science worksheet. Dean and Mary looked at each other. Mary gave her husband a brief, scant smile which he correctly interpreted to mean he should continue; she was not going to take over. "Deanna, the doctor called today and all of the results are back from the different tests they did on Grandma."

"Good. Will they be able to fix her memory?" Deanna asked as she reached down into her backpack on the floor to get colored pencils. She liked coloring the cover of her science homework packet more than doing the content pages. This week the front showed the stages of a butterfly's metamorphosis.

"I'm afraid not," Dean stated.

For the first time, Deanna straightened up and focused her full attention on her parents. Looking back and forth between them she demanded, "What do you mean? Aren't doctors supposed to help people? It sounds like you didn't pick a very good doctor. No wonder she didn't want to go."

Dean laid a hand on his daughter's shoulder. Gently and calmly he continued with his well-constructed explanation. "Grandma has dementia. That means her brain is wearing out and the parts that have quit working cannot be fixed. They have put her on some medication that will help the rest of her brain to wear out more slowly, but that is the only thing the doctors can do for her."

Deanna jumped up, pulling away from her father's touch, and stared her parents down. "Then take her to a different doctor who can fix her."

"The doctor Grandma saw is a specialist. She's the best. She knows what she's talking about," Dean said.

Deanna braced her hands on her hips in defiance. "You have to do something else. We can't just give up on Grandma"

Mary could remain silent no longer. "We're not giving up; we're being realistic. Her memory is starting to have problems. I know you've noticed it too."

"Yes, of course I've noticed and that's why I want to help her. I won't just write her off. I love Grandma. We can't just let her get worse. Doctors don't know everything. I'm going to find a way to help her remember things so she won't lose her shoes and her mail and buy the wrong things at the store anymore." Dean and Mary made eye contact again, communicating their mutual surprise. They had not anticipated anger nor knowledge of the pervasiveness of Greta's memory loss. During their conversations earlier, they'd discussed the best way to handle a tearful reaction or stubborn denial from Deanna. They never considered awareness and anger as possibilities. Dean was the first one to reorganize his plan of attack. "I want to encourage you to do everything you can to help Grandma remember things. Aren't you the one who thought of putting a hook for her keys near the kitchen door into the garage?"

"Yes." Deanna tipped her chin up defiantly, exuding both pride and suspicion.

"That was a great idea. You're a very creative girl, Deanna. You can apply that creativity to developing memory aids for grandma. You're with her the most so you're the best person to identify problems and then you can develop creative solutions."

"Yeah," Deanna said, relinquishing her distrust. "I've been worried that she's starting to forget people. Not us, but her friends. If she talks to someone on the phone, even if she has a nice long conversation, when I ask her who it was she always says she doesn't know. She thinks it was just some stranger. Maybe if I make a photo album with all of her friends in it, that will help her remember them. Grandma and I can look at the pictures in the afternoons so if they call, she'll know who they are."

Already, Deanna was visualizing the attractive page layouts she would use with old pictures, identifying people, and describing related stories or events. She and Grandma would make the albums together. This sounded like fun as well as being good for Grandma's memory.

Over the next few months, Mary spent a small fortune on Creative Memories supplies. Deanna and Greta assembled and decorated six different scrapbooks of old photos. Greta reminisced as they cut and glued and Deanna listened to stories about white Christmases and long, lazy summer days by the lake. The afternoons together, more than the completed books, turned into gems that Deanna would treasure for the rest of her life. Years later, Deanna occasionally pulled the photo albums off the shelf. With the pages open in front of her, Deanna would stare off into space and listen to her grandmother recounting a happy episode from a well-lived life. During the immediate future, however, Greta's teacup still disappeared and mysteriously reappeared in strange and unpredictable places, and the perplexing cat food bag would either be empty within a few days or would remain half full at the end of the week when it should be empty.

12:00 Noon Time to Eat

The Wedding Day

Since the beautician had spread out her products across the kitchen, Mary set trays of cheese, meat, rolls, and two types of salad on the seldom-used dining room table. No one was officially invited, but Mary expected relatives and a few friends to drop in before the wedding. She wanted to have something to offer them. She also anticipated Deanna and her friends would be satisfied with a light, self-serve lunch. Mary was right on both counts. The girls rolled slices of meat and cheese together and nibbled while they chatted and primped. All of the relatives from Nevada and several neighbors stopped by to offer congratulations and get a sneak peek of the bride. The offer of lunch added incentive for them to stay and visit and enjoy the building excitement.

Mary dropped spoonfuls of potato salad and broccoli salad onto two printed Christmas tree paper plates. She assembled mini turkey and Swiss sandwiches on dinner rolls and added them to the meal along with a few squares of cheese and some crackers. Carrying a plate in each hand plus plastic forks and the coordinating Christmas napkins, Mary entered Dean's office, next to the master bedroom. She placed their lunch on Dean's dark mahogany desk, between the meticulously organized in and out trays. Pulling up a light-weight chair he kept in the corner, she sat down across from him. It looked like she was a nervous interviewee called before the high-powered CEO. Dean placed his uncooperative cufflink next to the pencil jar and scrutinized Mary. "Are you doing okay?"

Mary shrugged noncommittally. "I'm not sure if I'm happy or sad that the wedding day has finally arrived."

Dean nodded in understanding.

After a moment of reflective silence, Mary continued, "I have to admit, I've enjoyed the months of planning. Mostly, I've enjoyed Deanna calling and spending more time with me than she has since she started college. Once she's married I assume that will end. All of her time will be devoted to Hank, which it should be, but I'll miss her. And then if they move away..." Mary's voice trailed off.

"Do you think it's harder to let go because she's our only child?" Dean asked solemnly.

"We'll never know, but I imagine a parent feels nostalgic at each child's wedding, regardless of how many other kids there are."

"I wish we'd had more children, but I could not have gone through that day again." Dean shuddered as the horrible memory surfaced. He could still vividly picture Mary laying in a pool of blood as three nurses rushed into the room and whisked her off to the OR, leaving him alone, fearing he'd lost his wife and baby. It may have been only minutes until someone had come to reassure him, but it'd felt like hours. A soft, whimpering groan escaped from Dean. "I don't think you knew how close of a call we had until after Deanna was born."

"You're right. They put me to sleep so quickly I didn't know what was happening, and when I woke up, Deanna was there. I was so happy, I didn't care about anything else.

Dean tapped his short, clean nails on the polished desktop. He cleared his throat, a preamble to something important. "Since you were under general anesthesia I had to make the decision about the tubaligation." He caught and held Mary's gaze, then timorously asked, "Have you ever questioned my choice?"

Mary laughed, relieved at the absurdity of his question. "Of course not! You made the right decision, Dean. I had three miscarriages before Deanna and I turned thirty-eight during my pregnancy. Having one healthy baby seemed miraculous. Don't you remember, once I was into the third trimester, we agreed that we weren't going to try for any more children."

"I know, but for some reason, today I need to know that you never held that decision against me."

Mary reached across the desk and squeezed his long, fidgety fingers. "Never."

Dean turned his hand over to encompass Mary's and returned the squeeze. "Thank you."

Mary slid a plate closer to Dean and arranged the other in front of herself. Dean tucked one corner of the napkin into his collar and spread the red and green decorated paper across his chest. He ate carefully in order to avoid spilling on his tuxedo shirt. Mary barely ate. She stared at the food on her plate, but focused on scenes in her mind's eye of a toddler chasing bubbles in the driveway, and a little girl running and splashing through sprinklers in the back yard. Here, hidden away, she allowed herself to sink into melancholy. In front of guests she played the happy hostess. Around her daughter she was the efficient event coordinator and excited mother-of-the-bride. But here, for a brief half hour, she could wallow in her erratic emotions with the only other person who felt the poignancy of the moment. In the past twenty-three years there had been many difficult, overwhelming days raising a daughter and caring for an aging parent, but somehow, those long days had added up to short years.

"Remember the Christmas we went to Nevada and Deanna saw falling snow for the first time?" Dean asked, a thin smile playing at the corners of his mouth.

Mary puckered her forehead and pinched her lips, trying to remember. "I guess it did snow. What I remember most was Deanna hid at the top of the stairs and watched my cousin in his Santa suit scatter presents under the tree. I'll never forget the tears that followed when she caught him in the spare bedroom changing out of the costume. At one in the morning I was trying to convince a seven-year-old that Santa was running behind and Cousin Charles was helping him out. She wanted to believe me but just couldn't. Her first snowfall occurred the same Christmas the magic of Santa ended. I guess that's the way with life. The good and the bad are inseparably bound together." Dean gave a slow, contemplative nod of agreement. Silence followed as they both meandered through sentimental memories, enjoying the brief respite from the forced smiles they were wearing in front of Deanna and company.

Initially, Mary's thoughts centered on Deanna, but then disjointedly began branching out to her own wedding, her childhood, and finally to her mother's failing cognition. She stabbed a square of cheese and placed it in her mouth. Was that cheddar or jack? She had failed to notice the color and could not discern any taste. The benign meal reminded her of another unsatisfying lunch a decade earlier. The memory brought a faint twinkle to her eyes today. During the original lunch, however, Mary had not been amused.

Ten Years Before

"Mom, where are you?" Mary called as she pushed open the front door with her shoulder. In her left hand, she carefully held a quart of clam chowder from The Seafood Grotto. With her right hand she awkwardly dropped keys into the purse hanging around her wrist and bumping against the briefcase slung over her shoulder. Thursdays were an easy day at work for Mary. She had an early class followed by an office hour and then a free afternoon. On short workdays she would come home and prepare a nice lunch to share with her mom, then dedicate the afternoon to grading papers and prepping for classes. Today, she'd fit in a fast trip to Fresno to pick up some clothes Deanna put on hold yesterday. Deanna's long-sleeved shirts from last winter were now three-quarter length and her pants exposed two inches of sock. It was the first time Mary and Dean had allowed Deanna to go shopping at the mall with a friend. The other mother dropped the girls off and picked them up, but left them to their own devices for several hours. In Deanna's excitement over the new taste of independence, she'd forgotten to bring money. Dean insisted it proved Deanna was not mature enough to go to the mall without direct adult supervision, but Mary was certain it was typical junior high school behavior.

As soon as Mary entered the store, she wanted to escape from the aggressive electric guitar and percussion reverberating off the cement floor. She glanced around for a sales associate. A purple-haired, lip-pierced girl wearing morbid black lipstick appeared to be the only help available. In Mary's opinion, the girl needed more help than she could possibly give. Mary purchased Deanna's outfits as quickly as possible. When asked if she had found everything she needed, Mary laughed out loud. "Oh yes. I've gotten more than I wanted from this store." Mary rubbed her temples at the beginnings of a noise-induced headache.

Back in the mall corridor, Mary found a bench to recover and let the ringing in her ears dissipate. If this was Deanna's new favorite store, then she would be shopping without Mary, regardless of Dean's approval or disapproval. Mary had no intention of spending time inside that discotheque charading as a clothing store.

Mary threw the bags in the trunk and wove through the

mall parking lot to locate an exit that allowed a left turn. She passed one of her favorite restaurants. There was an open parking spot in front designated for pick-up only. Impulsively, she turned into the empty space. Warm soup would take the chill off the October cold snap and make up for lunch being late today. Forty-five minutes later, Mary arrived at Greta's house.

"In here dear," Greta responded from her bedroom at the back of the house.

"I stopped and got clam chowder for our lunch," Mary called as she deposited the food on the kitchen counter and her purse on an extra chair at the far end of the table. She had to first swing her bag over the chair to shoo off the sleeping cat who stretched, yawned, and repositioned his feet several times before finally relinquishing his place. He slowly sauntered out of the kitchen with his tail held high, ensuring Mary understood the depths to which she had inconvenienced him.

Greta wandered down the hall and into the kitchen. She sat down in her chair at the head of the small table. She had been sitting on the same chrome and vinyl chair at the same end of the white speckled Formica kitchen table since Mary was an infant. The only changes were the cracks on the seat covers that exposed yellowed foam padding and a few scattered scratches and areas of uneven fading on the table top. When Greta had moved to be near her daughter, son-in-law, and infant granddaughter, she'd arranged the new kitchen to mimic her old house in Clovis. It struck Mary as ironic that someone as independent and self-reliant as Greta was so resistant to change.

Mary divided the soup between two bowls, then sliced sourdough French bread to add to the meal. Stacking the bread plate on top of the bowls, Mary cautiously turned and crossed the kitchen to maintain the precarious balance. She carefully placed the meal on the table, set the bread in the middle, scooted one bowl in front of Greta, and arranged the other in front of the chair to her mom's right. Mary retraced her steps across the small kitchen to retrieve soup spoons and a butter knife from the silverware drawer and butter from the refrigerator. As she turned back toward the table, she saw the blue and white sugar bowl, usually in the center of the table, close to her mother, and a heaping spoonful of sweet white crystals poised above her mother's soup. "Don't add that. It's sugar," Mary cautioned her mom.

"I always add sugar. I like my soup with sugar," Greta stubbornly insisted as she sprinkled the sweet additive into her clam chowder and refilled the spoon for a second helping.

"Mom, don't add more. At least taste it first." Too late. Two heaping doses of sugar had already been added to the briny meal. Mary took her seat. She pulled the sugar spoon from her mom's grasp. Picking up the sugar bowl and stretching across the table, Mary relocated it out of her mother's reach. Then, Mary buttered the bread. Greta hungrily ate her slice and requested more. Mary got up to cut another slice. She was quite hungry herself, so she cut two. The tangy sourdough nicely augmented the creamy chowder. Mary popped the bread into the toaster thinking the crunch would allow for dipping without the bread becoming soggy. It would taste similar to a bread bowl. Mary returned to the table and handed a slice of toast to her mom. Greta took it and asked, "Is there anything else for lunch?"

Mary pointed to the nearly full bowl in front of her mom. "You have soup that you've barely touched."

"This!" Greta said with disgust. "I can't eat this. Someone added sugar into it when I wasn't looking. It tastes terrible. Can I have yours?"

Mary eyed the bowl of now tepid soup in front of her. She had been anticipating this delicious lunch since she left Fresno. She was willing to sacrifice a lot for her mom, but not her soup, not today. "No," she snapped. "I'll make you something else." Pinching her lips together tightly to trap the expletives that were trying to escape, Mary stood up quickly, causing her chair to skid back and wobble precariously before it settled back onto all four legs. Mary's arm darted forward, grabbing the offensive bowl in front of her mother, sending some of the contents sloshing over the rim. She strode across the room in three long, determined steps and dropped the bowl into the sink with a thud. Surprisingly, the inexpensive, everyday china did not break. Mary scowled as she turned on the water, overflowing the bowl of sweetened soup, washing it down the garbage disposal. Then she opened the refrigerator, retrieved turkey meat, provolone cheese, and mayonnaise. Mary methodically and silently made the sandwich that she made for her mother almost every day. Usually, she made it in the morning, covered it with plastic wrap, and put it in the refrigerator. When Greta got hungry she would find it ready and waiting. Today it was going straight to the table to replace the special treat that was supposed to have been lunch. As Mary prepared the cold sandwich, she silently repeated her mantra of the past year: "It's the Alzheimer's. She's not doing this on purpose." Taking a deep breath and consciously relaxing the muscles in her face and shoulders, Mary put the sandwich onto a plate and turned around to deliver it to her hungry mother.

"Mom, here's a sandwich for you."

"Oh, no thank you," Greta replied contentedly. She pointed with her spoon toward Mary's empty bowl. "I just finished this delicious soup."

The Wedding Day

The hairdresser fluffed and teased until each girl appeared to have three times her natural tresses. Then, each girl's long hair was plaited and twisted into a complex knot at the nape of her neck. The bride and her maids could have passed for young English women on their way to a ball in one of Jane Austen's novels. The girls admired their hairdos and completed their makeup as they nibbled lunch.

"I'm surprised that one mean statement from his mom could split up you and Hank," Brittany commented, returning to their earlier conversation.

"Well, his mom's meddling started it but there were other things that made it escalate," Deanna replied, being intentionally vague.

"Like what?" Ashley asked. "It's time you gave us all the juicy details."

Deanna shook her head adamantly. She refused to talk about this any more today. Ashley had no idea she was partially responsible for escalating the misunderstanding between Deanna and Hank. It hadn't been intentional, but Ashley had held a key role in the whole painful experience. Maybe someday Deanna would enlighten her to the part she'd played, but for today, discussion of that episode was closed. "We all overreacted. Let's leave it at that," Deanna said with finality. A smile blossomed on her face and Deanna's eyes twinkled. "This is my wedding day! Today, I want to remember all the good times I've had with Hank and why I love him. There's no time for bad memories today." Deanna's friends easily acquiesced and moved on to other topics, beginning with the pros and cons of liquid eyeliner for the wedding pictures. Next, the girls spread out a multitude of lipsticks and began a debate about the appropriate boldness of red. Deanna picked a plum red from the same family of color as her favorite everyday lip gloss, just a tad deeper and bolder. The girls puckered and dabbed amidst inconsequential talk, but Deanna's mind reverted back to the painful events of three years ago, like a driver who cannot help but take one last look in the rearview mirror after passing a horrific wreck.

Three Years Before

On Friday, two days after her heart was shattered, Deanna crawled out of bed to the buzz of her alarm. She tugged on the lightweight, gray pants crumpled on the floor next to her bed, slid her feet into flip flops, and headed to her grandmother's house. Deanna did not brush her teeth or her hair. She wore a baggy Fresno State t-shirt that she'd caught when the rally committee threw shirts into the bleachers at a basketball game last year. It was the same shirt she'd slept in last night. And wore yesterday. And the night before.

Deanna drove cautiously and pulled over at one point when the constricting lump in her throat threatened to choke her and blurred vision made driving dangerous. Today she was scheduled to care for her grandmother. Deanna was not going to let Hank's inconsistency undermine her commitment to Greta. Yesterday she did not get dressed or leave the apartment, but today was different. Greta needed her and she would not let her grandmother down. It was fortunate Mary had called and left a message last night. Usually Deanna came every other Saturday, but weeks ago, Mary asked Deanna to switch Saturday for Friday this week. Mary was part of a curriculum revision project and today was the culminating meeting. She and two other faculty would present their recommendations to a high-powered campus committee. Deanna had agreed willingly when asked, but she would not have made it without her mother's reminder. Her head was blurred by pain, leaving her unconscious of the time or date.

Deanna's determination to care for her grandmother lasted for approximately ten seconds after entering the house. Rather than making Greta breakfast and gently reorienting her, Deanna collapsed onto the front room couch, totally spent.

Mary pushed the front room curtain aside and peeked out the window. Deanna's car was parked oddly askew in Greta's driveway. With a quick glance at her wrist watch, Mary determined she had enough time to pop in and say hello before leaving for work. She wanted to show Deanna the new light gray suit and dark gray sling pumps she had bought for today.

Mary let herself in the front door. She opened her mouth to call, announcing her presence, but stopped short.

Sound evaporated in the eerie quiet, like light in a black hole. Two bodies huddled in painful silence in the gloomy room. Deanna lay in a fetal position on the couch. A brown and orange hand-crocheted afghan was pulled up to her red nose. Her flat, greasy, dark hair and red puffy eyes emerged from under the thin protection. Greta sat next to her, squeezed between Deanna's bare feet and the arm rest, agitatedly picking at the crooked hem of her misbuttoned blouse as her lower lip quivered. Immediately, Mary knew everything except the specifics. She rushed to Deanna, squatted down, and pulled her daughter into a protective embrace. Deanna clung to her mother and sobbed like a small child, breaking the oppressive silence with the sounds of grief. Greta joined in with sniffs and trembling breaths. They were a trio of misery.

Mary's new outfit went back into the closet. She called in sick and stayed home to care for both her mother and daughter. The three women spent a long day in Greta's small front room, sipping tea, eating macaroni and cheese, talking a little, and crying a lot. The details of the situation eluded Greta, but she related to the raw emotions around her with tearful sympathy.

During the next two weeks, Deanna had trouble accomplishing the routine tasks of each day like climbing out of bed and ingesting food. Sitting through a class was impossible. Mary called her daughter every morning and evening. Deanna did not notice a change to the thick, gray depression consuming her, but Mary noted that each day their conversations lasted a little longer. Deanna's voice grew less apathetic, even occasionally containing some animation. Mary never scolded nor gave advice. She was satisfied with the slow but continuous progress she perceived in her daughter. Knowing Deanna was going to make it through this was enough. They would deal with the consequences later.

By the third week, stubbornness triumphed devastation. The fear of flunking out broke through the sadness and motivated Deanna to attend class despite the constriction of her chest and the gnawing pit in her stomach. Deanna focused on trying to resurrect a dismal semester. She found having a goal made it easier to suppress the pervasive gloom and nagging preoccupation. Ashley, whose philosophy was multiple inconsequential flings were the remedy for one intense relationship gone array, was sure Deanna needed to go on a date. To implement her theory, Ashley called every few days, inviting Deanna on a double date to a bonfire, or dinner, or dancing, or some type of activity. Every time Deanna declined.

"Come on, Deanna, I'm tired of seeing you mope around. It's just dinner. You have to eat anyway and you don't have to dance with him if you don't want to," Ashley prodded. It had been months since Hank had moved and weeks since the painful conversation with his mom. Contact between Deanna and Hank was infrequent, mostly because Deanna rarely answered his calls. When she did, the conversation was stilted and uncomfortable. Deanna could not have explained how it happened, but when she hung up after talking to Ashley, she was scheduled to go out Saturday night. It was a double date of sorts. Ashley said she had no preference so she would let Deanna take her pick of the two young men they would be dining with. Deanna's choice was up in Oregon with some woman named Kathy.

Deanna called Ashley half a dozen times on Saturday. Her first calls were attempts to cancel the date. She said she was not ready to see other people. Ashley rejected that idea before Deanna finished voicing it. Next, Deanna claimed she was too far behind in her classes to give up a night of studying. Ashley found the idea of studying on a Saturday night scandalous and she would not let her friend sink to such depths. During another call, Ashley scoffed at the possibility that Deanna was too tired to go out. After all, Deanna had done very little other than sleep during the past few weeks. Deanna's last excuse was that she did not own an appropriate outfit to wear. Ashley offered to lend her a halter and leather mini skirt.

"Really, Ashley, if I'm going to go, you have to help me," Deanna pleaded. "How do I dress to show I'm not interested without looking like the girl who got dumped and fell to pieces?"

"You are the girl who got dumped and fell to pieces."

"I know. I just don't want to look like it."

Deanna could not tell if Ashley was trying to be helpful or not, but her fashion suggestions were too risqué. By the time Deanna settled on an outfit, most of her wardrobe was heaped on her bed. Deanna turned side to side in front of the full-length mirror on the closet door, evaluating her final choice. She wore comfortable but snug fitting jeans and two layered tank tops. The yellow tank had a scoop neck edged with a thin cotton lace and a racerback which showed under the spaghetti strapped, v-necked pink tank. Since it was late fall and the weather had turned cool she grabbed an off-white sweater with a bias cut that hung long in the front and to the top of her back pockets on the rear.

Deanna spent more time debating over the shoes than she had on the rest of the outfit. She switched between heels, flats, and sneakers multiple times, but ended up wearing blue heels. She pulled her long, layered, brown, hair back into a ponytail at the last minute. If the spiked heels looked like she was coming onto this guy, the ponytail would say not-tonight-buddy.

That evening Deanna surprised herself by having a good time. Both Luke and Sam were good-looking business students in their last year at Fresno State. Luke was tall and thin with sandy blond hair. Sam was stockier with darker hair and a little boy face that probably only needed to be shaved once a week. Ashley worked as a receptionist at an accounting office where the two were interning. She alternately flirted with each.

Luke and Sam were kind, funny, and enjoyable to be around. They had been friends since second grade. After graduating from a small high school in the foothills, they'd come to Fresno State, where they'd roomed together all four years of college. They would be graduating in the spring. Luke planned to move to Oakhurst and join his dad's accounting practice. Sam wanted to go straight into an MBA program. He was applying to schools in the San Francisco bay area and Los Angeles. It would be the first time in more than a decade these best friends had been separated.

During dinner, Ashley described the time she and Deanna had pretended to be sick in high school. They'd fooled the nurse who sent them both home, but instead of going home they went jet skiing. What they didn't know was they were on the river right behind the principal's house and for some reason the principal came home early that day. Of course, Ashley embellished the story, so Deanna interrupted to correct inaccuracies and point out that they'd only missed the last period of the day. Ashley blamed all their troubles on Deanna, but Deanna insisted Ashley was the real culprit--the instigator who'd dragged her along as an unwilling participant. In the end, it was a lively dinner with entertaining conversation.

After dinner, they moved to the bar at the back of the restaurant. It was recessed three steps below the dinner tables. They squeezed four stools around a small, chrome table which would have been cozy for two. Since Deanna was still twenty, the guys ordered drinks at the counter and brought them back to the table. Deanna was not a heavy drinker; in fact, she usually volunteered to be the designated driver. Tonight, however, she was not driving, she was having fun—and for the first time in months she was not moping and pining after Hank. She enjoyed a glass of red wine. After the wine, Ashley ordered Deanna a "big girl drink." Deanna didn't know what was in it, but she liked the burn it left in her throat and the warmth that tingled in her fingertips. About the time they finished their second drinks, the advertised live music started. A mediocre tenor and soprano duo sang soft-rock oldies to canned music piped through low-quality speakers. To Deanna, after two drinks, it sounded much better than it actually was. The four got up and danced. They switched partners regularly until Ashley and Luke danced a slow song together and refused to allow the others to cut in.

Deanna and Sam left the dance floor to sit out the next few songs. Scanning the crowded bar, he spotted an unoccupied table in the farthest back corner, partially hidden by a pillar. Sam grabbed Deanna's hand, and at a trot, threaded his way through the congestion to stake their claim before someone else grabbed it. They sat down and ordered another set of drinks. A relaxed, mellow, contentment flowed through Deanna. She rested her elbows on the small, round table, and supported her chin in her hands, basking in the delightful sensation of enjoyment--something she had not experienced in a very long time. Pleasure played at her mouth and sparkled in her eyes. Her rosy cheeks glowed from alcohol and exertion. For the next half hour, she talked freely, smiled warmly, and laughed frequently. Deanna and Sam enjoyed their intimate conversation, but neither felt a romantic attraction for the person they bumped knees with under the tiny table. However, to an outside observer, especially a suspicious one, the scene appeared very different. He saw flushed lovers having a *tête-à-tête* at a secluded table in a seductively dim establishment.

The next morning Deanna had a mild headache and two new friends. Ashley was right; going out had been good for her.

Also the next morning, Hank received a phone call from his brother.

"Hey bro. What's up with you?" Bill asked.

"Trying to illuminate illiterate imps to the joys of reading. How about you? Made your million bucks yet so you can retire?"

"Naw, that's too hard. I've decided to marry well instead. I will happily be a kept man."

"So, you're dating someone new?"

"Nope. But I'm in the market for a smart, funny, tall,

thin, bombshell, with millions. If you find someone who meets my specifications, you have permission to give out my number."

"Wow, with such low standards I would expect you to have a whole lineup of girls to choose from. Oh wait, you didn't say girl. I guess that's not one of your requirements."

"You used to be funny. Just wait 'til I find her; then you'll be jealous. Hey, speaking of girls…I saw Deanna last night." Caution entered Bill's voice. "What's going on between you two?"

Hank cleared his throat. Guardedly he asked, "What do you mean?"

"Are you still dating?"

"Yeah, of course. Well, I think so. I mean, things have not been great lately. She was pretty upset that I moved. And now she's been really busy--we both have--so we don't get to talk all that often. Honestly, when we talk it's pretty awkward, but I think it's just the distance. I'm planning to spend Christmas in California and I'm sure when we have some time together everything will be fine."

"Oh man." Bill took a slow deep breath and scratched the morning stubble on his chin. "I was hoping you were going to tell me you two broke up."

"What! Why?"

"I hate meddling, but I gotta tell you. I saw her last night."

"Yeah, you said that. How was she?"

"She was looking really good. The problem is, she was looking at some collegiate hunk across the table."

"Did you talk to her? Maybe it was a study group or something. She's in education, you know. They do lots of group projects."

"Well then, this group project involved two people grinning at each other and whispering across a small table in a romantic corner of a dark bar. I hate to be the one to break the news to you, but she's seeing someone else." After a long silence, Bill put all joking aside and asked, "Are you okay,

Hank?"

"Not really. To tell you the truth, I'm angry rather than surprised. She's been really distant and distracted whenever I talk to her. What makes me mad is that I offered her space when I left but she assured me she didn't want it. She swore her undying love to me and now, within a few months, she's found someone new. And, she doesn't even have the decency to tell me the truth. Well, I'm glad I know. I don't need to make a fool of myself any longer."

"I really am sorry, bro. I liked her."

"I loved her."

"Yeah, I know you did."

1:00 p.m. Let's Go

The Wedding Day

The girls exited the house. With precise and delicate steps, they drifted toward Mary's Toyota. Their legs moved while their torsos, necks, and heads remained rigid and elongated, like a flock of flamingoes cruising along the water's edge. They layered the plastic-shrouded dresses in the trunk by squatting and reaching with their arms rather than bending forward. There was no way a defiant lock of hair would find an opportunity to escape its assigned arrangement. Slowly and deliberately, the five girls slid into the vehicle and Deanna turned on the car. Fog hovered thirty feet above them, creating dull light which cast no shadows, but their bright anticipation blinded them to the gloomy sky.

Deanna and her friends arrived at the church. They exited the car assuming the same formal carriage as when they entered, and proceeded into the nursery, which was designated as their changing room for the day.

As the girls donned their dresses, the photographer

paced the sanctuary, glancing at his wristwatch and voicing his annoyance. He needed them in their satin gowns and stationed across the front of the church half an hour ago. Even a bossy, perfectionist photographer could not stop Ashley from making periodic inappropriate comments and the other girls from giggling like thirteen-year-olds.

Deanna's parents and aunt and uncle arrived to take family photos about ten minutes after the girls' pictures began. The photographer, mumbling disgruntled comments throughout the shoot, finished his shots of Deanna solo and grouped with her bridesmaids in less than half the required time. Then, he positioned Mary on the right and Dean on the left, sandwiching their daughter, as he clicked away standing, squatting, from one side, and from the other, to obtain the perfect angle. Mary smiled for the pictures but disappointment welled up inside her heart and joined her chaotic emotions as she realized her mother would not be in any of Deanna's wedding pictures.

Every click taunted Mary, teasing her for spending this much money on professional family photos which would not contain the entire family. Why hadn't they taken more professional pictures over the years? Their albums were filled almost entirely with informal snapshots taken by one of them. They had pictures of Deanna's jack o'lantern smile at the Grand Canyon with Mary and Greta. Dean was not in those photos. There were pictures of Deanna as a toddler splashing in the shallows of the Merced river in Yosemite Valley. Dean and Greta supervised her in the cold snow melt as El Capitan loomed in the background. Mary was not in those pictures. In all of their pictures someone was missing. These photos would be no exception, except Greta's absence today was not because she was on the other side of the camera.

Mary's favorite photo album was from their family vacation to Hawaii when Deanna was fourteen. It was special because it was the last trip they had taken with Greta.

Nine Years Before

"Mom, we haven't told Deanna yet, but we're planning a trip to Hawaii this summer," Mary said as she escorted her mother home one evening. Wrapping her thick, navy cardigan tighter around her body as protection from the damp evening fog, Mary continued, "Everyone tells us this is probably the last year Deanna will enjoy vacationing with us. After this we'll have to go somewhere that has a teen room, so we can spend a lot of money and never see our daughter." Mary paused but received no response from her mother. "I know you prefer to not fly, but we'd like you to come."

"Oh, I don't know. We'll see."

Mary stopped and laid her hand her mother's arm. "I'm serious. We want to make sure you'll come before we talk to Deanna about it."

"Well, I'm not sure if I can. For one thing, who would take care of my cat?"

"The vet boards animals. We can take the cat there, or we could leave him home and have a neighbor come and feed him.".

"How much will it cost? I'm on a fixed income, you know."

"Don't worry about that. If you don't have enough we'll help out. We really want you to come." It was true, Mary and Dean did want Greta to accompany them on vacation, but in all honesty, there was no other option. Last night in bed they'd talked for an hour, considering different possibilities, and concluding there was no other viable solution. They could not go and leave Greta home alone. She was not used to preparing her own meals. And if she did have to cook, she would not remember to turn the stove burner off after every use. Also, she needed the reassurance of someone to call during episodes of confusion about the current time or date or schedule for the day.

Over the next week Mary coaxed, arranged, and secretly subsidized her mother's checkbook, until Greta finally agreed to accompany them on vacation. Greta's one requirement was that she pay her own way. Well, Dean and Mary made sure she thought she did.

Once Greta was committed to the trip, it was time to inform Deanna. Mary turned toward her husband during dinner on a cold night in February. She tried to maintain a deadpan appearance, but a sneaky smirk pushed up the corners of her mouth and twinkled in her eyes. Speaking directly to Dean and ignoring the presence of her mother and daughter, she commented, "Stew sure tastes good on a winter night, but it's not something you want at any other time. Poi must be the same kind of thing. I bet it's refreshing in the hot Hawaiian weather but wouldn't be the same anywhere else."

"Well then, it's a good thing we'll be eating it in Hawaii this summer and not here," Dean responded.

Deanna popped out of her chair like a jumping jack. She hopped up and down emitting shrill, excited screams.

Greta was soon infected by her granddaughter's enthusiasm. Over the next few months, a portion of each afternoon was spent perusing travel brochures and ignoring Deanna's waiting homework. Greta and Deanna gazed at images of white sand beaches and enormous green sea turtles, many with shells wider than their outstretched arms. The warm, clear, azure water and brightly colored fish of the coral reefs beckoned to them from the glossy pages. They discussed all the beautiful tropical sights they would see and the exciting adventures they would have on Maui.

School ended and the blistering summer hit, bringing long uncomfortable days of anticipation before the trip finally arrived. After an uneventful flight, they stepped off the jet onto the tarmac and inhaled the warm, hibiscus-scented breeze. Greta was convinced this trip was her best idea ever.

They collected their bags and rental car. Driving past sugar cane fields and bougainvillea-draped buildings, they reached the touristy side of the island and found their hotel nestled in palms, situated on an expansive stretch of sparkling white sand and impossibly blue shimmering water. Deanna jumped out of the car the second it came to a stop. She ran around to the opposite side of the vehicle, pulled Greta's door open, grabbed her grandmother's hand, and led Greta toward the continuously burning tiki torches that bookcased the double doors of the hotel entrance. Inside the taupe and wicker lobby of the Pacific Islander Hotel, Mary registered and collected their room keys as Dean lugged their bags into the lobby. Greta and Deanna ogled the large tropical flower arrangement on a small round table and touched the large waxy orange bird of paradise bloom and its spiky gray-green leaves.

A slow elevator transported them to the fifth floor. Pink and yellow painted flowers alternated with mirrors covered the interior walls of the small lift. Deanna grinned like a Cheshire cat at her grandmother's reflection. Greta responded by crossing her eyes and puckering her lips into a fish face. Dean watched his daughter and her grandmother make silly faces at each other, and then he joined in by stretching his large ears farther out and opening his eyes and mouth wide in an Alfalfa impersonation. The elevator stopped with a bump and opened its doors, exposing a long hallway painted with geometric shapes in sherbet tones. Dragging their heavy suitcases to the end of the hallway, Dean and Mary entered one room and Deanna and Greta continued next door.

After transferring the contents of his suitcase to the dresser drawers, Dean plopped down on the red, vinyl chair that overlooked their veranda. The sliding glass doors framed tranquil blue ocean under fluffy white clouds. He reached for Mary's hand and pulled her onto his lap. They gazed at the natural beauty outside as Dean entwined their fingers. Mary whispered that booking two rooms was the best idea of the whole vacation. Their attention was suddenly drawn away from the sky and sea and each other by aggressive rattling of their door knob followed by determined thumping. Dean eased Mary off his lap and went to open the door. Deanna thrust the door fully open, banging it against the wall. With wild exaggeration, she indignantly pointed at the wall separating her room from theirs. "You should see what she packed! There's nothing she can wear in that suitcase. We'll have to buy her all new clothes. You should have packed for her mom. What were you thinking!"

"What? But I did...I mean, I washed and laid out her clothes.... They were right there...on her bed.... I took the suitcase into her room.... She had to.... How could she not..." Seizing control of her stammering tongue and tumbling thoughts, Mary asked, "What did she pack?"

Deanna propped her hands on her hips and with a sassy sway answered, "Well, she didn't pack what you laid out, unless you laid out lots of pajamas and dirty underwear."

Mary groaned. "That sounds like the basket of dirty laundry I left next to the washing machine." Mary shifted her vision from her daughter's insolent stance to her husband's face which was pinched in frustration. A sudden determination to defend herself arose. "There was a lot to do to get ready for this trip. I ran out of time to finish her wash so I left a load waiting for when we get home." Puzzling up her face Mary tried to remember details. "Did she pack her ugly orange sweater?"

"Yep. Right on top."

"Oh no." Frustration and self-condemnation berated Mary. She slumped onto the bright floral bedspread and supported her chin on her right fist, resembling a Michelangelo statue. "That's the dirty laundry. She must have found the dirty clothes instead of packing the clean ones."

"Umm. No duh," Deanna said rolling her eyes and bobbing her head. Then she dramatically spun about face and marched out.

Mary jumped up and yelled, "Watch how you talk to me, young lady."

Deanna made no verbal response, but gave a brief, squinty-eyed glance over her right shoulder as she continued to stomp away and slam the door.

Mary swiveled, yelling at Dean, "She can't talk to us like that! She hasn't even started high school yet." Emphasizing each word with a violent extension of her arms, Mary enunciated, "Her behavior is totally unacceptable."

Dean restrained Mary's flailing arms, pinning them to her sides. "I think you're both upset and taking it out on each other, since we can hardly hold Greta responsible."

Mary, too angry to consider or accept his insight, spat out, "She said 'duh' to my face."

Dean slid his hands up to Mary's shoulders and gently pushed her down to sit on the edge of the bed. Seating himself beside her, he said, "We can talk to Deanna about her attitude later when no one is upset, but first things first. Right now, we need to get your mom some clothes. I'll call the front desk and ask if there is a store close by where locals shop. I don't want to pay tourist prices for a week's worth of clothing." Even on vacation, Dean could not stop being an accountant.

Fortunately, the hotel concierge found the story sweetly sentimental--a family vacationing one last time with Grandma, who suffers from early Alzheimer's--so he directed them to a nearby K-Mart. They bought inexpensive undergarments, plus several t-shirts screen printed with Hawaiian flowers, and coordinating solid-colored, elastic-waist shorts. Since they were scheduled to attend a luau, they also chose a lightweight pair of khaki pants with a breezy floral blouse.

A Hawaiian vacation requires a swimsuit. They left the women's department and entered beachwear. The store offered racks of simple, flattering one-piece bathing suits in various Hawaiian prints, but Greta's stubborn streak suddenly surfaced. She refused to consider any swimsuit except the plain black one with an attached gathered skirt. Deanna and Mary quickly agreed, not because they liked the suit, but to avoid the brewing argument.

The entire shopping trip was completed in a little over

an hour. Greta, Mary, and Deanna were pleased with their purchases. Dean was pleased with the price. After recovering from the difficult beginning, everyone was happy, Greta had clothes, and the vacation was underway. Fun and sunshine were in the forecast.

Morning light peeked through the curtains and chirping birds welcomed the new day. Mary woke to a gentle kiss on her neck followed by an off-key Don Hoe imitation ringing softly in her ear. She smiled without opening her eyes as the "tiny bubbles in the wine" blew her hair and tickled her face.

Knock, knock. "How does she always know the wrong moment to interrupt?" Dean grumbled, rolling out from under the sheets. "Give me a minute," he called, pulling on a white undershirt and baggy black gym shorts over the blue plaid boxers he'd slept in.

Dean opened the door and Deanna bounded into the room and hopped onto the luxurious king-size bed. The string ties of her pink, flowered bikini top were visible under her purple terrycloth cover up. "Are you ready for the beach yet?"

The vacation passed enjoyably. They developed a habit of scouring architectural and archeological sites in the mornings, which pleased Mary and Dean, and lazing in the sunshine at the beach during the afternoons, which pleased Deanna. Greta wandered through the vacation in wide-eyed bewilderment. Multiple times each day she asked where she was and what she was supposed to be doing. They patiently reoriented her and explained she was on vacation in Hawaii. "Oh, Hawaii. How lovely. I've always wanted to visit Hawaii," was the recurring answer.

After returning home, the Miller-Nilsson family settled back into their previous routines. Dean went to work in the morning and returned in the evening, since the financial office of the college worked year-round. Mary and Deanna spent a lot of time together, shopping for back to school supplies, painting two bedrooms in their house, and supervising Greta to ensure she dressed, bathed, and ate on a regular schedule.

Greta contentedly lived her low-stress life. She had a friendly tabby cat for company and a loving family who listened to her stories, regardless of how many times she repeated them. She recounted childhood birthday celebrations as if they were recent events, while last week's activities were depicted as ancient history. Meandering through the decades of her life brought Greta joy. Her family kindly ignored the chronologic chaos. Greta occasionally brought up the time she traveled to Hawaii, describing it as if it happened a lifetime ago. Her traveling companions changed with each rendition of the story.

Labor Day arrived, signaling the official end of summer (even though school had been in session for two weeks) and providing the best of the fall sales. Mary and Deanna planned a day of shopping in Fresno. They invited Greta but she declined and instead provided a shopping list of items she wanted. Deanna scanned the paper. "Grandma, you don't need any of this. I put two large packages of napkins in the bottom cupboard next to the stove just the other day. I'm sure you don't need any more."

Greta crossed her arms and nodded her head with certainty. "I always need them. I use a lot of napkins. If they are on sale I want you to buy them. It's best to stock up when you find a bargain."

"We can get them if you want, but really it's clothing that is on the best sales today," Mary interjected. "Maybe we should get you some new pants and sweaters for winter."

Greta shook her head. "I just got some new things. I don't need any more clothing."

"Grandma, you did not," Deanna said. "You wear the same old things every day. Don't you want something new?"

Fearing increasing tension, Mary countered, "We can get you whatever you want, Mom. You know Deanna is becoming a clothes hound."

Deanna glared at her mother.

"Then just tea bags like I asked for," Greta said.

Before Deanna could say anything else, Mary grasped her firmly by the elbow and ushered her out of the kitchen and into the front room. Mary whispered rapidly, "Go and look in her drawers and closet and make a mental list of what she needs. I'm quite sure she needs new shoes and socks and probably some warm sweaters for winter. Check how worn her pants are. She may need those as well." Mary saw an argument brewing in Deanna's piercing blue eyes, so before any words escaped from her daughter's mouth, Mary sent Deanna down the hallway with a shove. "We'll get her what she needs and if you want to get her the things she asked for we can do that too." To herself Mary snidely mumbled, "By the time we get back, she won't remember what she wanted anyway." Deanna's shoulders slumped and her lips pouted in a sour expression as she continued down the hall to her grandmother's room. She hated tricking her grandmother, even when her grandmother did not know she was being tricked.

Mary and Deanna returned from their shopping trip with a mountain of bags. They'd each bought a winter jacket at a bargain price and outfits for the cooler fall weather they hoped was coming soon. Deanna's purchases followed the current fashion trend of earthy shades of mustard, orange, and beige. Mary stuck with her old faithfuls--shades of blue and business gray along with one chocolate brown dress Deanna had convinced her to buy. After depositing their new clothing in their bedrooms, Mary and Deanna grabbed the bags for Greta and walked to her house.

Greta slid her feet into new, rubber-soled, black leather slip-on shoes and declared them the most comfortable shoes she ever owned. Pulling the thick knit pants and warm tops out of the store bag, Greta admired the winter scenes and snowflake designs on the sweaters. "Oh, thank you," she said. "I need these because it has been so chilly lately."

Ezaki

Deanna glanced out the window and watched distorted waves of heat radiating off the cement driveway. Greta continued, "I don't really have the money, but I needed new clothes. I'm glad I asked you to get them for me."

2:30 p.m. Commitment

The Wedding Day

The girls finished their pictures. The wedding coordinator whisked them out of the sanctuary through a nearly-camouflaged door on the side of the platform into a secret storage area filled with altar vestments and silk flower arrangements. In a stealthy crouch the coordinator ushered the bride, protected by her maids, out the other side of the storage closet, through a seldom-used back hallway, past the kitchen and a children's Sunday school room, and finally, full circle back into the nursery, where they'd started an hour before. Deanna was determined Hank's first glimpse of her today would be on her father's arm as she descended the aisle toward him and their future together. Last night he'd asked her to break the long-held wedding tradition and spend some time with him before the ceremony. When she'd refused, he swore he would die if he had to go all day without seeing her. Then he teased that he would sneak a peek while she dressed because he was more interested in what she would be wearing underneath than in the wedding gown itself. Hank learned that when a woman spends months finding the perfect dress a man should not say, even in jest, that he does not care what the dress looks like. Finally, Hank threatened to find her no matter how hard she hid from him because, really, it was too much to ask him to go through the whole harrowing day without at least one reassuring kiss. Deanna was adamant and steadfast in her convictions (her parents called her stubborn) and no amount of whining or cajoling was going to get him a glimpse of the bride prior to the ceremony. As a teenager, Deanna had directed the same dogged commitment to caring for her grandmother.

Eight Years Before

Mary slammed her car door, tramped across the garage, kicked the laundry room door open, burst into the house, and proceeded straight into the kitchen. With an accentuated groan, she tossed her briefcase full of poorly written, unimaginative student papers onto the table. "I'm thinking of changing my syllabus so I don't have to read any more essays. These are final papers and they're no better than the first ones," she said to no one in particular. "I've been reading essays for twenty-five years now and I have not read an original idea yet." She crossed into the adjacent family room and dropped onto the La-Z-Boy with a sigh, kicking off her sensible, low-heeled, gray shoes. Deanna sat on the opposite side of the room in a matching chair. Pretending not to hear her mother's monologue of complaints, Deanna focused on her textbook, intensifying her examination of the diagram identifying bacterial intracellular organelles.

Mary scanned the room, taking in Deanna's pile of clean laundry on the coffee table and Dean's shoes and socks lying on the floor next to the couch. Deanna was required to do very few chores but she couldn't even manage to put her laundry away. And Dean, a man who never put a paperclip into the wrong section of his desk organizer, somehow didn't mind leaving his shoes and dirty socks strewn all over. Mary realized that even though three people lived here, only one cleaned. Nothing in particular had gone wrong during the day, but unmotivated students, a confused elderly mother, a teenage daughter, and menopausal hormones had combined in a volatile mix. "Where's Grandma?" Mary demanded of her daughter.

"Taking a nap in the spare bedroom," Deanna answered, switching her focus from the textbook to the photocopied pages of her take-home quiz, judiciously avoiding her mother's gaze. "Lately she's been doing that this time of day."

Mary leaned forward. Finally, an opportunity to talk to Deanna without Greta around. Even though Greta lived two houses away, she was in Mary and Dean's house most afternoons and every evening, making a private discussion nearly impossible. "Your dad and I think you should get involved in an extracurricular activity after school," Mary said without preamble, aware that her time alone with her daughter might be limited. Deanna's head popped up, her eyebrows raised in surprise and confusion. "Huh?"

"Deanna," Mary continued, "you spend a lot of time alone here in the house. We think…"

"I'm not alone," Deanna interrupted.

Mary discounted Deanna's statement with a wave of her hand and a shake of her head. "Grandma doesn't count. We think you should find and pursue an activity you enjoy. Something where you interact with kids your own age. I know you have always been comfortable around adults, but your grandmother is getting older and more confused, and I think you need to develop interests to share with your peers. You won't always have your grandmother to spend your afternoons with." Deanna's mouth opened but no sound came out. Incredulity radiated from her face. Mary continued, somehow missing Deanna's overt nonverbal cues. "Really, Deanna, we worry about you. You spend so much time with Grandma, that you haven't been able to have a normal teenage social life. This summer you'll get your driver's license. Next year you'll be a junior, which means high school will already be half over for you. You need to participate in activities that don't revolve around your grandmother."

Deanna took a deep breath and answered, speaking slowly at first, formulating her ideas with difficulty, "I don't spend time with Grandma for *me*. I spend the afternoons with her for *her*. She needs me." Deanna flipped her textbook closed with a thump and threw it aside. Her words poured out faster and louder. "You aren't here to take care of her so I have to. She needs structure and predictability. If I come home even a little late she's flustered and extra confused." Now it was Mary's turn to look abashed. How could she have so misinterpreted her daughter's motives? She assumed Deanna was isolating herself from peers over some high school drama or teenage angst. It was too late to start the conversation over.

Deana was shouting. "You think I don't want to be a normal teenager? Well I do, but I can't. You don't seem to realize how bad Grandma has gotten. She can't be left alone all day. Leaving her alone while I'm at school is too long as it is."

Mary jumped in, attempting to redirect the conversation. "I know. That's what I'm getting at. I think it's time we hire a home health aide to stay with Grandma so she won't be alone. It will also allow you to enjoy what's left of your high school years."

Deanna stood up and faced her mother. Her eyes flashed and her pulse surged through her head, pushing words out of her mouth before her brain could stop them or evaluate them. "I love Grandma. She practically raised me while you were busy teaching your students instead of me. I'm not going to turn over her care to some stranger that she doesn't know and won't like. If that means I miss out on some of high school then so be it. Do you think I stay home with Grandma because I'm some sort of awkward, social hermit like Dad? Well, I'm not. I have friends but I choose to be with Grandma instead of them because it's the right thing to do—not because it's fun. Half the time she thinks I'm you. Do you really think that's fun for me?" Deanna threw her arms in the air, accentuating her sarcasm. "Oh, how wonderful to be confused with a frumpy, middle-aged professor. It's every teenage girl's dream."

The argument woke up Greta, who came ambling out into the family room. "Why are my girls yelling?' she asked innocently.

"My shift is done. It's your turn now. Or, are you going to hand it off to some stranger?" demanded Deanna, intentionally hurtful. "I'm calling Brittany and Ashley so I can have some fun and learn to do things that normal teenagers do, and let me tell you, you won't approve. You should have been happy with me staying home with Grandma." Deanna stomped out of the room, marched down the hall to her bedroom, and slammed the door. Mary was not finished. She took two angry steps after her daughter but was blocked by her grinning mother. Greta yawned, stretched, and patted Mary's shoulder, in total oblivion to the palpable tension.

"Mom, don't just stand there looking stupid," Mary snapped. Greta's smile instantly transformed into a frown. Her lower lip trembled like a frightened child. Indecisively, Mary shifted her focus between her daughter's challenging door and her mother's quivering face. After a deep breath to set her resolve and to get her emotions under control, Mary spoke to her mom in a calmer, but still harsh tone. "Come over to the kitchen with me. I need to start dinner. Dean will be home in about a half hour." Greta meekly followed Mary across the family room to the kitchen and settled into her usual spot. With her head bowed, Greta twisted the hem of her blouse one way and then the other. Occasionally a tear ran down her cheek and dripped from her chin onto her lap, or she would brush her jaw line against her shoulder to absorb the drip before it fell. For the next half hour, Greta was silent except for a periodic tremulous gasp as she continued to manipulate the bottom of her shirt.

Even though Mary had spoken only one short, harsh sentence to her mother, the effect lasted the entire evening. Mary discovered how negative emotions produced a depression in Greta that lifted slower than Central Valley tule fog in January.

Greta remained quiet and sullen throughout dinner. A moist, shimmering line ran down each of Greta's cheeks and she frequently sniffed or wiped her nose with the back of her hand. On the few instances when Greta spoke, her voice quavered and she mistook the people around her. Deanna was Mary, and Mary became Susan, Greta's older sister. Greta's fingers trembled, causing her to drop her spoon. The metal clanged against the tile floor. Greta slumped, drooping her head in shame, and whimpered, "Oh no. That thing, that thing hit the bottom."

Mary started to rise. "I'll get you a new spoon."

"No. I'm done. I'll just finish the milk in this book." Greta reached for her glass.

Deanna sat at the table during dinner as required, but kept her arms crossed, jaw clenched, and glared at her food. She refused to eat. She refused to look at her mother. She refused to speak in anything more than a grunt, or at best, a monosyllable. Dean, sensing the discontent of the females around the table, ate quickly, silently, and promptly retreated into his study.

After dinner Mary washed the dishes and arranged the leftovers in the fridge, surrounded by profound silence. She had suggested Greta watch TV, but Greta stared into her lap as she shook her head "no". To fill the long evening Mary opened her laptop and edited some lecture notes. Several times she attempted to engage Greta in small talk, but the only answers she received were sniffs or quick, minimized head movements.

Finally, bedtime approached and Mary walked her

mother home in dour silence. Greta entered her snug, familiar bungalow and shed her depression like an unneeded jacket. She chatted animatedly, describing the funny antics of her cat, as she handed Mary lettuce and a tomato from the refrigerator to add to tomorrow's lunch. Mary had an early class and would only be able to check in on her mom briefly, not enough time to prepare lunch, so they were making tomorrow's midday meal tonight. Mary also made sure there was cereal, milk, and fruit for breakfast. Satisfied that everything was ready and her mom was safe, Mary headed home. Her last action before leaving was to engage the house alarm. The alarm company touted their product as an effective way to prevent break-ins, but Mary and Dean employed the alarm because of the potential of a break-out. Fortunately, Greta seemed to sleep well at night, or at least if she got up, she never attempted to leave her house.

Mary trudged heavily past the neighbor's house and stopped on the sidewalk in front of her own home. A wreath with happy pinks and yellows on the carved wooden door welcomed spring. To the right of the door, a genial golden glow shown through the sheer curtains of the front room. The light was softened and subdued by distance as it radiated out from the family room. Mary remained outside looking in, replaying her argument with Deanna from a different vantage point. She sifted through their angry words, retrieving the grains of truth hidden amidst the chaff.

It was true, Greta functioned better with people she knew and a consistent, predictable routine. However, Greta had Alzheimer's and Alzheimer's was progressive. Aricept had seemed like a miracle cure for a few years, but its healing properties had lost their potency. Greta's daily habit of reading the newspaper in the morning, eating the prepared lunch waiting in the fridge, then rereading the paper and marveling over the ever-new headlines, was no longer adequate. Greta was not safe. Her confusion left her gullible and vulnerable. If Deanna was committed to babysitting her grandmother in the afternoons, then the hours after three thirty were covered. The time between eight am and three thirty pm was the problem. Mary sighed. Only one feasible solution existed: they needed to hire help. She had been abrupt and insensitive when she'd presented the idea to Deanna, but the reality remained the same. Somehow, she needed to broach the subject with Deanna again, and soon.

Dean rose early the next morning. He showered quickly and dressed in dark gray slacks and a light blue shirt before heading to the kitchen. He grabbed the box of Bisquick from the cupboard and eggs from the fridge. Then, he looked down at his clothes. To prevent the need to change before heading to work, he put on Mary's green floral apron. The ruffled edge ended a few inches below his crotch, while the breadth wrapped around his entire torso. It fit him like a mini dress. Before Mary or Deanna began their daily routine, Dean was stirring batter in a large silver mixing bowl, preparing waffles for breakfast. It was his peace offering to the god of discontentment, who had invaded his house the night before. Dean made waffles because waffles were the only thing Dean ever made. Somehow, even though he'd lived on his own until he was past thirty, he'd survived without learning to cook anything that required a pot or pan.

Mary entered the kitchen as Dean was spooning creamy batter into the sizzling waffle iron. Three white plates sat on floral placemats around the square kitchen table. In the center was another plate containing several golden-brown waffles. Leaning her briefcase against the wall by the laundry room door, Mary pulled syrup, butter, and lingonberry jelly--Deanna's favorite--out of the fridge. At the same time as the last waffle finished cooking, Deanna dashed into the kitchen, snatched a banana off the bar, and spun around to grab a breakfast bar out of the cupboard. But then, seeing the waffles on the table and appreciating her dad's unspoken gesture to restore family harmony, Deanna replaced her hasty breakfast and walked toward the table, preparing to sit down. With a quick glance to her left, she made fleeting eye contact with her mom. Deanna wanted the fight to be over and forgotten, but she still felt justified in her position and was unwilling to apologize first. Mary also wanted to restore her relationship with her daughter but was unsure how to begin. Dean spread his arms, displaying the waiting feast, and said, "Let's eat." The simple sentence broke the tense silence. Apologies poured out of Mary and Deanna simultaneously. They reached out and hugged each other. No one really had enough time, but they all sat down to eat one of Dean's waffles.

After a few bites, Mary turned to her daughter and tentatively began, "I know I went about everything in the wrong way yesterday, but I'm worried Grandma may be getting to the point that we can't leave her alone during the day anymore." Mary scrutinized her daughter's face. Deanna remained silent, with her jaw set and eyes averted. Was this disagreement or capitulation? Cautiously, Mary continued, "Dad and I have talked it over and I'm going to cut back my class load to eighty percent next year. That means I'll have every Monday off to stay with Grandma. And, I won't have classes on Friday, just an office hour which I can schedule after you get home. If you don't mind coming home in the afternoon that's great, but I think we need to start looking for someone to stay with Grandma during the mornings we won't be there."

Deanna forced a swallow, trying to dislodge the lump in her throat. "I thought about it a lot last night too. You're right. We can't be with her 24/7. The important thing will be finding the right person." Deanna stared at her plate, unable to look her mother in the eyes because of the threat of tears in her own.

Mary reached over and placed a comforting hand on her daughter's knee. "This is not something we are going to do immediately or without a lot of consideration," Mary reassured her. "But, it's time to start planning for the next stage and looking for help. We can get everything in place this summer. That will give Grandma some time to get adjusted while we're around so there won't be a big transition in the fall when school starts." Deanna nodded. Her eyes brimmed with tears and her throat constricted as she consented to both hiring a caregiver and accepting her grandmother's increasing incapacity.

The three left for work and school in a rush, slightly late, dirty dishes still on the table, but satisfied with the resolution they'd reached.

As soon as school let out for the summer, Mary and Deanna applied themselves to the task of finding a caregiver for Greta. They called several agencies, looked through ads in the newspaper, and finally compiled a list of candidates. With Mary's new work schedule, she would be on duty watching her mother on Mondays and on Friday mornings. Deanna was committed to continuing her habit of coming home immediately after school to be with her grandmother on weekday afternoons. A caregiver would only be needed on Tuesday, Wednesday, and Thursday mornings. Even if the caregiver left right after lunch, Greta would only be unsupervised for a couple hours. This would be minimal compared to the number of hours per day she had been spending alone previously. Mary and Deanna considered this schedule an ideal beginning. It was not a drastic change, so Greta could adjust to outside help coming in little by little. As Greta's confusion increased, the care provider's hours would also increase. Dean, wisely, supported their solution but extricated himself from the decision-making process.

Both Mary and Deanna's top pick was a Mexican woman whose past references vouched for her excellent care, pleasant personality, and dedicated reliability. The cheerful, spunky candidate arrived ten minutes early for the interview. She wore a white peasant blouse embroidered with large red and orange flowers and a full, gathered, red skirt. She looked as if she should be taking their orders at a Mexican restaurant. Unfortunately, Greta took one look at her, turned to her daughter and said, "Why did you bring this Mexican whore into my house?" Mary and Deanna both gasped and stared at Greta wide-eyed and open-mouthed. Everyone--except Greta--stopped talking, moving, and even breathing for a moment. Unfazed, Greta continued, "I don't like her. She's mean. I don't want to see her ever again." Greta crossed her arms and glared challengingly at the woman. Trying to minimize everyone's embarrassment, the caregiver responded in her clipped English, "Dat es ok. I have other yob. I no want to work so much extra hours as you need. I tink tis is not a good yob for me." She left as Mary and Deanna apologized profusely and Greta, seated on her front room couch, stated emphatically, "I don't want that horrible woman here and I am not sorry."

Mary and Deanna found another home health aide whom Greta liked on first sight with the same intensity as she'd disliked the previous choice. However, the new caregiver did not have as many glowing reviews and satisfied clients as the candidate they'd sent away.

Six weeks after beginning to utilize paid caregivers, at seven thirty on Tuesday morning, minutes after Dean left for work, the phone rang. Mary was in the shower. Hearing the phone, she quickly stepped out of the shower and grabbed her towel. She dashed across the light beige carpet, tracking dark, wet footprints, to catch the phone before the answering machine picked up.

"Hello," Mary gasped, breathless from her haste. She wrapped the towel more securely around herself and, pinching the phone between her ear and shoulder, began to rub and pat herself in a poor attempt to dry off.

"Mrs. Nilsson, I'm calling to let you know I'm quitting. I wanted to let you know first. I'll call the agency and let them know too."

Mary stood up straight and let the water trickle down her legs. "You're resigning already? When will your last day be?"

"Ummm, I'm quitting."

"Okay. What day will be your last?" The dark spot on the carpet around Mary's feet grew.

"I told you. I'm quitting. I'm quitting today. Tomorrow I'm moving so I need to pack today. I won't be able to work for you anymore."

"You aren't coming beginning *today*?" Mary struggled to process this bizarre conversation.

Nonplussed, Mary examined the mini calendar next to the phone base on the small table by Dean's reading chair. The caregiver's name, Sandy, was written down on Tuesday, Wednesday, and Thursday for three more weeks until the end of the month. Could someone really quit a job without giving any notice? And moving! How did someone decide today to move tomorrow?

Mary placed a call, which was rerouted to the agency's answering service. Dressing quickly in khaki pants and a print silk blouse—a bit informal if she ended up going to work, but nicer than she usually dressed for days with her mom--Mary headed to Greta's house to await the next installment of this singular day. The adult care agency returned Mary's call and promised an emergency caregiver would be on her way to Greta's house within the hour.

An hour and ten minutes later Mary scowled at the white plastic clock on Greta's kitchen wall. To make it to class on time Mary needed to leave now. She wanted to stall and meet the new caregiver, but students are not forgiving of late instructors. And being late this early in the semester, when students did not know her yet, would set a precedent that tardiness was acceptable.

"Mom, I have to go to work. Sandy called me earlier and she won't be able to come visit you today." *Or ever again,* Mary thought to herself.

"Oh that's too bad. She is such a nice lady and we always have a good time when she visits, but I know everyone is busy." Greta continued in a singsong voice, "Except me and you, you lazy old bag of bones." Greta reached around the corner of the table and scratched the fluffy gray neck of the cat sleeping on an old newspaper on the next seat. The plump tabby was anything but a bag of bones.

"A new person is coming to stay with you today."

"I don't need anyone to stay with me," Greta stated harshly.

"It's a friend of Sandy's." Mary interjected quickly. "She wants to meet you. Sandy is sure you two will get along. Her name is," Mary glanced over her shoulder at the notepad near the phone, "Helen. Sandy's friend, Helen, is coming over."

"Oh, okay. Sandy is a lovely woman. I'm sure I'll get along with any friend of Sandy's."

"Great. She should be here anytime. The agency...um, Sandy gave her a key so she'll just let herself in. I have to leave now for work, but I'll call when I get to school to be sure Helen arrived." Greta nodded idly and continued to pet the purring cat.

Helen supervised Greta three morning per week, juggling it around her other job caring for an elderly gentleman three nights per week. Her other client had sundowner's syndrome with bouts of insomnia. Some mornings Helen arrived with droopy eyelids and dark circles under her eyes after a night of preventing her charge from sneaking into his shop in the garage, where he wanted to use power tools to build wooden lawn ornaments. Fortunately, his family had hired an electrician and disconnected the garage outlets.

Greta soon forgot about Sandy. Dinner conversations were filled with stories about Greta's new friend, Helen. It was obvious many of Greta's stories were the conflation of old experiences with Helen's presence superimposed on the memory, but no one in the Nilsson household corrected Greta. They had learned the futility of that long ago.

Deanna and Mary asked, and nearly begged, Helen to permanently accept the position as Greta's caregiver, but when a full-time position became available for a ninety-year-old wheelchair-bound woman, Helen moved on. In order to attract a new, and hopefully long-term aide, Mary offered the next caregiver employment three full days per week. The extended hours enticed more applicants, but none that matched Helen's kindness and commitment.

Mary and Deanna picked a satisfactory caregiver, who seemed to click with Greta, from their list of mediocre choices. Finally, life settled into a stable and predictable pattern. Mary stayed with Greta all day on Mondays, and until she cleaned up the lunch dishes on Fridays. Deanna was officially on duty only on Friday afternoons, although she insisted on coming straight home after school every day to check on her grandmother. The unexceptional aide from the agency sat on Greta's couch watching TV from breakfast until dinner every Tuesday, Wednesday, and Thursday, ensuring Greta was safe.

The only piece of the schedule that became unpredictable was Greta. Most days passed peacefully. Greta soon recognized her caregiver and considered her an old childhood friend. Many tales of Nevada were repeated until both women could contribute details during the retelling. There were occasional days, however, when Greta brooded on the couch, sitting catatonically next to her caregiver. Infrequently, Greta was anxious with no identifiable cause. Greta would pace and wander through her house, picking up and moving things. The sedentary caregiver had to leave her upholstered perch and follow Greta, retrieving the sugar jar from the closet and returning it to the kitchen, or collecting pencils from window sills and replacing them in the kitchen drawer of miscellaneous items. On rare, unpleasant occasions Greta adamantly refused care and scolded everyone who tried to help her. If Greta was set off by something in the morning, no one--caregiver, family, or otherwise--was able to improve her mood the rest of the day.

Throughout Deanna's junior year of high school, she maintained her routine of leaving school promptly and heading straight to her grandmother's house. Her presence was superfluous, but her emotions told her she needed to be available for her grandmother. To fill her afternoons, Deanna gossiped on the telephone or posted to Myspace on her dad's old laptop while the caregiver watched soap operas and talk shows from the couch and Greta fumbled with the newspaper at the kitchen table or reclined in her chair stroking the cat. The perpetually spouting TV in the front room forced Deanna to retreat into the spare bedroom.

The quantity of hours Deanna was physically with Greta remained unchanged, but the quality of their time together waned. Even Deanna and Greta's solo afternoons were substantively different. While remaining companionable, their time together was distant. Deanna communicated more and more with friends and less with her grandmother. Deanna never resented staying with her grandmother, but typically Greta reread the daily paper then napped for a couple hours. Deanna smiled warmly at her grandmother whenever she entered the same room, and Greta affectionately patted her granddaughter's shoulder or back whenever she passed within arm's reach, but no secrets were whispered and no plots were hatched.

Deanna signed up for an advanced placement class her senior year. The course required attendance at study groups and after school tutorials once or twice a week. To be successful in the class, Deanna was forced to relinquished Greta's afternoon care to the home health aide. Even with the increased academic rigor of an AP class, Deanna discovered she had more free time than she had ever had before--more than she could fill, so she signed up to keep statistics for the basketball team. The coach accepted her application gratefully, before he discovered she had never attended a game and knew nothing about the sport. But Deanna was bright and reliable, and by mid-season the coach joked around with her as much as he did the team members.

When Mary had reduced her workload by twenty percent and dedicated the extra hours to supervising and providing care for her mother, she'd never factored in, and could not have imagined, the additional time required to coordinate home health aides hired through an agency. In direct opposition to what was happening with Deanna, every day was overly full for Mary. Weeks passed quickly. A year was gone in a flash. Mary's jaw dropped in perplexed shock when Deanna asked her to go shopping for a senior prom dress. Too late, Mary realized the emotional stress of watching her mother's increasing decline had blinded her to the joy of witnessing her daughter's maturation into a highly competent young woman.

On Deanna's graduation day, Mary, who had already been out of school for a week, treated her daughter to a morning at a spa. They got pedicures and manicures, and Deanna's hair was cut and colored. The finicky hairstylist refused to continue the thick, chunky highlights Deanna had been adding into her mousy brown hair. Instead, he applied an allover chestnut brown with chocolate lowlights. The beautician finished, and with a dramatic flair, spun Deanna around toward the large mirror where, she stared with some confusion at the elegant brunette peering back at her. Her sparkling blue eyes were accentuated by the soft, dark fringe around her face. Her former straight, long, blunt cut now cascaded past her shoulders in gently flowing layers. Deanna had been considered neither pretty nor plain in high school; in fact, she had not been considered at all. Only a few kids outside of her small circle of friends would have been able to come up with her name if asked, and it would have taken them some time and effort. But today, there was no doubt the ugly duckling had become a swan. Deanna had always been tall and thin like her father, but her new look exuded poise and sophistication whereas just yesterday she had been gangly and lanky.

The Wedding Day

The girls were safely hidden in the church nursery, allowing Hank, his family, and the groomsmen to take their pictures. With nothing else to do, the girls poked around through the shelves in the nursery. They picked up different toddler toys and teased Deanna about needing them soon. Ashley, of course, incorporated inappropriate innuendo into her statements. Deanna's friends were unperturbed by the prospect of being trapped in this little room for the next hour. Deanna, however, was quiet and aloof. She leaned against the wall to avoid sitting and potentially wrinkling her dress. Plus, the toddler-sized, wooden chairs were uncomfortable. The girls found a few toys they remembered from their preschool years and demonstrated for each other the silly things they used to do. Deanna watched with minimal amusement. With nothing to do and little to distract her, the gloomy feeling that had accompanied the remembrance of the hard year she and Hank had spent apart resurfaced. In an effort to chase away those memories, she fast forwarded her thoughts to their reconciliation. *After all,* she reminded herself, lifting her left hand to admire the sparkle of her diamond solitaire, *we did get back together.*

Two and One-Half Years Before

There were four weeks left in the school year but Hank's students had already checked out. After attempting and failing to keep them engaged, Hank capitulated and revised their reading schedule to eliminate the last book altogether. He was tired of reading responses that matched Wikipedia word for word. Did his students really think he was so out of touch that he did not know how to Google? Shortly before lunch recess on Tuesday, his principal burst unexpectedly into his room. With an excess of words and lack of clarity she assumed his classroom duties and directed him to her office to receive a confidential, emergency phone call. Confused, he hurried down the hall to retrieve his call on the principal's desk phone.

His heart was pounding as he grabbed the phone and jammed it next to his ear. "Hank Floyd here. May I help you?" He said in one rapid breath.

"This is Fresno District Medical Center," a professional female voice stated. "We are notifying the family of Fred Floyd that he was admitted to the hospital a few hours ago with chest pain."

"Chest pain? He's barely over fifty."

"He was brought into the hospital by ambulance after collapsing…"

"He collapsed! When? How? Is he going to be all right?" Hank sat down in the low blue molded plastic chair designated for students receiving discipline. His throat tightened, his hands trembled, and his stomach roiled, the same as the students who sat in this seat. Hank could barely hear the voice on the phone above the escalating rumble in his ears, and he stared at, but did not see, the expensive frames on the desk containing photos of a well-groomed miniature poodle.

"I am sorry Mr. Floyd. I do not have a lot of details. I can tell you your father has been admitted and he is currently in the cardiac catheterization lab undergoing a procedure. His wife gave us the numbers of family members she wanted notified. You should contact her for more information." Hank's mind was entirely blank. He had nothing to say. The hospital nurse, social worker, receptionist, or whoever it was making this call continued after a prolonged pause. "I am very sorry to be bringing you this news. Please call your stepmother to get more information. She is currently in the waiting room in a portion of the hospital where cell phones do not work, so you may not get through to her right away. She said to leave a message. I can also tell you that while his condition is considered serious, he is stable and we will do our very best to care for him. Please contact his wife for more information." Hank made an unintelligible grunt that was neither thank you nor goodbye but sufficed for both, then hung up. He remained in the student chair until his back started to sweat against the formed plastic.

Forty-eight hours later Hank entered the hospital, located the telemetry unit, and burst into his father's hospital room. Multiple conversations with his stepmother and even a few with his dad, who was heavily medicated and would fall asleep mid-sentence, did not prepare him for what he saw. He knew a cardiac surgeon had inserted two stents into nearly occluded arteries in his father's heart. He also knew there was a small amount of permanent damage done to the heart muscle and that his father's lifestyle required a radical change in order to prevent a repeat hospital admit in the not-too-distant future. But the unimaginable shock came from seeing a familiar, pretty, young brunette sitting in the brown vinyl hospital chair next to his father's bed. With a smile and a chuckle, she handed back an entertaining get well card. Deanna looked up as Hank entered and the mirth in her blue eyes retreated into her suddenly pale face. Her eyes began to well up and the card in her hand started to tremble.

"Oh." Deanna gulped. "I'm so sorry," she began. "We expected you to call before you arrived. I shouldn't stay if you're here. There, um, aren't supposed to be very many visitors at one time." She stood up and indicated Hank should sit in the only chair. "I'll go. You stay." She forced her lips into a cold, artificial smile. Turning, she kissed Fred on the cheek, and said, "Please call again next time you're lonely. I have a lot of breaks so it's easy for me to come by." Passing Hank in the tight space between the hospital bed and wall required touching to maneuver their bodies past each other. Deanna flushed red and the tears in her eyes teetered on the brink of spilling over and running down her face. She needed to get out quickly. "Get well Fred. Bye Hank," she choked out as she hurriedly fled from the room. Hank remained where he was, staring at the door in bewildered silence.

"Well, you are a bigger idiot than I thought," his father said.

Drawn back to his father's ashen face above the blue checkered gown, Hank asked, "What kind of welcome is that?"

"The kind you deserve."

Fred Floyd was released from the hospital on Saturday, four days after his heart attack. He was to remain off work for two weeks and then go back incrementally as tolerated. Hank had arrived in Fresno on Thursday after requesting leave from school for Thursday, Friday, and Monday. With his father improving it looked realistic for him to fly back to Oregon Monday evening and return to work Tuesday morning. His stepmother, Stephanie, went to work on Monday and left Hank to assist and supervise his father. Bill, Hank's brother, planned to spend Tuesday with their father, and Stephanie would stay home the rest of the week if needed. It was a well-coordinated plan.

Fred was not a matchmaker. He had never before interfered in anyone's private affairs, but seeing Deanna and Hank's obvious emotions when they unexpectedly met in his hospital room had convinced him they had made each other miserable long enough. On Monday morning he called Deanna and requested she bring him Chinese takeout for lunch. He explained that his wife had returned to work and he did not have the energy to make his own meals. He conveniently neglected to say Hank was still in the apartment.

Deanna refused Fred's initial request for sweet and sour pork and countered with an offer to bring a bag of salad and low-fat dressing. After some bartering they agreed to Chinese chicken salad. "That's what I expected I'd end up with, but it was worth the try to get something better," Fred said.

Slightly before noon Deanna arrived with two orders of Chinese chicken salad as planned. Based on a hunch, she added an order of spring rolls, hoping it was as healthy as the name implied. Deanna's heart beat fast and loud as she rang the doorbell to the luxury condo. Her nervous stomach quickly dissipated and she had to suppress a snicker at the sight of Hank's gaping mouth and befuddled stammers as he stared at her on the doorstep. "Your dad called and asked me to bring him Chinese. I don't know if it's forbidden and he didn't think you would comply with his cheating, or if he wanted us to meet again." She was pleased with how calm her voice sounded as she passed Hank and headed to the kitchen, carrying a brown paper bag filled with white takeout containers.

"Oh, okay. I don't know. Is Chinese food low salt, low fat? Why does he keep calling you?" Hank remained where he was, with his hand on the doorknob of the wide open front door.

Deanna had been to Fred and Stephanie's place multiple times when she and Hank were dating, but she was not familiar with their kitchen storage. "Where are the plates and silverware?" she asked.

Hank closed the door in slow motion and warily crossed the plush carpet, giving his bemused brain time to reorient. He joined Deanna in the kitchen. Opening the upper cupboard left of the sink, he reached, paused, looked at Deanna for confirmation of whether she was eating with them or not. He received nothing other than an amused smirk. Turning his back on her to steady his hands, he proceeded to take out three plates. The possibility of her staying for lunch squelched his appetite but the option of her not staying escalated his discomfort to rival a violent flu. Since their encounter on Thursday, Hank had been eating poorly and sleeping fitfully. He needed to know if she was still seeing the guy his brother had caught her with. He wished he didn't care, but he did. Desperately.

Fred entered the kitchen, smiled at Deanna, frowned at his son, and plopped down at the table. He adjusted the plaid flannel bathrobe over his sweat pants and frayed t-shirt. "Well, are we going to eat or not?" he asked. Fred made small talk about the weather and the inadequate quality of entertainment on TV, ignoring the lack of response from his tablemates. While Fred ate and talked as if nothing was wrong, Deanna and Hank stared at their plates and poked at their food. After an uncomfortable quarter of an hour, Fred pushed his empty plate away, and slid his chair back from the table creating two distinct scratching noises. He stood up and said, "I'm going to sit down and take a rest. Hank, do you remember when you were little and you and your brother would fight?" Hank nodded, giving his father a look of confusion mixed with suspicion. "I'd make you two sit across the table from each other until you finally worked out your disagreement. Well, I'm doing the same thing today because, frankly, you are both acting like little children. Neither of you may leave this table until you've talked about whatever the problem is. I'll be sitting in my recliner in the front room, guarding the door to make sure neither of you leave before you're done." He turned around and shuffled off.

Clearly, Fred was serious. Deanna and Hank cautiously made eye contact. Hank said, "I haven't had to do this for at least fifteen years. I learned a long time ago that sitting silently only makes the ordeal take longer. So, how have you been?"

Deanna shrugged and looked away. "I've been okay. School keeps me busy." Her tone was guarded. "How about you?"

"School keeps me busy as well. My mom, my job, Oregon, all of it has been a good learning experience, but I don't plan to sign a contract for next year. I'm really thinking about going back to school for a doctorate. I prefer teaching at the college level. I think next year I'll just substitute and look into PhD programs. I'll probably come back here, although I guess it doesn't matter. They seem to need subs everywhere." His brown eyes probed her face for an answer to his unspoken question. "At least, I don't think it matters."

Unable to restrain herself or the tears she had battled for the past few days, Deanna blurted out, "What about Kathy?"

"Who's Kathy?" Hank asked.

Deanna dropped her head into her crossed arms on the tabletop as sobs took over her body. Reaching across, Hank gently stroked her silky brown hair and asked again, "Who is

Kathy?"

Hank's words slowly took meaning in Deanna's conscious. She lifted her head and sniffed. Wiping her eyes with the back of her hands, she smeared mascara across her face, almost to her hairline. She looked like an ancient Egyptian. Her voice cracked as she answered, "She's the girl you dumped me for."

Hank sprang out of his seat and moved around the table and cradled Deanna's face in his hands. He smiled into her blackened, smudged eyes. "I have no idea who Kathy is or where you got the idea that I dumped you for anyone, but I can assure you there is no one except you in my heart. This year has been miserable. I miss you desperately and I beg you to let me prove that I love you more than anyone else ever could. Whoever it is that you're seeing, give me a chance to win you back from him." Hank pulled Deanna to his chest and held her in a tighter embrace than was comfortable. Deanna responded into his rumpled t-shirt, "I'm not seeing anyone and I don't want to see anyone except you." Hank laid his cheek against the top of her head. Her soft brown hair caressed the side of his face as he whispered chivalrous promises. Deanna clung to him, trying to squeeze out the pain of the past months, and began crying again. This time the salt water irrigated and cleansed the wound that had been festering. When her sobs subsided, Hank tipped her face up and kissed her determinedly. If his words and embrace had not convinced her of his steadfast love, his kiss certainly did.

When both the weeping and kissing reached a lull, Hank asked again, "Who is Kathy?"

Five and One-Half Years Before

Mary was almost home after a contentious faculty meeting. She squeezed the steering wheel with residual frustration, her jaw clenched, tension radiating down her neck into her shoulders and arms. Today was Monday, her day off, yet a peer had persuaded her to attend a meeting and present current research correlating increased classroom participation with student success. Mary agreed on the condition she could give her spiel and leave, since this was a non-duty day. More importantly, her mother would be unattended while she was gone. Mary prepared a fifteen-minute presentation. Questions might stretch it out to twenty. Even with the drive and parking she would be gone less than an hour. Greta would be fine on her own for that long.

Mary entered the faculty lounge, expecting to present immediately. The department chair, however, handed Mary an agenda and pointed to the last item, "You're here." Mary started to disagree but the power-obsessed head of the department rudely turned her back on Mary and proceeded to the front of the room to begin the meeting. "We will follow the agenda as posted," she informed the faculty with a challenging nod toward Mary.

After more than an hour of futile discussions, during which Mary could feel her blood pressure rising, she finally had the platform. Then, instead of giving a brief presentation, she had to debate the merit of the research. Several instructors discredited the results simply because if the research was accurate, it had negative implications about the effectiveness of their teaching.

It had been close to three hours since Mary had left her mother reading the paper and drinking tea. There was no lunch waiting in the fridge if Greta got hungry. There was no one to listen to her stories or reorient her to the day and time if she became confused. As the distance from campus increased and the span to home decreased, Mary's tension shifted from vexation of the past few hours to guilt over abandoning her mother. She increased the pressure on the gas pedal, accelerating a fair amount above the legal limit. Mary turned into the cul-de-sac and came around the curve where Greta's house sat. A shot of panic pierced through

Mary. Her stomach lurched. Stepping hard on the break, Mary pulled to the curb, and jumped out. Scurrying up Greta's driveway she examined the gray Ford parked there. Her eyes bugged out and her tongue felt as parched as dry leather. Finding the car parked in the driveway instead of the garage was a concern, but the large dent beginning at the passenger side rear wheel and extending to the smashed taillight and drooping bumper trumped all other worries of the day.

Greta's driver's license had expired six months ago. Most days Greta remembered she was no longer a licensed driver, but nothing stayed in her mind every single day. A couple months before her license expired, Greta had picked up the DMV renewal study guide, but she never made an appointment. If Greta had shown up at the DMV, she would have been refused a renewal based on medical records submitted by her doctor, but she never knew that. During the last year that Greta's license was valid, she drove infrequently. Usually she went either five blocks to the grocery store or six blocks the opposite direction to the post office. Deanna, on the other hand, drove the car several times a week. Everyone, including Greta, referred to it as Deanna's car. In a few months, Deanna would head off to college in that gray Ford, but in the meantime, it resided in Greta's garage.

Mary rushed into the house. "Mom what happened to your car? Are you okay?"

Greta looked up, nonchalantly. "What?" She was comfortably reclined in her chair with the cat napping on her lap and today's news spread over the armrest to accommodate the cat.

"Were you driving today, or did Deanna have the car?" Mary asked realizing the dent could have been the fault of a seventeen-year-old, inexperienced driver just as easily as a confused eighty-year-old.

Greta scratched the top of the cat's head. He purred contentedly but gave no other indication of being awake.

"Tabby and I have been here reading the newspaper. I don't have anywhere I need to go."

"Do you know why your car is in the driveway instead of the garage or how it got the dent?"

Unperturbed, Greta answered, "It has a dent? The policeman didn't tell me it was dented."

"Were you in a car accident?" Mary asked, coming closer and scanning her mother for any evidence of injury. Mary was silently scolding herself for not hiding Greta's keys, as Dean had been recommending. Her mother had keys to the car and both houses attached to a single keychain. Mary had intended to remove the car key but hadn't done it yet. Dean had lobbied for taking away all Greta's keys. He did not want her going in and out of houses without their knowledge.

"I don't think there was an accident. The policeman just drove me home to be nice. He must have left it in the driveway," Greta answered and flipped the crinkly page of the newspaper.

"The police drove you home!?" Mary interrogated, her volume increasing with fear and frustration. Bringing her face close to Greta's in an effort to get her mother's undivided attention, Mary demanded, "Tell me what happened today!"

"Nothing happened." Greta pushed her daughter back, out of her personal space. "I was having a nice drive and a friendly police officer stopped to talk to me. He knows my parents. He asked to see my license, but I forgot my purse so I didn't have it. He wouldn't let me drive without my license so he drove me home." Folding the daily newspaper and draping it over the side of the chair, Greta lifted the cat off her lap, dropped him on the floor, and pushed herself up and out of the soft recliner. "Would you like some tea? I'm going to put a cup into the microwave for myself."

Mary stepped in front of her mother, obstructing the path to the kitchen. "There is a large dent in your car, Mom. The bumper is hanging down on one side and the taillight is broken." Mary put her hands on her hips and peered insistently into her mother's eyes. "Do you know how your car got that dent?"

"Oh, someone was telling me about that. I think he backed up into it, but I didn't think it was very bad so I told him not to worry about it." Greta stepped around her daughter and walked to the kitchen. She filled a cup with water and placed it in the microwave. She punched in seven zero zero and the hum of the microwave began.

"What are you doing?" Mary demanded. "That is way more time than you need to heat up water, and this is important. Try to remember what happened to your car."

"No it's not. Seven makes it perfect." Greta took a tea bag out of the bowl on the counter, pulled the sugar bowl and spoon forward, and prepared to wait patiently.

Mary had moved the things Greta used frequently to visible, easily accessible places. Items still got lost occasionally, but considerably less time was wasted on unnecessary searches. Over the last year, Mary also adhered labels around the house with messages such as "towels here" and "put mail here." Clearly, she would need to affix one onto the microwave saying, "tea 90 seconds."

After a minute and a half Mary took the mug out and set it on the counter in front of her mother. Greta plopped in the tea bag, added a heaping spoonful of sugar, and stirred. Mary asked again, this time with forced restraint that sounded patronizing, "Mom, do you know what happened to your car or how it ended up in the driveway?"

"I think that's where the policeman parked it."

"Why was a police officer driving your car?"

Greta smiled. "He was very nice. He gave me a ride home."

Mary was struggling to remaining calm. This was harder than explaining grades to an unreasonable student. In a saccharine-sweet voice Mary asked, "Why did the nice policeman give you a ride home?"

"I think it was because the mean man at the store hit

my car. My car needs to be fixed," Greta added. "Someone told me it has a big dent, but I haven't seen it yet."

"So, someone backed up into your car today and the police drove you home," Mary repeated for clarification and validation. "Were you in the grocery store parking lot?"

Greta blew on her tea before cautiously taking a sip. She looked up at her daughter with a blank, passive expression. "What, dear?"

"Did you go to the store this morning?" Mary asked sharply, trying to fit together the pieces of the disjointed story.

"Oh no. I haven't gone anywhere today."

"Did someone back up into your car?"

"Yes. My very first car. It was red. Do you remember it? I loved that car. I was so sad when someone hit it." Greta had a far away, dreamy expression as she drank more tea.

Mary sighed and rolled her eyes like a teenager. Then, in an attempt to bring her mother back to the present, she demanded, "Did a policeman drive you home today, Mom?"

"What? Of course not. I have never had a policeman drive me home."

Mary released an exasperated grunt, picked up the cordless phone receiver, sat down at the table, and called the local police department. They had no report of an accident involving Greta's car and no record of an officer driving her home today or any other day. Through the window, Mary could see the car in the driveway, its rear bumper a lopsided frown, mocking and challenging her. If it had a tongue it would have been sticking it out. Mary took her mother's key ring off the hook on the wall and said, "Your car needs some work. I don't think it can be driven until we get the bumper fixed. I'm taking your keys and I'll have Deanna or Dean help me get it to the repair shop."

Greta sat down at the kitchen table, across from her daughter, to enjoy her tea break. "You know that car belongs to Deanna now. I never renewed my license so I can't drive anymore. You should keep it at your house." Greta took another careful drink of hot tea.

"Yes, that's a good idea. I'll keep it at my house." Mary pocketed the keys. Taking Greta's keys had not triggered the expected catastrophic reaction, at least not today. There was no telling how many times in the next weeks and months Greta would complain of losing her keys or accuse Mary of stealing them and demand their return, but, as all of the literature supporting Alzheimer's caregivers recommended, take one day at a time. Today, Greta was giving up her car and her keys willingly, and that was a huge victory for Mary.

The mystery of the dent and the policeman was never solved. Over the years, the story turned into a staple at Nilsson family functions, with each family member holding to his or her own unsubstantiated theory of the events of that day.

The gray Ford was repaired. It spent the scorching summer parked on the street in front of Deanna's house instead of in Greta's garage, where the aging paint would have been protected from the intense San Joaquin Valley sun.

The third week of August arrived. Deanna loaded the car with all her clothes, new extra-long twin bedding, and a few random desk supplies stuffed into the corners of the vehicle. She took off for Fresno, music blaring and nervous energy soaring. Dean and Mary followed somberly with the rest of her possessions.

They arrived at Fresno State. Dean and Mary drove up and down the lanes of the nearly full parking lot in front of the three-story dorm building before finding two adjacent spots. They pulled into one and Deanna, behind them in the Ford Focus, took the other. Before getting out Dean and Mary eyed each other. Dean gave Mary a reassuring nod and she responded with a tight, forced grin. "I know we have to let her grow up, but it's gone so much faster than I expected," Mary said. She opened the car door and found her daughter already waiting on the blacktop. "Let's go find my room before we get anything out," Deanna said brightly as she leaned back and bounced against the side of her car.

Deanna's roommate had not checked in yet, so Deanna picked the bed, closet, and desk on the right-hand side of the institutional-white, rectangular dorm room. Then, Deanna and her parents began the slow, heavy unloading of two cars followed by a futile attempt to fit all her college gear into half of a tiny room. With many students arriving at the same time, the elevator was crowded and slow, so the Nilssons used the narrow staircase as they made the trek between the parking lot and the second story a dozen times. Mary and Dean had wanted to take Deanna and her new roommate out to lunch, but the roommate had not checked in yet, and Mary, unused to so much physical labor, was exhausted. Deanna flitted from room to room, meeting her floormates. Currently she was three doors away introducing herself to two girls from the San Francisco Bay Area. Not wanting to dampen her enthusiasm, Dean and Mary found their daughter, restrained their tears, hugged her goodbye, and headed home in depressing silence to their big, empty house.

Deanna's first week of college passed in a blur of spirit-filled rallies and orientations. She lost her voice cheering the Bulldogs on to a win at the first home football game. After a month, however, Deanna was annoyed by her roommate's excessive use of the snooze alarm. During midterms, the minimal floor space of the textbook-strewn dorm room made Deanna feel claustrophobic. November arrived, bringing an uncomfortable chill. As Deanna threw away a full serving of soggy noodles and watered-down tomato paste that the dining commons called lasagna, she fantasized about the scrumptious turkey and stuffing she would be eating at home in two weeks. But rather than the hoped-for respite, Thanksgiving marked the beginning of the sprint to the end of the semester. Deanna spent the long holiday weekend alone in her bedroom with her nose in textbooks. When the last final of her first semester of college was over, Deanna headed home for a much-needed break.

During the first few days of vacation, Deanna slept until noon, then camped out on the couch in baggy sweats, catching up on TV shows. By Wednesday, she was ready to rekindle old friendships. Walking past the TV without even a glance, she found her phone and dialed a high school friend.

At eight p.m., a group of girls gathered at Starbucks, greeting each other with screams and hugs. Deanna soon felt left out from the local gossip and defensive over their complaints about community college; the college where both of her parents worked. Deanna caught them up on her life. She described the infectious energy in the student section at football games and the camaraderie of the dorms during midterms and finals. Her friends listened politely, unmoved by her stories.

At ten pm Starbucks locked up and kicked out Deanna and her friends. Keeping their goodbyes brief in the chilly air, they made vague suggestions but no concrete plans to meet again. Deanna climbed into her car and pulled her cell phone out of her purse. She dialed her roommate. They each apologized to the other for their end of the semester irritability and selfishness.

Deanna spent New Year's Eve in Modesto with new college friends and joined them on a road trip to go shopping during the January sales in San Francisco. During spring semester, the days lengthened and warmed, along with Deanna's appreciation of collegiate life.

3:00 p.m. Waiting

Two Years Before

"I talked with the agency this afternoon and they're going to assign two caregivers to Mom. The agency will still handle the scheduling but this way we'll have someone to call as a backup when one of them doesn't show up," Mary informed Dean as she changed into cotton pajama pants and an old t-shirt. "I know consistency helps Mom and she would do better with a single caregiver, but I can't keep changing my plans and cancelling classes at the last minute to cover for their problems. Initially, I thought we just had bad luck picking people. We somehow chose aides with an unusual amount of family crises. Now, I'm thinking it's normal for caregivers to have chaotic lives and multiple family members they're responsible for along with their client caseload." Mary plopped down on the edge of bed. She elevated her right foot onto her left knee and began kneading the sore spot on the ball below the big toe. "I sure am tired. I'm about at my limit of handling problems with Mom and her caregivers."

Dean was sitting in the leather chair tucked into the back corner of their bedroom. He lifted his gaze up from his book for the first time. "I've been at my limit of all of this for at least two years."

"What are you talking about? You don't help care for Mom," Mary said rather sharply. "I don't think you've even been listening to me," she accused.

Dean methodically inserted his bookmark, closed his book, and set it on the little table next to his chair. Then, he took off his reading glasses and peered straight into Mary's eyes. Leaning forward with his elbows on his knees and his hands hanging down between his legs, he swung the black plastic glasses back and forth, as if he was winding himself up to speak. "Quite honestly, Mary, I quit listening several years ago." Doubt and confusion crossed Mary's face. Dean's glasses continued to keep time like a metronome. "I keep telling myself 'this isn't permanent. Things will change and then our relationship will get better.' Well, things do change, but always for the worse. I'm not sure it will ever end and I can't wait patiently any longer."

"What are you talking about? My mom has Alzheimer's. I can't make her well. I would if I could but I can't. You're my sounding board. I rely on you. I need you to listen when I vent that her caregiver didn't show up or canceled at the last minute..."

"Or your mom steals and hides the mail. Or she refuses to bathe or change her clothes. Or she puts eye makeup all over her face. I know your mother has Alzheimer's and that's very stressful for you, but I am your husband. You seem to think I'm nothing more than a one-way call center for you to list your grievances. I'm not. This is supposed to be a marriage. I think you've forgotten what that looks like."

Mary reeled back like she had been hit by a physical shock wave rather than an unexpected verbal explosion. She regained her balance and leaned forward on the edge of the king-size bed, staring at her husband, panic rapidly spreading from her gut to her trembling fingers. "Are you unhappy with our marriage?" she asked in breathy shock.

Dean stood up, instinctively ready to take a comforting step toward Mary, but he stopped himself. He dropped his glasses on top of his book and pushed his hands into the pockets of his khaki pants. His head hung sorrowfully as he spoke to his sneakers. "I'm not happy, Mary. I still love you, or at least, I love the person you used to be, and the life we had in the past. But, that life and that person seem like a long-lost memory these days."

"Dean, I'm sorry. I really am. I guess I've been so worried about my mom I didn't think about you." Mary's eyes begged him for reassurance. "Why didn't you tell me sooner?"

Dean shrugged. In a dejected monotone he said, "I've tried, but you don't listen to me."

"Yes I do."

"Really?" He looked up, challenging her. "What report am I creating at work?" No answer. "Where did I suggest we go on a vacation?"

"I remember you talking about that. It was somewhere in the US—the East Coast."

"Not the US. Canada. I really want to see Nova Scotia and the bay of Fundy." Some animation returned to Dean's voice. "I've watched several documentaries on the area and I find it fascinating. I asked if you would like to go in the summer or wait until the fall to see the trees in full color. Of course, the question is, can you take time off work in the fall?"

"And can I make arrangements so we can leave Mom for that long."

Dean threw his hands up in the air, frustration returned. "Every conversation turns to your mother! I am sick of your mom being the central theme in our lives. She has lived next to us practically since the day we got married. Deanna's gone—this should be our chance to reconnect and enjoy each other, but we can't because of your mother." Dean stomped across the room headed toward the doorway, passing Mary without a glance.

"Where are you going?" Mary stood and reached toward her husband, her outstretched hands open and pleading. "Dean, please. What do you want me to do?"

Turning back toward his wife, Dean answered, "I am going to sleep on the couch in my office. What should you do? Well, for one, don't fixate on your mom all the time. And two, consider me...us. Eighty percent of what you do and say relates to your mom. The rest is about work. Less than one percent pertains to our relationship. Do you have any idea when we last made love?"

"It wasn't that long ago. Last week I think."

"No, last month. It was after we went out for my birthday. Mary, don't kid yourself, things are really bad between us. Maybe bad is the wrong word. Empty might be more accurate, because we don't have a relationship anymore. The fact that you haven't noticed is a sign of your disinterest in our marriage. I've wondered what would happen if I left. I was estimating how many days it would take before you even noticed I was gone."

Dean's long, thin face blurred and distorted in Mary's vision. Her throat constricted. Sound would not have escaped through the narrow passage if she had tried to speak. During all the emotional turmoil related to her mom over the last few years, Mary had depended on Dean's steadfast support and understanding, taking it for granted. She'd never imagined he was feeling neglected. She'd certainly never entertained the idea that he might leave her, and she was not sure she could survive if he did. Deanna was grown and out of the house, her mom was gone in most ways except physically, and now Dean was talking about being dissatisfied with their marriage. Mary's entire existence was spiraling into dark, cold, airless outer space. *So the Elizabethan writers were correct after all,* Mary thought. *A person can die from shock and emotional pain.* Shakespeare's leading lady, Hero, was never faking death; she really was dead—

emotionally expired, even if not physically deceased.

Mary took a slow, faltering breath through her trembling lips, squeezing past the mass obstructing her airway. Surprisingly, her heart beat despite the crushing pressure on her chest, circulating the inhaled oxygen from her lungs to her icy cold limbs. The heart is a remarkable organ. It can keep a body alive when the soul has been mortally pierced by unexpected painful words, or when existence has withered slowly, overtaken by dementia, but nonetheless, is gone.

For Mary, her marriage was more than just satisfying, it was the solid foundation that gave her world stability and prevented it from flying apart into a million irretrievable pieces. "Is it too late?" squeaked out of Mary's mouth around the swollen lump in her throat.

"I don't know. I've been rehearsing this dialogue in my mind over and over and every time I want to talk to you, you are upset about something. So, I wait. Or, a crisis happens with your mother and you have to run off. So, I wait. I think I may have waited too long. I don't know what's left to save."

"How can you have been feeling this way and I didn't know?" Mary asked.

"That is my question for you. After twenty-three years, do you really know me so little that you can't tell when I'm unhappy? Or do you not care? You're so caught up in your mother's health and Deanna's romance that you never have time for me. I need time too, Mary. I'm tired of being last on your to-do list. Just below scrubbing the toilets."

In a tremulous, breathy whisper Mary asked, "Are you leaving me?"

"I think you left me a long time ago." Dean walked out of the bedroom.

Mary's legs gave way. She collapsed onto the bed, buried her face in her hands, and allowed the cascade of tears to flow unhindered.

The next morning, when the sun's first pale rays shone

through Mary's window, she untangled herself from the twisted sheets, slipped her feet into slippers, and tiptoed out of the bedroom. Quietly, she opened the door to Dean's office and peeked in. Dean's tall, thin frame was stretched across the short couch. His feet and lower legs extended over the armrest, unsupported and uncovered by the small brown throw blanket over his torso. His head was resting on the opposite armrest as if it was a pillow. He looked just like the Dr. Seuss character who can't keep his whole body inside the bed. Mary took a step back and silently pulled the door closed. She knew they needed to have a long and serious talk, but after a night of far more tossing and turning than sleeping she was in no shape for an intense discussion. And, despite the lengthy, solitary night of thinking, she could not identify her feelings and certainly could not express them.

Needing something to do, Mary decided to check on her mother. She threw a robe over her pajamas and padded across the front yard, past the neighbor's, to her mother's house. Turning the front door key as gently as possible, Mary entered and crept to the master bedroom. Greta lay curled up on her side, facing away from Mary. Her hair gleamed like strands of silver thread embellishing her white lacy pillowcase. The old-world lace of the matching comforter, embroidered with scattered pink rosebuds, was pulled up to her chin. The bedding rose and fell with a steady, peaceful pattern. The gentle and predictable rhythm comforted Mary, like watching waves wash in and out on the sand. Occasionally, Greta's cheek would twitch into a momentary smile or she would release a contented sigh. Compassion and protectiveness swelled in Mary's breast as she watched her frail mother rest.

Greta lay near the edge of the queen-size bed. The lazy cat occupied the rest. He was stretched across the extra pillow with his white belly exposed and his gray striped legs extended to their fullest.

Mary observed her mother's breathing for several minutes in soothing silence. It was still early, barely past dawn, so Mary left as quietly as she had entered, and went home to wait and fret. She found a full-sized blanket in the closet, silently entered Dean's office and stretched it over his body. Dazed and only half-conscious, he mumbled "thanks" and repositioned himself, immediately back to sleep. When he passed Mary in the hallway later that morning, he gave her a peck on the check, but said nothing. Mary and Dean remained distant but civil to each other.

Dean continued to cram his tall frame onto the short couch in his office for the next two nights. Mary was still evaluating and processing Dean's complaints about their relationship and Dean was emotionally spent. He was relieved that his building frustration had finally been expressed, but he was not ready for another emotional encounter. And, Mary could not yet talk without her feelings overtaking her reason. They both knew a discussion was necessary and inevitable, but for now they were in the calm eye of the storm. They were not on safe ground, but they had some time to regroup and prepare before the next onslaught.

They were not able to devote all their time to pondering their relationship, however, because they had responsibilities. Their jobs demanded attention and Greta required supervision.

"Hi Mom. It's Saturday morning. Let's go in. I'm going to help you take a shower." Mary reached for Greta's elbow in an attempt to escort her mother inside. Even though today was Deanna's day on the schedule of alternating Saturdays, Mary needed to get Greta bathed and dressed before Deanna arrived. Deanna accepted her grandmother's confused conversation and odd behavior with grace and love, but she angrily held Mary accountable when Greta looked unkempt, or smelled musty. Both of which were true today.

"I already took a shower this morning," Greta said, pulling out of Mary's grasp and reaching to pick an expired flower off the gardenia bush in her front yard.

"No, I just arrived. You, ah...you wore that to bed," Mary said, eyeing the odd mismatch of color and texture on her mother. Greta wore a red and green plaid flannel Christmas pajama top paired with summer-weight pajama pants, on which two shades of orange geraniums climbed a soft yellow background. *She just needs some fall leaves to have the whole calendar covered,* Mary thought.

After getting up, Greta decided she wanted to garden, so she put on undergarments. Unfortunately, she put them on over what she was wearing. She hooked the bra in front, but then got confused and did not twist it around. She proceeded to slip her arms through the straps of the backwards bra. The clasp under her bust pushed her breasts up as if she was wearing a corset. The cups protruded from her back, resembling some kind of mythical double anterior human.

The underpants were worse. Both of Greta's legs went through the same leg hole. From the right side, it looked like she was wearing a tight, but old and frayed, white mini skirt over loose cotton print leggings. The opposite side appeared to have a large tumor protruding from her hip, cradled in a white cotton dressing. Her tangled, flat-backed, high-topped hairdo added to the comical disarray.

"Come on Mom. We need to go inside." Mary grasped Greta's arm firmly, biting into the flesh of her upper arm, and pulled her up the front walk. Mary succumbed to the temptation to look up and down the block. The neighbors understood. In fact, most had offered to help, but Mary was still embarrassed by her mother's appearance. With relief, she noted no one was mowing the grass or playing with their kids on the front lawn yet. Hopefully, the entire neighborhood had slept in and missed her mom dressed like a bizarre, unkempt clown.

"Where are we going?" Greta asked.

"It's time for a shower."

"I don't want to shower. I don't need a shower," Greta

insisted and tried to pull her arm out of Mary's grasp. Mary pushed her mother through the front door.

"Mom, let's check the calendar. Look. This is today. It says shower on your calendar. That means you need to shower today." Mary pointed at Friday even though it was Saturday. She would cross Friday off on the calendar only after Greta received the shower intended for that day. As of yet, she had not.

"I already had a shower. I took one this morning. Now, I want to go out and take a walk."

In January, Mary had hung up the glossy, month-at-a-glance calendar advertising Ted and Ned's auto repair. Each month featured a photograph of a classic car and provided a daily box for Mary and the caregivers to write "shower" or "take medicine" or other necessary activities. For the past six months, the calendar trick had worked like magic. If something was written down, Greta believed it was important. Every Monday and Friday listed shower. If Greta adamantly refused to bathe, which she sometimes did, the caregiver would not cross out the day on the calendar. The next day when the caregiver and Greta looked at the calendar "shower" would still be written on what appeared to be the current date. When Greta did bathe, whether it be Monday, Tuesday, or Wednesday, the caregiver would cross off Monday on the calendar in front of Greta, and slyly return later to cross off the other days, making the calendar accurate. In reality, the hired help bathed Greta sometime between Monday and Thursday, and Mary gave her the second shower of the week sometime between Friday and Sunday.

Recently, however, the calendar trick was losing its power, like soda gone flat. Greta had refused to shower all week, regardless of how many times she was shown the calendar. She gave off a stale odor. Her matted hair made it obvious she was the origin of the bad scent. Mary moved on to the next tactic she'd kept in reserve for weeks like this. She reached out and removed the exterior brassiere, then began unbuttoning her mother's pajama top. "We need to unbutton your top, Mom," Mary said. No request. No explanation. No preamble. And absolutely no mention of the word shower.

Mary occasionally attended an Alzheimer's caregivers' support group. At every meeting, the longest discussion revolved around ideas to coax confused loved ones into bathing. Some members had horror stories. One woman's mother called 911 to report she was being held hostage by a murderer. Crouched in the corner, she'd whispered to the emergency dispatch operator that an intruder was in her bathroom preparing the murder scene to look like an accident. Fortunately, or perhaps unfortunately, 911 knew the phone number well and helped talk the woman into taking her shower. An obese Alzheimer's patient had refused her bath all morning. In the afternoon, she'd finally climbed into the tub, where she'd stayed for four hours. The caregiver, who was outweighed by a hundred pounds, could neither pull nor coerce her charge out of the water. All the caregiver was able to do was refresh the warm water until the woman finally grabbed the tub lip and safety rail with her pruney hands, lifted herself up, and said, "My, that was refreshing." The general principle Mary had gleaned from the meetings and stories was if a person with dementia does not want to bathe, the caregiver must avoid speaking the words bath, bathe, or shower at all costs.

"What are you doing?" Greta asked, pushing Mary's hands away from her chest.

"Unbuttoning your top."

"I can do that," Greta stubbornly asserted and began undoing the buttons Mary had not yet loosened.

Mary ushered her mother, now topless, into the bathroom and guided her to sit down on the fuzzy, faded-pink toilet seat cover, undoubtedly a gift from Deanna a decade ago. Mary started the shower and adjusted the water temperature. Turning back toward her mother, she pulled the underpants and pajama pants off before pushing Greta, with a bit of force, into the spray of warm water. Greta had been much younger when she'd bought this house, but even back then, she'd appreciated the walk-in shower in the master bathroom. She said stepping over the side of a tub would get harder and harder as she got older. In recent years, Mary was especially grateful for her mother's foresight.

The Wedding Day

After finishing his pictures, Dean plopped down on the front pew. He stretched his long, skinny legs out and crossed his ankles. Nothing to do from now until the wedding began. The forced air of the heater whistled through the vent, making the candle flames on the right side of the altar stand taller and flicker brighter than the left. It already looked like they had burned more wax than the candles of the left. Dean wondered if there were extra candles, in case they melted down before the ceremony. The stiff, unforgiving leather of the shiny black dress shoes pinched his feet. He wiggled his toes and rubbed an imaginary scuff on the top of his right shoe against his left pant leg. Next, he examined his fingers and nails. He massaged the callus on his right middle finger where his pencil rested. It was harder, rougher, and lighter in color than the surrounding skin, like a granite boulder protruding from a meadow, only in miniature. Deanna had loved to climb the granite boulders scattered around Yosemite Valley when she was a girl. She would clamber up the largest rock and declare herself queen of the mountain. Yosemite had been their favorite getaway destination. Dean sighed, rested his hands in his lap, and stared off at nothing. Staying focused today was a challenge. The fact that his attention span seemed shorter than a toddler's was not helping to make the time go faster. Maybe he had something to do or read in his car. He pictured the box of files in his trunk. Were any of them appropriate to work on while he waited? Most had some level of confidentiality, so probably not. He tried to remember if his latest copy of *Business Week* was in the file box. Maybe a Grisham thriller was stuffed in the glovebox. As he considered where he could find reading material, doubt surfaced and soon trumped his desire for a book or magazine. Dean was certain an unspoken rule existed prohibiting the father of the bride from working or pleasure reading on his daughter's wedding day. He groaned and slumped lower into the pew. The next hour was going to be interminable.

The wedding coordinator ushered Hank, his parents, and his groomsmen into the sanctuary through the side door, and turned them over to the photographer. Dean was pleasantly distracted by the groom and his friends teasing and pushing each other around as the photographer attempted to catch the rare moments when they were all where they were supposed to be and no one was making rabbit ears on someone else's head. Dean smiled. Nervous men always act like junior high boys. He wished he could join them. Perhaps that would take the edge off his own anxiety.

Hank's mom joined Dean, a little too closely, on the front pew. The red silk of her tight dress brushed Dean's thigh. He inched away. She grabbed his upper arm, encircling it with her manicured hands, and pleaded loudly for Dean to talk some sense into her ex-husband, who's back towered in front of her. Fred had to have heard her, but he remained as impassive as a brick wall. Dean mumbled something and stood up, tugging his arm out of her resistant grasp. Last night Dean had ignored their bickering, but he could not tolerate it today. More accurately, her bickering, because Fred rarely even acknowledged she was talking to him. He would stare right through her, then rudely turn and walk away which, unfortunately, escalated her shrill demands.

Dean left the sanctuary and wandered around the church. Each part of the building brought back images of Deanna as a child. He could picture her skipping down the Sunday school hall in white Mary Janes and lace-edged bobby socks, showing off a new pink polka dot Easter dress and coordinating pink hat. Today's dress was created by a fashion designer out of exquisite fabrics, but that Easter dress from the girl's department at Mervyn's was the image he would treasure every time he walked this hall.

Dean passed the nursery and heard Deanna laugh. Not very long ago that sound would have sent him rushing to find Mary. She would want to know Deanna was having fun in the church nursery rather than crying. It had been twenty years ago that Deanna was a toddler reluctant to leave her mother. How quickly those twenty years had passed!

Dean tapped on the nursery door and a sudden quiet ensured. "Deanna?" he called gently. The door opened a crack and his daughter's sparking blue eye, perfectly outlined in charcoal, peeked out. "Hank isn't around, is he?" she asked.

"No. Just me. He's taking pictures with the guys and then his family will do some pictures after that." The door opened partway, Deanna grabbed her father's arm, pulled him in, and slammed the door behind him. "I was worried that you were Hank trying to sneak in," she explained.

Dean looked around at the young women in matching dresses. He should remember their names but his mind was too scrambled to even attempt it right now. After an awkward silence Ashley said, "Time to infiltrate the enemy ranks. We'll gather intelligence, and let you know what is happening on the front lines, Deanna." The four bridesmaids left. The swish of satin and twitter of giggles receded down the hall.

Dean looked at his daughter. He knew Mary had been on the verge of tears all day, but his enemy today was confusion. The vivid mental image of his little girl skipping in the hallway did not match the beautiful, elegant young woman standing before him. He loved this woman in front of him, but he knew in his heart, he would never love her again with the same intensity as he'd loved that little girl in her Easter dress. His consolation was that he was certain Hank loved her now with the same protective and self-sacrificing love as he had loved her then. She would be okay. She would be happy. Knowing that, he could let go.

"Dad, don't just stand there and stare. You're making me feel self-conscious."

Dean shook his head. "You have no reason to be self-conscious. If anything, you should be aware you're the most beautiful bride in the history of the world."

Deanna smiled with pleasure. "Thank you, but we both know that's ridiculous."

"Well, the only brides I ever really looked at closely were Aunt Audrey--and I wondered why anyone would want to marry her--your mom, and now you. Don't tell your mom, but you are even prettier than she was on our wedding day."

Deanna laughed. She relished the compliment but countered with, "I spent ten times more money on my dress, hair, and makeup than Mom did. I guess that should make me look ten times better."

Dean took her hand and solemnly said, "You do."

"Your wedding was entirely different," Deanna defended her mother. "Mom would have looked ridiculous with a dress like this and two guests."

"I suppose you're right," Dean conceded. His wedding had included eight people total: the bride, groom, mother of the bride, sister and brother-in-law of the groom with their two children, plus an officiant. That was all.

Dean and Mary had both worked at the college for many years prior to their marriage. She knew all the faculty and educational administrators. He'd worked in the accounting department at the district office and was acquainted with most of the non-educational personnel, including vendors, the college president, chancellor, and board of trustees. They had two choices for their wedding. They could invite coworkers along with relatives and have several hundred guests, or they could have an intimate family-only celebration. Since Mary was an only child and Dean had one sibling but had already lost both of his parents, a family wedding for them was smaller than for most people. Mary took a day to rule out the big wedding. Dean listened with dread as she considered it and concurred with relief when she realized a small, simple ceremony suited them better. She rationalized they were older and established. Combining two households would be hard as it was. They certainly did not need a lot of gifts. For Dean, being the guest of honor at a large traditional wedding sounded like torture.

There were so many things Dean wanted to tell Deanna today, but expressing emotions left him tongue tied at the best of times, and currently his emotions were more perplexing than any he had previously experienced. Finally, he looked down at his polished black shoes so Deanna's image would not hinder his ability to think or speak. "You know that your mom and I love you. We are very proud of the woman you have become. Today is hard for your mother because she feels like she is letting go of you. I don't feel the same. I believe it is time for you to move ahead with your own life, and I know you're ready. I've given you everything I can; I've finished my job. I tried to be a father and a friend, your champion and your protector. The one thing I can never be is your knight in shining armor."

Deanna blinked rapidly trying to dissipate the developing tears. "Stop, Dad. You're going to mess up my makeup before the wedding even begins."

"Let me finish. I'm almost done. What I'm trying to say is, giving you away today is easy because of the quality of the man you are marrying and the depth of love you have for each other. He is kind and devoted to you, and I can see how happy he makes you. There is nothing in this world that means more to me than your happiness, so giving you away today will be my greatest honor." Dean looked up from his shoes into Deanna's glistening eyes. "I love you and I wholeheartedly approve of Hank." They hugged without words. Deanna could not speak because of the threat of tears, and Dean was finished. He had said exactly what he wanted to say.

Ezaki

4:30 p.m. Entrance

The Wedding Day

At the front left of the sanctuary, behind the altar rail and in front of a row of artificial ficus trees, a cello rested on its side, its bow laying across the top. An elegant harp posed next to it. A young woman with untamable hair, no makeup, and gauzy black palazzo pants emerged from a barely-discernable door on the platform behind the greenery, and unobtrusively went to the harp. An older man in a well-worn, basic black tuxedo followed her. He stepped over the cello and seated himself. Methodically, he picked up the bow and tightened it, then lifted the cello, fitting it between his knees. Wiggling his bottom and shifting his weight, he attempted to establish his usual position in the unfamiliar chair. When satisfied, he nodded at the harpist who lifted her hands with trained grace, and they began a duet of "Silent Night" as the groomsmen ushered the first guests to their seats. "The First Noel" followed. The musicians performed a repeating medley of Christmas carols in which "We Three

Kings" followed "Angels We Have Heard on High" every five minutes or so. The only variation was an occasional unwritten grace note, trill, or run inserted by the professional musicians to break up their monotony. The guests, who had come to see two young people exchange vows, never noticed they heard each carol four times.

Twenty minutes later, all the guests were seated, the carols came to an end, and selections from Tchaikovsky's ballet began. One of Deanna's favorite childhood memories was accompanying her parents to the Nutcracker Ballet in San Francisco during Christmas break of first grade. Six-year-old Deanna carried herself with aristocratic maturity on the way to the theater as her red satin dress swished and the half-inch heels on her black patent leather shoes clicked on the pavement of that exciting city. As soon as they chose a Christmas wedding, Deanna began listening to recordings of Tchaikovsky's ballet to pick her favorite movements and associate the music with the various parts of the ceremony. The groomsmen escorted family members down the center aisle as "The Sugar Plum Dance" played slowly, accentuating the deep, somber bass line on the cello. Hank's mother grasped her oldest son's arm and walked with a brisk, bouncy step, out of sync with the music. She surveyed the groom's side of the church acknowledging as many friends as she could with a grin and a nod. The melancholy music contradicted her form-fitting, blood-red dress, bold demeanor, and theatrical expressions.

The music changed and the first bridesmaid glided in on the flowing strains of the "Waltz of the Flowers." Each girl waited for a dramatic run of eighth notes before entering from the foyer. Deanna's attendants carried bouquets containing three long-stem red roses surrounded by variegated holly leaves. They were clad in golden, strapless, floor-length dresses cut in a simple A-line. A four-inch ivory satin ribbon encircled each waist. The dresses were identical, but each girl added her own personal flair using the ribbon to accessorize. Jenna, being the most conservative, tied a classic bow in the center back. Artistic Katie created a loopy knot which resembled a flower resting above her left hip. Ashley's sash hung in a loose twist at the front. The belt rested low on her hips and the long tendril ends swished as she walked. She looked both more modern and more medieval than the other bridesmaids. Brittany doubled the ribbon, creating a belt without trailing ends. Initially, Deanna agreed to the variations with reservation. But today, seeing the combination of coordination and individuality, she was pleased her friends had talked her into it.

The girls assembled in a line across the left front of the church at the base of the altar platform, the minister, groom, and groomsmen completing the line to the right. Once more the music changed. Bold, heavy double-stops on the cello introduced the fanfare of the "March of the Toy Soldiers." Mary, in a two-piece golden lace dress, stood, turned, and focused on the closed doors separating the sanctuary from the foyer. The rest of the assembly followed her lead. The initial phrase of music finished, the harp joined the cello, and the doors opened, revealing Deanna to the congregation, grasping the crook of her father's arm. Deanna wore a winter-white satin gown with playful, modern detailing on the bodice. Her veil emerged from the asymmetrical bun of her hair like a frothy white waterfall erupting around brown boulders and spreading out in a translucent trail of mist. Several layers of netting cascaded behind her, extending beyond the short train of the dress.

Deanna's favorite part of the dress was the bodice. From a dropped waist to the strapless, sweetheart neckline the fabric was almost completely covered by a random pattern of multi-sized rosettes made of varying fabrics and textures. Some were simple ribbon roses, while others were created petal by petal from fabric that coordinated with the gown. A few larger flowers were made from shimmering tulle in playful, modern, expanding circles. Each flower was anchored to the gown with a shiny crystal rhinestone at its center. Below the fitted torso, the skirt flared and another cluster of fabric flowers sat at her left thigh where the top layer of satin joined together in a gathered crisscross. The exposed under layers revealed thinner, lighter chiffon over polyester. The fabrics of the linings could be found incorporated into some of the floral bodice adornments. Upon seeing the bride, most guests returned her smile and snickered at her ashen, shaking father. A few, including Mary, began crying at the first sight of Deanna's beaming face.

Hank inhaled slowly and deeply, taking in everything-- every sight, sound, and feeling of this moment. A married friend had told him to pay attention to how he felt when he saw Deanna coming down the aisle. "That memory is what you want to think about whenever you two fight. If you can remember how much you loved her when you saw her on your wedding day, it will make whatever you're angry about pale and recede into its proper place," his friend had advised. Hank glanced at his right knee which just now, for the first time in his life, had developed a rapid twitch. He wiggled his fingers, which suddenly felt like plump sausages. He attempted to swallow but there was no saliva in his mouth. This was not the gushing romantic feeling he had expected. He was not nervous and he had no reservations about the vows he was about to make. What was wrong with him? He focused again on Deanna. She smiled tenderly at him with unveiled love and vulnerability. She was sweet, young, innocent. That was his problem: he felt guilty. No question he was getting better than he deserved. "Marrying above yourself," as his brother had commented earlier in the morning. *What is she thinking marrying an overeducated, underemployed goof like me?* Hank wondered. Yet the closer she came toward the front of the church, the less his leg shook. His fingers returned to near-normal size. Hank reassured himself, *She said yes. She knows what she's getting and she still said yes.* Dean reached out and shook Hank's hand. He kissed his daughter tenderly on her check and extracted her hand from his elbow, placing it into its new niche, inside Hank's elbow

Ezaki

instead. Hank still found it inexplicable that Deanna had chosen him, but she had, and she was here today to make it official. Hank inserted lucky into the list of adjectives he used to describe himself.

5:00 p.m. I Do's and Special Music

The Wedding Day

"Do you take this woman to be your lawfully wedded wife? Do you promise to love and to comfort her, to cherish and to keep her, and forsaking all others, to keep only unto her as long as you both shall live?"

"I do." Hank declared with bold certainty, squeezing Deanna's hand.

The minister repeated the words of intention, this time, questioning Deanna.

"Do you take this man…" Deanna lost track of the minister's voice. Hank's response brought to mind a scene from years ago. It was a hot summer afternoon. She was eating popsicles with Greta on the patio in the backyard. Funny how her mind was wandering today. And such seemingly unrelated connections.

"Oh my, this is too cold for my teeth. I don't think I want it," Greta said. She held her juice bar out toward Deanna, knowing a missing bite would not deter her granddaughter from finishing it off. With the fingertips of her left hand, Deanna precariously grasped the base of the stick which protruded below her grandmother's hand. "What are you doing?" Greta questioned, pulling her Popsicle out of her granddaughter's hold. "You still have yours," she said, pointing toward the grape juice bar in Deanna's right hand.

"I thought you didn't want yours."

"Well, I do."

Deanna resumed licking her own popsicle. Greta followed her granddaughter's example, stuck out her tongue, and licked from bottom to top of her sticky, purple, frozen treat. "Oh, these are good. Grape is my favorite," Greta said.

"Mine too," Deanna agreed, unaffected by Greta's abrupt reversal of opinion.

Greta took another small bite from the top and began to chew the cold, crumbling frozen juice. "Oh, I don't like this. This hurts my teeth."

Deanna lifted her hand toward her grandmother but stopped halfway, ready to take the unwanted treat if it was offered to her again. She waited, watching for a clue from Greta. Greta did not eat any more but neither did she hand the frozen juice bar to Deanna. "Do you like your popsicle, Grandma?"

"I do."

"Do you want the rest of it?"

"Yes, of course, I do."

A large drop formed at the bottom of Deanna's popsicle, threatening to run down her hand. She caught it on her tongue, then licked around the entire base, preventing the next wave of drops.

"Oh my, this is too cold. Do you want mine?" Greta asked. Deanna waited to see what was coming next. When her grandmother made no motion to eat her Popsicle, Deanna asked, "Do you like your juice bar?"

Greta nodded. "Mmmm, yes, I do."

A palpable silence brought Deanna back to the present. "I do," she blurted out, with a snicker in her voice, partly from embarrassment at missing her cue and partly at the irony of quoting her confused grandmother.

The minister led Deanna and Hank up the three small steps onto the platform, inside the alter railing. He directed them to face each other, clasp hands and gaze into the other's eyes as they recited the ancient and holy vows of marriage. They sealed their vows with golden rings. Stepping aside, the minister motioned for the couple to proceed forward toward the altar and light the waiting unity candle.

Hank gently placed his hand on Deanna elbow, escorting her as he whispered, "Listen. This is for you." Deanna tilted her head and puckered her perfectly tweezed eyebrows. It took a moment for her to understand what he was referring to. Deanna had picked all the music for the wedding except the song during the unity candle. Hank had asked to choose that one selection, but then refused to give Deanna even a hint about what would be playing during that portion of the ceremony.

Hank's friend, Dave, picked a simple melody on an acoustic guitar and sang as Deanna and Hank combined the flames of two small tapers to ignite one tall, white pillar in the center of the red roses and baby's breath arrangement on the altar. Blowing out their individual candles they turned around and, hand in hand, walked to the front of the platform where they could see the faces of their guests. Deanna tipped her head toward Hank and whispered, "This song is perfect. I've never heard it before."

Hank grinned proudly. "No one has ever heard it before. I wrote it for you. For today. Dave put it to music." Surprised and flattered, Deanna said nothing else so she could listen attentively to her wedding song.

"Your eyes hold the sparkle of the stars,

you heart, the purity of new snow,
my life is complete with you at my side
and forever I want you to know...
You are my beautiful Christmas bride.

My beautiful, beautiful, beautiful,
My beautiful Christmas bride.

White gown, misty veil, red roses,
You approach and reassuringly smile,
It's hard to believe you could really love me,
This beauty who floats down the aisle,
You're the most beautiful Christmas bride.

My beautiful, beautiful, beautiful,
My beautiful Christmas bride.

I asked for your hand and held my breath
Fearing the end to my dream
You professed your love and our happiness
Heaven touched earth it seemed
Giving me a beautiful Christmas bride.

I love my beautiful, beautiful, beautiful,
Such a beautiful, beautiful, beautiful,
You'll always be my beautiful, beautiful, beautiful,
My beautiful Christmas bride.

As the song ended Deanna used the knuckle of her index finger to put pressure against the inner canthus of one eye and then the other, struggling to hold back sentimental tears. Her voice cracked slightly as she whispered, "Did you really write that for me?"

"Well, it didn't seem appropriate to write it for anyone else," Hank responded with a jovial tilt of his head and a playful smirk.

Breaking the solemnity of the ceremony, Hank

acknowledged and thanked Dave with a nod and a long-distance knuckle knock. Dave lifted the guitar strap over his head then mimicked Hank by extending his clenched right fist. He followed the motion with a thumbs-up before retreating down the side aisle to his seat at the back of the sanctuary.

Hank and Deanna turned around once again, facing the pastor with their backs to the congregation. With a booming voice and a broad grin, the officiant pronounced them husband and wife. Then, he encouraged Hank to kiss his bride. Hank wrapped his arms around Deanna. With one arm supporting her back and the other cradling her neck and head, he twisted her around into a slight dip, as if they were ballroom dancers. Slowly he brought his face down to meet hers. When their lips touched, he kissed his wife greedily. After a few long seconds, the guests from the senior age group shifted in their seats or looked away from the couple up front. One of the older guests cleared his throat in obvious disapproval. In response, one of Hank's friends let out a whoop of encouragement. Ashley added her support with a sports-style arm pump of her rose bouquet. Finally, Hank brought Deanna back to vertical. He loosened his embrace, but kept his hands on her sides and a tender and sincere smile focused on her beloved face. He wanted to leave no doubt that he meant everything he had promised today.

The pastor introduced Mr. and Mrs. Henry Floyd to the congregation. Everyone cheered and the instrumentalists played a few quick measures of Handel's "Hallelujah Chorus." Deanna had not requested that musical touch but it was the most appropriate piece they could have played and she appreciated their impromptu addition. A few years before, there was a day where Greta had added an unexpected musical surprise. The difference being, Greta's contribution was neither appropriate nor appreciated.

Two Years Before

It was late morning on Saturday. Deanna's open textbook rested on her lap while her notes spread out around her on the floral couch cushions. Heavy gray clouds obstructed the sun from shining through the front room windows. Deanna attempted to reread the highlighting in her textbook and review her notes for a twentieth-century US history midterm on Monday. Greta perched on the edge of her chair, leaning forward, watching Deanna. Then, Greta stood up and scanned the area. She meandered around the room, humming under her breath, stopping at the end of the couch near Deanna. Greta peered over her granddaughter's shoulder. Deanna applied a fake smile, looked up, and asked, "Do you need something, Grandma?"

"Oh, just wondering what time it is." Greta patted Deanna's shoulder affectionately and returned to her seat. A few minutes later the conversation repeated itself except this time Greta asked, "What day is it today?" The same scenario had been running on rewind all morning. The only variation was the question Greta asked. Deanna remained committed to helping care for her grandmother, but today proved that studying could be not done concurrently with caregiving.

Mary and Deanna alternated Saturdays at Greta's house. According to the schedule, today was Mary's day, but Deanna, realizing there were issues between her parents that had been escalated, if not created, by the demands of caring for Greta, had offered to spend an extra Saturday supervising her grandmother.

"Buzzzzz." Deanna's cell phone vibrated in her pocket. Pulling it out, she saw Hank's grinning face on the screen.

"Hi there," she answered.

"Hey good-lookin', what you got cookin'?"

"That's cheesy even for you," she replied with a laugh in her voice.

"It's an oldies saying and I'm in an oldies mood. And the good news is, there's an oldies movie special at some little theater in Hanford. It might be fun to go and see a black and white forties musical, complete with tap dancing and a grand waltz. Maybe we'll get up and waltz along with Fred and Ginger, or whoever the stars are."

"Do you know how to waltz?" Deanna asked, surprised and a bit doubtful.

"No. But no one else does either, so they won't know we're doing it wrong."

"As exciting as waltzing badly sounds, I can't. I'm at Grandma's today. My parents are off enjoying some boring exhibit at a museum. Why don't you come down here? We can find her transistor radio for you to listen to your oldies music. That should satisfy your need for nostalgia."

"Why don't I come and get both of you. We can grab some lunch then go to the movies. This is from her era. She's sure to love it. I might even learn how to waltz if I dance with her."

Deanna looked over at her grandmother. Greta's stocking-clad feet were up, her hands limp in her lap, and her eyes closed as she relaxed in her usual brown, faded recliner. The occasional repositioning of her head and shifting of her neck and shoulders proved she was not sleeping deeply. The fat, gray-striped cat curled up like a fuzzy throw pillow next to her.

"Okay. Let's try it. If things go badly we can always leave."

They arrived at the movie theater and found seats in the first row to save Greta from climbing up and down steps in the dim light. Greta fit right in with the gray-haired clientele at the cinema.

Hank was accurate about the dancing scenes. The opening act had a musical number that led into a tap dance. He took Deanna's hand and swayed their entwined fingers to the beat. Greta sat up straight when the music began. She was soon tapping her feet and patting her thighs in rhythm with the song. This looked like it was going to be a good outing.

It was clear the two men who had opened the movie as partners were destined to become rivals over the lovely young protagonist, who entered during the second song of the show. She had big eyes, short hair with pin curls, dark lips, and desperately needed their help to solve a crisis which had yet to be explained. Even in black and white her lipstick was obviously bright, ruby red. The first bachelor evaded his partner and arranged a clandestine meeting with her as a new song began. Hank rocked their clasped hands. Greta swayed in her chair. When Deanna was a child, Greta had frequently played old show tunes on the radio, but in recent years, Greta was confused by the knobs on the stereo system, and no one thought about putting music on for her very often. Bringing her to see an old movie was a good idea, especially since Deanna hadn't been getting any studying done anyway.

The second verse of the song began. Greta stood up. Oblivious to her surroundings and the two dozen or so moviegoers in the theater, Greta joined the couple on the screen in singing the lyrics. Deanna grabbed her grandmother's arm and pulled her back into the theater seat, then turned on Hank. Her large, aghast eyes demanded a response. He smiled, shrugged, and said, "Apparently, she likes this song." Before Hank finished speaking, an elderly, slightly off-key alto on Deanna's right was singing again. Deanna turned toward her grandmother and said in a stage whisper, loud enough for Greta's aging ears to pick up, "Grandma, just listen; don't sing." Greta must have misinterpreted the statement because she smiled at Deanna, nodded, and increased her volume. She stood up again, the third voice in the duet.

Deanna forcefully yanked Greta back down. Maintaining her hold on Greta's upper arm, Deanna turned an angry glare on Hank and demanded, "What are we going to do?" Hank answered with an unconcerned shrug and a soft chuckle. Fortunately, the song ended and Greta made herself comfortable in the padded theater seat to await the next musical number.

A Day to Remember

The movie progressed through a prolonged section of dialogue without any song and dance numbers. Greta remained in her seat. As the dialogue continued, her head bobbed forward until her chin rested on her chest and her breathing became slow and regular. Deanna relaxed and finally released her grip on her grandmother's arm. It was preferable to have Greta sleep through the movie than contribute to it. Deanna crossed her legs so that her lower leg was against Hank. She slipped her foot behind his calf and leaned against him, snuggling into his warm, comfortable side. He responded by wrapping his arm around her and placing a reassuring kiss on the top of her head.

In a little while the second lead male discovered his partner had secretly wooed the lipsticked beauty and a loud chase scene followed. Both men swung fists and objects that the other easily avoided. The first man tried to apologize and explain as he darted in and out from behind various props and ineffective hiding places. His rotund partner refused to listen. Deanna was warm and comfortable under Hank's protective arm. She nestled into his side as the charming actor made his escape. Unbeknownst to them, the heavy sound effects of the fight scene woke Greta up. The first actor, of course, proceeded to his sweetheart and together they sang a love song. It was a popular song. Deanna had heard this song many times before and knew a few of the lines. The couple on the screen twirled together off the set and reemerged in a lovely, twilight garden, clad in formal wear. A few older couples proceeded down the aisles to the open floor below the screen and directly in front of Hank, Deanna, and Greta. Deanna watched the couples inside the theater as they copied the dance on the screen step by step. One pair, who were slightly younger than the others, performed it with grace and agility that rivaled the original professional dancers. The other three couples used minimized movements as they performed a slightly arthritic version of the dance, but beamed with enjoyment and love for their life-long dance partners. Hank pulled Deanna up,

181

drew her into his arms, and began to sway in a gentle
embrace. They did not know the choreography, but the older
couples willingly opened a spot on the makeshift dance floor
for them. The partners on the concrete theater floor
continued to dance as the actors paused in their dancing and
broke out in song.

Greta was awake and watching. She was on her feet
now. She knew every word of this song so she sang, and she
sang with gusto. Deanna pushed Hank back a step, and
reached for her grandmother. She thrust Greta down into
the seat, then turned to Hank with panic across her face. As
soon as Deanna removed her hands from Greta's shoulders,
Greta was up again and singing just as loudly, and just as
badly as earlier. Deanna fixed her gaze on Hank, her eyes
pleading for help, demanding he devise a plan. Hank simply
shrugged and remained in place as the older couples waltzed
behind him. Deanna heard several people murmur
understanding. "Don't worry honey." "It's okay. We all get
confused." "Everyone our age likes to sing and dance." They
may not mind, but Deanna certainly did. She was on the
verge of tears. Now, everyone in the theater knew that Greta
had dementia. Deanna grabbed Hank's arm with her left
hand and Greta's arm with her right and marched them out
of the theater.

As they drove home, Hank apologized for taking them,
but Deanna crossed her arms, scowled, and refused to
answer. Next, he told her it had not bothered anyone in the
theater because they all had friends or relatives with
Alzheimer's. Deanna gave him a squinty eyed glare for that
comment. Still feeling a need to make amends, Hank
attempted to reassure Deanna that Greta had enjoyed herself
and was not the least bit self-conscious or embarrassed by
what she had done. He reasoned, perhaps Greta would not
have behaved that way in the past, but she enjoyed singing in
public now.

"Don't you get it? I had to watch my grandmother, who
practically raised me, make a complete laughingstock of

herself. Nothing you can say will change that. We should never have come!" Deanna fixed her gaze out the front window of the car and scowled at the passing street lights. Hank continued to offer reassurance and support, which elicited curt, annoyed responses from Deanna while Greta hummed pleasantly from the backseat.

Ezaki

5:15 p.m. Leaving

The Wedding Day

The harp and cello played the rapid, syncopated, staccato of "The Russian Dance" as the newlyweds led the recession down the center aisle and out of the church. Dean and Mary stood and fell in step behind the last bridesmaid and groomsman. Hank's immediate family and then extended family queued up next. The rest of the guests followed in an orderly exodus. Greta had similarly followed a stranger, or perhaps a whim, several years earlier.

Three Years Before

Mary's cell phone vibrated and rattled against the wooden podium, bouncing and jittering like a Mexican jumping bean. She grabbed it quickly to stop the surprisingly loud noise in the quiet classroom. Slowly and carefully, she opened the flip phone to avoid the click it usually made. "Yes?" she whispered.

"Mrs. Nilsson, I'm so sorry. I went to the bathroom and I was only gone a few minutes. I swear it was only a minute or two, but somehow, she got out of the house. I ran out looking for her because she couldn't have gone far, but I couldn't find her. I don't know how she could have gotten away from me. It was only a minute. Really." Sniffling and ragged breathing continued over the line. Carol was a backup home health aide they had used a few times in the past, but not recently. This morning, Mary had stopped by Greta's to talk with Carol and stress the difficulty they were having preventing Greta from wandering off. Carol adamantly insisted Greta would not be left alone; there would be no opportunity to escape.

Turning away from the students before answering in an emotionless whisper, Mary asked, "Have you called the police?" Mary inched her way into the farthest corner to isolate herself, but even as carefully as she moved, her low-heeled pumps clunked and the leather soles scuffed on the white tile floor. She had begun keeping her cell phone on vibrate even in class, because calls about her mom came at unanticipated and inconvenient moments. At least today's call did not interrupt Mary mid-sentence during a lecture. Students, however, might consider interrupting a test equally disruptive. A couple students looked up from their exams to glare disapprovingly. A young man in the second row sighed loudly. Mary knew she was causing less of a disturbance than the student in the back who intermittently tapped a cadence with the side of his pencil on the edge of the desk, but still, she hated answering her phone during a class but felt helpless to do anything else. School policy, as well as logic and experience, prevented her from stepping outside and allowing students to continue the exam unproctored.

"No, I didn't want to call unless..." Carol began, then stopped and swallowed audibly. As she continued, her voice threatened to crack, "unless you knew what was going on." A raspy gulp of air followed, undoubtedly accompanied by streaming tears. Greta's recent escaping was upsetting and a nuisance, but crying was not a solution. Why did care providers always react like teenage girls in horror movies? They made incompetent, incomprehensible decisions during a crisis and then crumbled into a nonfunctional, weepy heap precisely when their help was needed.

Mary cupped her hand over the phone's mouthpiece, attempting to prevent her voice from carrying across the room. "Call the police and get them looking. I will be done here in," Mary glanced at the clock on the wall, "about forty minutes. I'll be home shortly after that." Click. Mary snapped her phone shut, cutting off a prolonged and tearful apology. Two months ago, Mary had yelled at the first care provider who'd lost her mom, but now it was practically routine. For some inexplicable reason, Greta would dash out of the house at the slightest opportunity. Then, she followed an irregular, untraceable route. Shaking her head, Mary wondered where her mother was so determined to get to anyway.

Two students continued to stare at their tests until time ran out. Then, they slowly trudged to the front of the class and surrendered their blue books with visible reluctance. Mary grabbed their exams and shooed them out of the room. She rushed to her office, dropped the pile of exams on her desk, grabbed her purse, and hurried to her car. As she drove, Mary tapped her fingers nervously on the steering wheel. She needed to talk to someone. Her purse lay on the passenger seat, so she rummaged around blindly in it with her right hand as she steered the car with her left. She felt the smooth metal and rounded corners of her phone. She pulled it out, then hesitated. Should she call Dean? She did not want to embitter him and add more distance to their relationship, but neither did she want to exclude him from her life, and right now her life centered on finding her mother. With quick resolve, she flipped the phone open using her thumb in a practiced motion and hit his speed dial. She listened through four rings before his recorded voice came on, over-enunciating a request for the caller to leave a message.

Mary snapped her phone shut, and threw it forcefully against the passenger seat. It bounced off the padded brown leather and whacked into the dash. The phone, battery cover, and battery flew in different directions. Mary's second call would have been to Deanna, but now that was impossible without stopping and reassembling her phone. Getting home quickly was the highest priority. Besides, neither Dean nor Deanna was likely to be available to help, and refusing Mary's request would induce guilt without providing assistance.

Mary arrived at Greta's house and found Carol agitated, squirming in her spot on the couch with the telephone in her lap, while Dr. Phil scolded a dysfunctional family on the television. Before Mary said anything, Carol defensively stated, "The police told me to stay here. They said they wanted me to be here when they found her and brought her back." Carol's face crumbled. She dropped her head into her hands and whimpered, "I'm so sorry. I've never lost a client before." Lifting her tear-stained face she pleaded, "Please don't report me to the agency. I promise you I've never had this happen before and I'll make sure it never happens again. I'm very careful with my clients." Carol returned to her sobs. Mary left Greta's house to begin searching. The police would follow the most likely routes an individual without Alzheimer's would take, which left Mary to do all of the real hunting on back roads and dirt paths where her mom was most likely to wander.

Almost two hours later, Mary spotted an elderly woman wearing a light-blue, short-sleeved blouse in the cool evening air of early spring. She was sitting on a berm, one hundred yards or more off the road, facing a field of grape vines. She seemed to be contemplatively observing the early, light green shoots of life emerging on the gnarled, barren wood. It would have made an intriguing painting. Mary stopped the car and went to retrieve her mother. When Mary got close, Greta clumsily pushed herself up to standing from her dirt

Ezaki

seat and said, "There you are. I've been waiting for you." As they walked along the tamped down tractor path to the car, Mary smelled a fishy whiff of old urine. She peered at her mother's crotch and discovered a wet stain on the inner thighs of her mom's blue double-knit pants. Mud, created by urine and the dusty top soil, clung to the seat of Greta's trousers. Mary told herself she should feel sorry for her mother—after all, Greta had been lost for at least three hours. It was not surprising her mother was unable to control her bladder for that long. However, the reality that Greta had peed her pants was appalling. The closest Mary could get to sympathy was embarrassment. At least no one was out her to see. Mary came to an abrupt stop, hit by a wave of disgust. She had no towels or paper in her car. Greta would have sit in the passenger seat with the grime and urine getting embedded into the leather upholstery. Lifting her gaze to her mother's face, Mary noticed dirt smudges under Greta's right eye and along her chin. What had her mom had been through in the last few hours? "Where were you going and what happened to you?" Mary asked.

"I was waiting for my mom to come get me."

Mary sighed and tersely responded, "Your mom has been dead more than fifteen years."

"She has not. I saw her today. She told me to wait for her at the store."

Mary surveyed the landscape. Her blue Toyota was the only object, other than grapevines, in every direction as far as she could see. "What store?" Realizing the futility of logic, Mary changed tactics, "Why didn't you stay where you were? You should not have gone off looking for her."

"I was looking for you. Please let me go to the lake with you. I'll be good." Greta pulled on Mary's arm and continued to beg. "I won't get in the way at all and I won't tell on you, even if you have boys there. Please let me come." This change of identity might work in Mary's favor. Playing along as Greta's sister, Mary said, "Okay. You can come with me. Get in the car and I'll drive you there."

"Really? Oh, thank you!" Greta eagerly rushed to the car, crumbs of foul mud falling from her bottom. She climbed into the passenger seat, eager to embark on an adventure she had been excluded from nearly three quarters of a century earlier.

Mary turned in at a fast food drive-through since it was past dinner time. Her voice ordering into the static of the speaker was the only break of the silence inside the car until they reached Greta's house. As soon as they arrived, Mary helped her mom into clean pants, but decided to save the thorough cleaning until after eating, because there was no telling how long getting her cleaned up might take.

Mary served them each a Big Mac and half of an apple. Greta was only halfway through her burger when her head nodded forward and her eyes fluttered until they stayed shut. She sat with her head bowed, chin resting on chest, breathing slowly and deeply through her open mouth; asleep in her chair at the table just like a small child. Mary smiled at her mom for the first time that day. Funny how watching a loved one in the vulnerable state of peaceful rest erases hours of frustration. Mary gently roused her mom and led her to the bathroom. After a quick shower, Mary helped her mom into pajamas, and tucked her into bed. Then, Mary headed to her own house.

Ezaki

6:00 p.m. New Beginnings

Two years before

Two days after Dean's emotional unloading, he and Mary made a mutual decision. They agreed things had digressed too far to be resolved without professional help. After checking with their insurance carrier and reading online recommendations, they chose a well-reputed marriage counselor and scheduled an appointment. Their initial visit would be next Thursday afternoon, one week from today. As soon as the appointment was scheduled, the pit in Dean's stomach dissipated. In just seven days they would deal with the root causes of their disintegrating marriage, not just treat symptoms or pacify superficial irritations. Mary, however, feared that maintaining a companionable truce for seven more days might give her an ulcer.

The week reached its end slowly and the weekend crept by at a snail's pace. Monday morning eventually came. Dean left for work and Mary headed to Greta's. She wore jeans and a t-shirt, no make-up, and let her short brown hair dry naturally with its unpredictable, asymmetrical wave. Today she would be with her mother and they had no plans to go anywhere.

"Good morning Mom," Mary called from the front door as she entered. A answering groan came from the other side of the recliner. Mary stepped closer to the sound. Two bare feet were visible on the ground beyond the extended footrest. The toes pushed against the beige carpet and the heels pointed toward the ceiling. Mary gasped and rushed behind the chair to see her mother's face. Greta was on her hands and knees like a crawling baby. She reached one hand out to Mary for help and bobbled while trying to balance on only three limbs. Mary took her mother's hand and the two women struggled to get Greta onto her feet.

"Who moved my chair?" Greta demanded. Mary kept her grip on her mom, pivoted, and eased Greta's bottom onto the recliner. Greta then swung her legs up unaided and rubbed her sore knees. Mary pulled out her phone and called Dr. Gonzalez, who was now in her list of contacts.

Greta was evaluated by the doctor and x-rayed on all four extremities, which confirmed there were no fractures, only painful bruising. The doctor ordered a front wheel walker and scheduled a physical therapist to come to the house to train Greta on its use. Mary doubted Greta would comply with using an assistive device even if she could remember the directions on how to use it. Doctor Gonzalez insisted they try.

After long waits for short appointments and quick procedures, Mary and Greta arrived home. It was a little before three in the afternoon. The prompt therapist arrived exactly at four, as expected. He was thirty-something, average height and build, with the beginnings of a pot belly. He carried a shiny new stainless-steel walker, covered by clear plastic, into Greta's front room.

"Hello, Greta. I understand you had a fall this

morning," he said, and began stripping off the plastic wrapping.

"Students are expected to call me Mrs. Miller," she scolded with a disapproving scowl.

"I'm sorry Mrs. Miller. You're right. That was not very professional of me." Once the protective cover was removed, he opened the sides of the walker and clicked them into place. "Let me show you how to open and close your new walker first, then I'll have you walk with it."

Greta crossed her arms. "I don't need that."

"Your doctor wants you to use this so you won't fall again."

"I didn't fall. I was pushed. Those boys were fighting in the cafeteria and I was breaking them up. They listen to me better than the other ladies."

"I'm glad no one got hurt," he responded, without laughing or patronizing—he was clearly familiar with dementia patients. "For your own safety, it will be best if you use a walker from now on," he patiently insisted.

He demonstrated folding the sides in and opening them out as well as the proper way to walk and balance while using the new equipment. Greta watched, squinting with disapproval. She kept her arms wrapped tightly across her chest and refused to touch the horrible contraption.

Before leaving, the therapist reassured Mary, "Most confused, older people get the hang of using a walker instinctively even if they didn't understand the instructions. The important thing is to remind her to use it until it becomes a habit."

Mary responded, "I still have to convince her she needs it before I can remind her to use it."

Mary and Dean arranged to meet at the counselor's office on the day of their appointment. Dean arrived fifteen minutes early, as he always did, with his latest copy of *Business Week* in hand. The room was small but welcoming and arranged to maximize seating. Eight Queen Anne chairs upholstered in coordinating colors and prints encircled an elegant old chest, which displayed an array of magazines. The room was silent and empty except for one woman, whom Dean estimated to be around age forty, reading a novel in the chair farthest from the entry door. Engrossed in her book, she did not look up when Dean entered. He wondered what life crisis had prompted her to seek counseling--a struggling marriage, depression, or was she waiting while her troubled child met with the counselor? Choosing the most comfortable looking of the high backed, lightly padded chairs, Dean sat down and prepared to wait. He crossed his long legs and flipped through his *Business Week*, looking calm except for the rhythmic bounce of his right foot.

Two minutes before their appointment Mary burst through the door with her briefcase pinned against her chest, trapping loose papers on top of it. Relief flooded through her when she saw Dean was still in the waiting room. Slowing her step to pretend she wasn't panicked, she plopped down on the closest chair and set her load by her feet. Picking up the disarrayed papers, she shuffled through them, straightening and rearranging, but unable to make sense of how they should be filed. After shifting without effectively sorting the pile, Mary opened her briefcase and inserted the papers into a folder. Then, she snapped her briefcase shut, learned back in her chair, and took some deep breaths, trying to relax before the next ordeal began.

All day Mary had watched the clock, willing and dreading it to announce the time for this appointment. Unfortunately, four students had turned up at Mary's office hour fifteen minutes before it ended. They'd asked to review their papers, but really, they'd wanted to argue their grades. When her office hour was over and it was time for her to leave, they were not yet satisfied. Mary had picked up her briefcase, taken out her car keys, and asked for their essays back. It took ten more minutes to retrieve their work and shoo them out. Yes, her job was working with students, but they seemed to have an uncanny sense of how to show up at the wrong times and make her life harder.

A pretty young woman in a professional pink silk blouse and black pencil skirt stuck her head out from the interior door. Her soothing voice called, "Dean and Mary." They got up, glanced at each other, and with knotted stomachs and racing pulses followed her. Dean whispered, "She's got to be older than she looks, right?"

At the first session, they reassured each other of their desire for their marriage to survive and to thrive. Neither was too proud nor too inflexible to do whatever was needed, including difficult changes, in order to restore affection and harmony. The counselor got Dean to express his feelings and admit that his emotional withholding had contributed to their problems. The counselor also got Mary to acknowledge she was neglecting Dean due to the urgency of her mother's needs. By the third counseling session a consensus was reached that Greta needed to move to an assisted living facility. Greta's illness was an excessive strain on their marriage. Because Dean had built up a lot of resentment toward Greta's care over the past years, Mary agreed to ask a friend and colleague to go with her to preview potential sites for her mom.

After several afternoons of visiting nursing homes and interviewing administrators, Mary chose an Alzheimer's care facility. It was a large, homey house in a quiet, older neighborhood. On clear days, the Sierra Nevadas painted a majestic background to the trellises of blue morning glories and red climbing roses in the well-groomed backyard. Mary imagined her mother staring at the mountains and reliving childhood memories of Sparks, Nevada. The facility had been built as a family home, but was remodeled and rezoned, authorizing eight Alzheimer's patients to occupy its four bedrooms. One licensed vocational nurse and a home health aide remained on the premises at all times, keeping the residents clean, fed, and safe. A calm, soft-spoken registered nurse with years of hospice experience was the facility's administrator.

A few days after previewing the home, Mary returned alone to inform the administrator of her decision and inquire when Greta could move in. "Your timing is perfect," the nurse responded cheerfully. "We have an open bed right now. If you complete the paperwork today, we'll be ready for your mother tomorrow." Mary signed the forms with conviction. On the short drive home, silent tears rolled down her cheeks. By the time she entered her house, doubt had joined and overthrown sadness. She needed to talk to someone. Someone who would understand her conflicted reaction and assure her she was doing the right thing. Calling Dean was out. She had promised him and the counselor that she would develop a new support system for concerns related to her mom. Unfortunately, the co-workers she had in mind had full lives and were not necessarily available the moment she needed someone, and she needed someone right now. She glanced at her watch. Deanna should be getting out of class. She hit the automatic dial and waited, hoping her daughter's sweet voice would answer.

"Hey, Mom."

"Hi sweetheart. How's school going?" Mary began, successfully hiding the tremble in her voice.

"It's good," Deanna answered. "I've been doing classroom observations and I've definitely decided I like fourth, fifth, sixth grade kids the best. Kids in K and one are really cute, and they say such funny things, but I think I'd get frustrated trying to teach them. They're just so immature. Second/third is better, but it's not very interesting curriculum." Mary gave an occasional murmur of acknowledgement or agreement as Deanna talked cheerfully about her classes, her friends, and especially about Hank. Hank was back in Fresno living with his brother, and their relationship was progressing happily. Deanna finally realized she had been doing all the talking even though her mother had called her. "So, what's up? Why'd you call?"

"It hasn't been a good day for me. Listening to you helps to cheer me up."

Deanna stopped walking. Her stomach constricted. Between her parents' marital issues and her grandmother's illness, she had no idea what to prepare for. Bracing every muscle in her body she enquired, "What's wrong?"

"You know I've been looking at care homes for Grandma?"

"Uh huh."

"Well, I found one."

Realizing her family would no longer be the ones providing for Greta's needs created a wave of guilt which crashed over Deanna like an Atlantic nor'easter storm swamping a small fishing boat. "Where is it?" she breathed. "I'd like to go and see it."

"You can go see it," Mary said, "but I've already signed the forms and paid them for the first month. They have an open bed. We can move her in as soon as tomorrow." Mary spoke slowly and carefully, successfully controlling the emotional waver of her voice, even as one last determined tear got loose and rolled down her right cheek.

Deanna's legs went limp, like a distance runner at the end of a race. She needed somewhere to sit, and fast. The central fountain danced and bubbled happily, unconcerned with her family's problems. The fountain was surrounded by benches, designed for students to relax and let the cool spray ease the central valley heat. One bench had a couple sitting close, holding hands, carrying on an intimate conversation, unaware their private happy oasis was surrounded by a desert of pain. Deanna took four wobbly steps to the closest bench and dropped onto it with a thud. She pressed her phone to her ear with her right hand and support her woozy head with her left. "Wow," was all she was able to articulate. Her grandmother had been a pillar in Deanna's life; the first pillar to give way under the erosion of time. "I knew you were looking, and I know she needs more care than we can give her, but I can hardly believe this is real. I feel numb; like I'll wake up and this conversation won't have really happened."

Mary and Deanna talked for another quarter of an hour. Mary described the facility to Deanna and Deanna concurred it sounded like the right choice.

"What's your class schedule tomorrow?" Mary asked. "I assume you want to come when I bring Grandma to her new place, and honestly, I would like to have you with me."

"Of course, I'll come. You wouldn't be able to stop me. I have a class at ten but I don't mind missing it. I doubt I'll be able to concentrate anyway. When are your classes?"

"I only have one class and then an office hour, but I'm not going in. I already posted an alternative assignment for my students and cancelled my office hour. I'll probably spend more time answering student emails than if I had gone into my office, but like you said, I won't be good for much tomorrow. I don't want to have to face students and pretend it's just another day."

Shortly before noon the following day, Mary, Deanna, and Greta parked under a shady magnolia tree. The large, healthy tree with smooth, deep green leaves larger than an open hand must have been the inspiration for the name of Magnolia Assisted Living Center. "What a lovely home," Greta commented. Turning to Mary she asked, "Do you live here?"

Mary and Deanna exchanged glances, unsure how to proceed. "I have friends here," Mary replied after a pause. Gathering momentum, she continued, "And they have invited us for lunch. Let's go in."

"Oh, how nice," Greta said. She fumbled with the passenger side door lock and window control in an unsuccessful attempt to find the handle. Mary reached across her mother, released the seat belt, then pulled the door latch. Greta swung her legs out of the car. She rocked forward and right back to her original position. Again, she leaned forward, moving her hands from the seat to the chair back and dashboard, then to the doorframe. Greta was unable to pull or push her body out of the car. Deanna brought the walker from the trunk. Greta scowled at it and stated, "That's not mine. I don't need that thing." As if she hadn't heard, Deanna opened the walker, snapping the sides into place, and positioned Greta's hands on the top. Deanna stabilized the device with a foot on the lowest horizontal brace, placed one of her hands under each of Greta's arms, and said, "Pull yourself up Grandma." Shifting her weight back as Greta made a feeble attempt to pull, Deanna leveraged her grandmother out of the car. Greta stepped forward, oblivious of the dramatic change she was walking into.

The facility's administrator had suggested Greta arrive in time for lunch in order to get acquainted with the other residents during a routine, daily event. Mary and Deanna brought lunch for themselves. They planned to stay and eat with Greta before leaving, hoping their presence during her first meal would ease the transition. The staff had warned Mary that most residents displayed increased confusion and angry, frustrated outbursts during the first few days, until they adjusted to their new surroundings.

Mary, Deanna, and Greta slowly ambled up the slight grade of the front walk and entered the facility. Lunch was about to be served so they went straight to the large dining table. Mary and Deanna sat stiffly and stared at their dry, tasteless sandwiches. Neither was able to get down more than one bite of the cardboard and paste that had been sold to them as pastrami and cheese. The nurse's aide did her best to remain positive and reassuring. She offered them tomato and rice soup with sourdough bread and chocolate pudding for dessert. Most of the residents consumed it with gusto, as if it was a gourmet meal, but to Mary and Deanna it appeared even less appetizing than their uneatable sandwiches.

"Is this your house?" Greta asked a wrinkled, stooped, man with a large hooked nose. The few, scattered tufts of long, thin, white hair on his head made him look like a mad scientist on chemotherapy. His bread was cut into small, crustless squares and dropped into thickened soup, creating a meal of gooey mush.

"What?" he yelled back at Greta.

"My friend made us lunch. Isn't it good?" she asked.

"Don't know why they can't make decent coffee on this damn ship," the man complained. "Look at this. It's so thick you can eat it with a spoon." He sunk his spoon into his cup of honey-thick water. It stood in place for several seconds before gliding in slow motion to lean against the side of the cup. "I've been on ships in every ocean and none served us slop as bad as this." Having voiced his complaint, he dropped his chin onto his chest and emitted a soft snore. Mary and Deanna watched wide-eyed and aghast as thickened red spittle with scattered grains of rice made a slow trek from the corners of his mouth through the deep crevasses down to his chin. Greta turned to Mary and stated, "What a nice man." She proceeded to eat every bite of her institutional lunch.

The Wedding Day

The wedding day schedule included an hour between the ceremony and the reception for pictures with the bride and groom together. The photographer requested an hour and a half, but both families refused to leave guests idle for so long, nibbling hors-d'oeuvres and waiting for the evening to begin. Due to the time pressure, the photographer barked orders at Hank and Deanna, posing them in front of the altar. Then, he pointed his camera at them. They remained in position, stiff and artificial. He yelled at them to smile and enjoy themselves. Their plastic smiles morphed into grimaces. Nearly the entire photo session was a waste. A couple pictures of the bridal party were acceptable. The combined family shots were few and poorly staged. The photographer usually spent as much time positioning people for one shot as he spent in total on Hank and Deanna's family pictures. Fortunately, the photographer reminded himself, no one has to look great in a group photo as long as no one looks terrible, and his pictures were never terrible. The highlights from the rushed session were close ups of Hank and Deanna's clasped hands with shiny new rings. When the photographer looked back at the proofs, he discovered one gem amidst of the rubbish. Deanna looked down at her bouquet of cream roses with the hint of a dreamy smile. From behind her, Hank encased her in his arms, his hands enfolding hers, as he observed her profile. The tenderness in that one picture made up for all the others.

Mary and Dean left the sanctuary together. It was already dark. The hazy yellow of the street lights illuminated the world without adding warmth or happiness. Dean took Mary's hand. He idly traced circles on her palm with his thumb. In melancholy silence, they crossed the street to the public parking lot, where Deanna had left Mary's blue Avalon many hours ago. Mary unlocked the door with her car fob, squeezed Dean's hand before pulling her's free, and got into her car. She inserted the key into the ignition. *Tap, tap, tap.* Dean's face was peering in, inches from the passenger window. Mary hit the control on the door handle, unlocking the other doors. Dean climbed in.

"I thought you were taking your car," she explained.

Dean shrugged. "We can get it later. Or even leave it until tomorrow. The car will be fine here. I don't want to be alone right now."

Mary swallowed the lump in her throat and nodded.

"You know," Dean continued, "I like Hank. In fact, I think he's the right man for our daughter. I guess my melancholy is because I'm in shock that she's grown up. I certainly don't disapprove of her marriage or harbor regrets from her childhood."

"My only regret..." Mary began, then trailed off.

Disagreements about her mother were infrequent since Greta had entered assisted living, but Mary's emotions were raw and unpredictable today. She would not risk discussing her mother with Dean.

"You wish your mom could have been part of this day," Dean supplied. "I wish that too, Mary. I honestly do. In fact, I wish your mother's memory was not impaired. And, I wish she could know Hank the way we've come to know and love him. And, I wish she could have celebrated with Deanna today." Dean shifted in his seat, repositioning himself to face his wife. "And above all else, I wish I had not made things harder on you while you were dealing with your mother's illness."

"Thank you," Mary said with sincerity. "But, it wasn't all your fault. I think we learned during our sessions with the counselor that neither of us dealt well with the stress we were under at that time."

"Yes, that's what she said. But, I'm not sure it's true. If I'm honest, I have to say I acted like a baby. Deanna was pulling away and leading her own life, and her life was becoming entwined with Hank rather than us. At the same time your mother needed you. I felt like I was losing both you and Deanna and I didn't like it. I was jealous. I wanted both of you to myself. You should know, Mary, that I love you. I've always loved you, and I am so proud you are my wife."

Mary leaned over the center console, plopped her face on the black tux covering Dean's bony shoulder, and sobbed.

After taking pictures in the sanctuary, the bridal party piled into the back of a limousine. Hank signaled to Deanna with an open hand to wait and let their friends enter first. Once everyone else was inside, Hank slammed the side door and motioned for the driver to take off. He grabbed Deanna's hand and ran around the corner of the church to his waiting red Previa. Hank had bought the Previa during his year in Oregon in an effort to fit into the ecologically minded community, but he chose glaring red, subconsciously declaring himself to be a Californian.

"Please tell me we're going to the reception. My parents will kill us both if we ditch our wedding now," Deanna said with mock scolding in her voice.

Hank pulled Deanna close, "Just five minutes alone. That's all I'm asking for." Hank kissed her smiling lips. Then her ear. Then her neck. Then her exposed shoulder. He drew back to examine her face. Her eyes were closed and her lips were slightly parted in desire and satisfaction. Deep contentment shown on her face. Deanna's eyes fluttered open. "What?" she asked his self-satisfied smirk.

Hank slowly released her and opened the passenger door. "Now I'm ready to go face all those people." He helped Deanna collect the layers of her dress inside the vehicle.

"You sound more like my father than my husband right now," she accused, expecting him to laugh at the absurd comparison.

Hank gave a sideways glance as he shut her door and trotted around to the driver's seat. "I may have more of your father in me than you think," he warned. "I just hide it better. If your parents wouldn't kill us, I'd drive off into the sunset with you right now. Just you and me, baby."

"Figuratively speaking," Deanna clarified, "Since the sun set an hour ago."

The reception venue was a gorgeous Victorian rose garden. Meandering cobblestone paths outlined by twinkling Christmas lights led to white trellis gazebos. Wrought iron benches were tucked into corners. Even in the crisp December air with the foliage nearly dormant, the old-world ambiance called to the romantic spirit of the attendees to come and wander and dream. Dinner and dancing were to be inside a simple, rustic structure in the middle of the garden.

The DJ called for everyone enjoying the garden to enter

the building and take their seats. Then, one couple at a time, he introduced the bridal party. The audience clapped as each pair entered and crossed the dance floor in the center of the room, making their way to the head table. Last, the DJ presented the newlyweds. When Hank and Deanna entered the cozy room, guests rose to their feet, cheering and applauding loudly. Deanna had removed the two floor-length layers of her veil, leaving one layer of gathered netting that reached the small of her back. The short train of the dress did not require bustling, but did require caution not to trip or step on it if she turned quickly.

The standard wedding reception buffet was served. Guests chose either marinated beef or chicken breast, accompanied by green salad, rice pilaf, mixed vegetables, and a roll. The bridal party ate first, allowing Deanna and Hank to finish first and circulate among the tables, greeting their guests who were still enjoying dinner. Deanna was surprised by the number of Hank's extended family and old friends she was meeting for the first time. Since she came from a small family, she could not imagine traveling to the wedding of a cousin or nephew whom you had not seen in years and meeting his bride on her wedding day. His family, however, seemed to treat weddings and funerals as family reunions. At least six times someone she had never met, or even heard of, grabbed her in a slightly tipsy and overly affectionate embrace, as Hank make introductions and the person offered congratulations. Then, the distant relative would pump Hank's hand and slap him on the back saying, "Haven't seen you since Uncle Pete's funeral." Deanna loved Hank, but she still had a lot to learn about joining his family.

After the dinner plates were cleared away, champagne was poured. One by one, the wedding party rose and toasted the couple. Guests chuckled at the funny speeches and clinked their glasses in approval, but immediately forgot the exaggerated stories. The tingling Champagne bubbles on their tongues contained less gas than the outrageous speeches.

Next, the DJ called the bride and groom to the dance floor. Deanna and Hank held onto each other and swayed back and forth to a gentle beat. In the middle of the song, the bridal party joined in around them. The song finished and the bridal party scattered, allowing Dean onto the dance floor. Dean said nothing but sniffed loudly and bit his quivering bottom lip as he took his daughter in his arms. After a few long measures during which Dean looked miserable, Hank invited his mother to join him on the dance floor. He wanted to spare Dean from being the only focus for two hundred pairs of eyes. Initially, she held up her hands and refused. She wanted an entire song to herself. But when she realized the crowd had witnessed her rejecting her son on his special day, she reluctantly consented. Kenny Loggins sang about Pooh's Corner and the fleeting sweetness and innocence of childhood while Hank danced with his mother, whose disgruntled sense of being cheated was evident in her piercing eyes and tight lips, and Deanna danced with her awkward father, patting his back, comforting and reassuring him. It was a dance well remembered by the guests.

Once the specific arranged dances were over, Hank and Deanna cut their cake. Hank circled a handful of white cake around in the air inches from Deanna's face. She followed it with her open mouth like a bobble-head doll. Remembering the strict warning Mary had given him about no cake shoving or smearing, Hank relented and carefully fed his bride a bite. Mary sighed in relief as Hank's friends booed. The dance floor and the dessert table were opened up to everyone. Deanna and her girls moved back to the head table to enjoy their cake. Hank and the groomsmen stayed in a clump near the dancing, pushing and teasing each other.

After half a slice of cake, Ashley pushed the plate aside, turned to Deanna and whined, "Did you have to have such a stiff first dance? You made me lose my bet with Jenna."

Deanna snickered, understanding what Ashley was implying, "I told Hank I would be nervous with everyone watching just the two of us. I told him no turns or twists, nothing but straightforward back and forth swaying."

Ashley exaggeratedly slumped her shoulders and said, "Please tell me he will do his crazy dancing at some point tonight or this wedding will be completely perfect and therefore a total bore and failure for me." The girls all began to laugh, picturing Hank's thin arms and legs waving wildly to no discernible beat. Brittany covered her mouth with her napkin to prevent spewing cake. When she finally swallowed successfully she mumbled from behind the white paper, "I love when Hank dances. It was always the end of the party for me when he would stop dancing and begin a long, dull conversation about old books with someone."

"He dances like a jellyfish" Brittany said and giggled.

"An uncoordinated, skinny jellyfish," added Jenna.

Joining in the laughter, Deanna glanced around to be sure Hank and his friends were out of earshot. They remained huddled on the other side of the dance floor, as far from the head table as possible. "He got mad at me when I told him he doesn't have any rhythm," she whispered even though there was no chance of him overhearing. "He thinks he dances just fine."

"He does." Ashley said. "He wiggles and flings his arms around better than any belly dancer I've ever seen or heard of." The laughter from the girls increased. "Most people try not to hurt others when they dance. I think dancing is Hank's passive-aggressive way to clobber those who have offended him."

"Seriously, he's not that bad," Deanna defended.

"Oh, yes he is!" Jenna and Ashley said in unison.

Poised to defend him, Deanna paused for a moment, then said, "You're right. He is." Hank had many great attributes, but rhythm and grace were not among them.

In a conspiratorial whisper Deanna confessed, "I told the DJ about Hank's wild dancing. He promised me all slow songs tonight."

Ashley exploded with a giant snorty laugh, grabbing her

stomach, and doubling over. It was fortunate her hair was in an updo or it would have landed in the frosting left behind on her cake plate. "Oh, you've ruined my evening. That is what I was most looking forward to today. Everything else will be beautiful and perfect. Hank jellyfish dancing would have been the comic relief."

Ten months Before

It was Monday morning. Mary sipped a second cup of coffee and considered her plans for the day. She perched on one of the kitchen bar stools, facing the family room, her back resting against the beige tiles. The national news ended and the television blared celebrity gossip.

When Mary had reduced her workload to eighty percent, she'd added the nearly full-time job of overseeing her mother's care to her responsibilities. For four long years, her dual roles left her no time for television or hobbies, and barely enough time to eat and sleep. Then, when Greta was admitted into the skilled nursing facility, Mary's hectic life suddenly switched from the fast lane to the slow lane, giving her too little to do and too much time to do it in.

If Mary left now to visit her mother, she was sure to wait outside the pulled curtain for half an hour. Even the Kardashians were more entertaining than an Alzheimer's care home during the morning bathroom rituals. Mary reached over and touched her mother's padded stool. It had remained in its place, unused for the past year. She knew Greta was never coming back, but disposing of the chair held a finality she had not been ready to face.

Every day, Mary stopped by Greta's nursing facility for at least a few minutes. Today there was nothing else on her calendar and she could spend the entire day there. Visiting Magnolia Assisted Living Center had become a routine but unpleasant task, like paying bills or scrubbing toilets. A full day at the home felt like scouring the entire neighborhood's toilets.

Mary spun around on her stool to scan the clean kitchen, hoping for a necessary task to present itself. None did. Mary drummed her fingers on the counter tiles, and took a sip of strong, black coffee. She was loitering. The TV continued to spout information that did not catch Mary's interest or attention. Mary stared at her mother's stool and knew it was time to get rid of the one mismatched item in the open kitchen-family room. Maybe she would take it to Goodwill this afternoon. That would give her a reason to leave the nursing home. Finally, with a sigh, Mary set her empty cup in the sink, turned off the irrelevant discussion on the TV, and grabbed her purse to head to the purgatory that was Magnolia Assisted Living Center.

A short time later, Mary rang the bell for admittance. The staff greeted her warmly but briefly as they continued the arduous task of getting eight confused and sometimes combative residents cleaned and dressed. Mary headed to her mother's room. An aide guided Greta to the waiting wheelchair by holding onto the waistband on the back of Greta's pants. Greta sat down in the chair willingly but then pushed at the aide's hands, resisting the seat belt that anchored her in place. "Stop that. What are you doing?" she demanded as she yanked at the woven belt and the young woman's nimble fingers.

"I'm helping you to remember to ask for help before you walk anywhere."

"I don't need help walking."

The aide secured the clip at the back of the chair, away from Greta's probing fingers. "When you want to get up you let me know and I'll walk with you," she said, reinforcing an important safety consideration that Greta always failed to remember.

"Good morning, Mom," Mary said from the doorway.

Greta tried to stand to see who was talking behind her. After hitting resistance from the restraining belt a couple times, Greta rotated the chair by side-stepping with her feet. Upon viewing Mary, she smiled broadly. "Oh hello. How wonderful to see you."

Mary returned a shallow smile.

"I'll take her out to the main room," Mary told the aide.

As Mary rolled her mother down the hallway, Greta continued, "How's your family? I haven't seen them in such a long time."

Answering the same question as yesterday and the day before, Mary said, "My family is fine. Today is Monday so Dean is at work and Deanna is at school. Deanna graduated from college in December and now she is working on a teaching credential. Do you remember that Deanna got engaged? They've decided on a Christmas wedding."

"Really? How exciting. No, I didn't know that. I wonder why Mary never told me."

"I have told you," Mary stated with exasperation.

"Maybe you did, but Mary certainly did not."

They entered the comfortable, well-lit front room. Two relatively agile residents sat on the couch while the other residents arrived in wheelchairs or supported by walkers. The residents were arranged to form a circle, allowing for comfortable, albeit nonsensical, conversation. Many verbal exchanges were in progress but few of the individuals thought to be taking part were actually present.

Mary positioned her mother next to a sniveling, paranoid woman who was accusing the dozing man next to her of stealing her jewelry. Large, brightly-colored plastic gemstones glinted on the woman's fingers, wrists, neck, and ears. She was wearing more adornments than a princess, but was sure many were missing. Mary dragged one of the simple wooden visitor's chairs away from the wall and joined the circle of residents. Greta glanced toward the scraping noise of the chair gliding across the hygienic laminate floor. With wide-eyed surprise she exclaimed, "Oh my goodness. I didn't know you were here. I haven't seen you in such a long time. How are you?"

"Just great." Greta missed the dripping sarcasm.

"Have you met my friend?" Greta pointed to the angry,

bejeweled woman on her right.

"Yes. We've met before," Mary said.

Greta turned back to Mary, surprise wrinkling her brow as she said, "Have we really? I don't remember you. What did you say your name was?"

For a moment Mary considered introducing herself as Jackie Onassis or Marilyn Monroe to break up the monotony of the day, but teasing her mother felt cruel rather than funny.

"I'm Mary."

"My daughter's name is Mary, but she never comes to visit me."

Mary sighed. "So I've heard."

9:00 pm Last Things

The Wedding Day

Hank held Deanna tenderly, swaying to a Sinatra love ballad. Some of the guests who weren't dancers were starting to leave. Others were still chatting, catching up with old acquaintances over a second piece of cake and coffee. Most of the younger crowd, influenced by the romantic mood, were in pairs on the dance floor.

"Happy with today?" Hank asked softly into Deanna's ear. The contented feeling in her soul let Deanna know the answer was yes, but she took a few seconds to inventory the day before answering. The ceremony, the setting, their friends, her dress that made her feel like a princess. Happy? It was a dream come true. The man holding her, whom she could now call her husband, made her heart race and her breath catch whenever he so much as looked at her. Happy? Exceedingly. Her father had radiated love and pride and had seemed relaxed and comfortable most of the day. Her mother had clearly enjoyed herself. Deanna had not seen her mom without a broad smile and ready laugh at any time during the day. Happy? Absolutely. The people she loved most were happy, which created a deeper happiness--a contented peace. The only part of the day that left a gap in her joy was her grandmother's absence. As Deanna thought about it, she realized that even though her grandmother was not physically present, her legacy was evident. Greta's belief in kindness and honesty and helping others, which she'd taught and modeled to her daughter and granddaughter, was here in the two women she'd loved and had poured her life into. The self-assurance tamed by humility she'd instilled into Deanna through years of gracious guidance was here. Even the hard lessons of the last decade, unknowingly taught and unwillingly learned, were here. Greta, in her illness, had taught Deanna that love is an action first and a feeling second. It means doing what must be done, regardless of how emotionally trying or unpleasant it might be. Genuine love requires sacrifice: putting another's needs before your own, even when it is painful and the benefits seem non-existent. Greta had taught Deanna the most important life lessons needed for marriage, even though much of the teaching had been done without Greta's awareness. The best of Grandma was here, even if she was not here in person.

Ready to give her answer, Deanna looked into her husband's eyes and said, "I feel as if, up until today, I have only had fleeting, elusive glimpses that hinted at what happiness might be. Now I know the full beauty and intensity of what happiness really means." Hank drew her closer into his embrace and kissed his wife with immense satisfaction.

When Deanna was able to speak, she said, "There's one more thing I would like to do before today is over."

Hank smiled a crooked grin, and his eyes twinkled brighter than the morning star. In a husky whisper into her ear, he said, "Me too."

Deanna giggled embarrassedly, then replied, "Make that two things." Hank drew back and looked at her quizzically, having no idea what she was proposing.

Even though it was nearly eleven o'clock, Deanna knew the staff at Magnolia Assisted Living would let them in. The staff would be thrilled to see her beaded, creamy white, satin dress and her tuxedo-clad husband, even if her grandmother was sound asleep and did not wake up to greet the newlyweds.

Just as Deanna had predicted, the nurse opened the perpetually locked door, took one look at her, and let out an excited expletive. Then she ushered Deanna and Hank in with a quick hug and not a single word about visiting hours or policies.

"I expected you to be a beautiful bride but you are even more beautiful than I imagined," said the middle-aged, heavy-set night nurse as she circled her finger in the air, motioning for Deanna to spin around and give her a three hundred and sixty degree look at the wedding gown. Deanna complied willingly, still enjoying the aristocratic feeling of being the best-dressed person in the room. After a prolonged moment of ogling over Deanna's dress, the nurse said, "Your grandma has been in bed for a while, but you can go into her room and see if she's awake."

Deanna proceeded down the hallway, gently opened the door, and stepped into the shadowy, night-time lighting of the bedroom her grandmother shared with a nonverbal, non-ambulatory woman named Bettie. Crossing the room, Deanna bent down and softly kissed her grandmother's cheek. Greta opened her eyes and turned her head toward Deanna. A smile spread across her face, demonstrating recognition, but whether she recognized Deanna as her sister, daughter, or granddaughter was impossible to tell. "Hello...ah...you, you there," Greta stammered.

"Hi Grandma. I wanted to come by and show you my wedding dress." Taking Hank by the arm and pulling him forward into the dim light Deanna continued, "This is my husband, Hank. We got married today."

"Oh, wonderful! I'm getting married…yes…me and George. I like George. You're married too. So happy. That's good. Mary should get married…oh, she did…yes, you did. Finally married." Pause. "Nice man. Mary married him. His name…ah…what's that name?"

"Dean. Mary married Dean and he is my father," Deanna said, hoping to gently reorient her grandmother.

"Hello, Dean," Greta said reaching out a withered hand toward Hank in greeting. Deanna had learned that correcting Greta would either make her stubbornly angry or withdrawn, ending the conversation. Wanting to keep her grandmother talking a little longer, she ignored the odd twist in their dialogue and went on, "Today is my wedding day, but it would not have been complete if I hadn't been able to see you. So, do you like my wedding dress?" Deanna stood up straight and took a step back so her grandmother could get a fuller view of the strapless gown with its playful detailing.

"Are you the bride…the bride and the…the boy?" Greta asked, struggling to identify the words she wanted. Smiling at the happy couple she said, "You…on the top…the cake… jumped right off." Greta snickered, enjoying her own joke. She smiled dreamily. "Oh, I like George…he delivers our groceries. A college boy. A college boy likes me. George. I want to marry George." Greta was back in the happy days of 1946 or 1947.

Deanna bent over the rail of the hospital bed that prevented her grandmother from falling or getting up unsupervised at night, and gave the best hug she could in that awkward position. "I love you Grandma. Good night."

"Love you too, Deanna. Beautiful. Happy bride," Greta said in one last short, nearly lucid moment. In fact, it was the last time Greta ever called Deanna by name.

Deanna turned to her husband, and with the same mischievous glint in her eyes that she so admired in his, said, "Now, one more thing to do to make today perfect."

ABOUT THE AUTHOR

Gretchen Nelson Ezaki is a pediatric nurse and certified nurse educator. She is also the daughter and granddaughter of Alzheimer's victims. A Day to Remember is her debut novel in which she draws on her medical knowledge, combining it with the experience of sitting at a confused loved one's bedside. Her hope is to offer an accurate portrayal of how difficult it is to lose a family member to Alzheimer's, but also to remind readers that even though life is hard, at the end of the day, life is good.